WHISPERS
AT DUSK

Also by *New York Times* bestselling author Heather Graham

SHADOW OF DEATH
CRIMSON SUMMER
DANGER IN NUMBERS

New York Confidential

THE FINAL DECEPTION
A LETHAL LEGACY
A DANGEROUS GAME
A PERFECT OBSESSION
FLAWLESS

Krewe of Hunters

THE UNKNOWN
THE FORBIDDEN
THE UNFORGIVEN
DREAMING DEATH
DEADLY TOUCH
SEEING DARKNESS
THE STALKING
THE SEEKERS
THE SUMMONING
ECHOES OF EVIL
PALE AS DEATH
FADE TO BLACK
WICKED DEEDS
DARK RITES
DYING BREATH

DARKEST JOURNEY
DEADLY FATE
HAUNTED DESTINY
THE HIDDEN
THE FORGOTTEN
THE SILENCED
THE BETRAYED
THE HEXED
THE CURSED
THE NIGHT IS FOREVER
THE NIGHT IS ALIVE
THE NIGHT IS WATCHING
THE UNINVITED
THE UNSPOKEN
THE UNHOLY
THE UNSEEN
THE EVIL INSIDE
SACRED EVIL
HEART OF EVIL
PHANTOM EVIL

Cafferty & Quinn

THE DEAD PLAY ON
WAKING THE DEAD
LET THE DEAD SLEEP

Look for Heather Graham's next novel
SECRETS IN THE DARK
available soon from MIRA.

* * * * *

For additional books by Heather Graham,
visit theoriginalheathergraham.com.

HEATHER GRAHAM

WHISPERS AT DUSK

mira

ISBN-13: 978-0-7783-0763-1

Whispers at Dusk

Mira
22 Adelaide St. West, 41st Floor
Toronto, Ontario M5H 4E3, Canada
BookClubbish.com

Printed in U.S.A.

For the Lee family, Kaylyn, Travis, Annabel, Elijah, Ezra
and, of course, Della, with lots of love!

CAST OF CHARACTERS

The Krewe of Hunters—
a specialized FBI unit that uses its members' "unique abilities"
to bring justice to strange or unorthodox cases

Adam Harrison—
philanthropist founder of the Krewe of Hunters

Jackson Crow—
supervisory field agent, Adam's chosen leader for the team

Angela Hawkins Crow—
original Krewe member, exceptional in the field
and with research

The Euro Special Assistance Team or "Blackbird"—
a newly formed group created to extend the Krewe's reach
into Europe to assist with crimes abroad

Della Hamilton—
late twenties, five-eight, light brown hair, green eyes,
with the Krewe almost a year

Mason Carter—
six-five, dark hair, blue eyes, FBI for six years, has been
working solo since the death of his partner in the line of duty

Jon Wilhelm—
early fifties, experienced law enforcement with
Norway's National Police Directorate, speaks English
with an American accent because he studied at Yale

Edmund Taylor—
early forties, London's Metropolitan Police detective
chief inspector

Jeanne Lapierre—
fifties, tall and solid, longtime Parisian detective,
excellent at his work

François Bisset—
forty-five, light blue eyes, friendly and professional manner,
the Krewe's Interpol liaison

Midnight Slasher—
a serial killer who has murdered across state lines

The Vampire/the Master—
organized serial killer, globe-trotting to bring his "kingship"
from country to country

Dr. Dag Andersen—
a specialist medical examiner, Norway

Ian Robertson—
Scottish detective

Dr. Calleigh Harper—
medical examiner, Scotland

Commander Anton Alexandru—
Romanian law enforcement

Alan Fremont—
Department of Criminal Investigation, the state of Louisiana

Gideon Grimsby—
a helpful Englishman who once sailed with Lafitte, died 1820

Orm Olafson—
a now-peaceful Viking, died 894

Sir Gordon Stewart—
former Scottish law enforcement, died 1490

PROLOGUE

For Della Hamilton, it began with the old cemetery.

And with Jose Garcia, her friend all through grade school, middle school and high school.

They lived on the same block. It was never romantic, just a true friendship that had been strengthened by years of shared local experiences and talks about everything: family, heart-throbs, and more. They shared everything that went into growing up.

And Jose was just a good guy. She didn't know anyone who didn't like Jose.

What killed him was a bizarre accident. Truly bizarre and tragic for all concerned. Another kid in high school would have the guilt of Jose's death on him for all the years of his life to come.

Della found out about it when she was at cheerleading practice during her senior year of high school. The blood bank called.

She gave blood with her parents' blessing several times a year. Gave. They weren't rich, but she wasn't selling her blood.

Her health and the coagulating wonder of her blood was a gift from a higher power, however one chose to see God. It was an amazing thing to give the gift of her blood to others. So she did.

Della was joking with the girls when the call came, and they were all laughing and calling her a vampire. She reminded them vampires drank blood; they didn't give it to others.

It wasn't until she arrived at the hospital and saw her parents and Jose's parents that she heard what had happened. She wished she could open a vein and pour her blood straight into her friend's heart.

It had been…ridiculous. A couple of the high schools in the area had friendly rivalries going. *Usually* friendly. Occasionally something might get a little physical, but it was broken up most of the time by an authority figure, or it simply petered out with the rivals laughing.

But this time…

Jose and some friends had been at a popular South Miami restaurant. "Rivals" had been at another table. They'd been playing around, throwing napkins, then someone had picked up something heavier, a mug. It had struck Jose in the head and cracked open his skull and…

Now, they were praying for his life. If not for the mug, the day probably would have ended with laughter and with the groups picking up all the napkins together. The rivalries weren't between the junkies and the thieves and the crew of kids headed for criminal behavior. These teens were on the sports teams, the debate team, into music, movies, and theater.

But the mug had flown.

They took Della's blood.

But neither her blood nor blood from any other donor nor any help from the medical community could save Jose.

He died that night.

Her parents had taken her home. Jose's mom and dad had stayed with him to the last minute.

She heard later his mother wouldn't let the funeral home take his body.

And at the funeral, the poor woman had tried to drag him from his coffin. If she could not do so, she wanted to be buried in it with him. Her husband kept her from doing either one.

Della wished there was something she could do to help. But there wasn't. The woman had lost her only son.

It was about ten days later, and Della had just left the pool where she worked part-time as a lifeguard after school until dusk. She was heading toward the cemetery where Jose was buried. She knew the area well. Her friend's father was the caretaker, and their home was on the cemetery property. They'd often had sleepovers and spent the nights trying to scare each other and outdo each other with ghost stories. The cemetery had never scared Della. She had felt *something* strange; oddly, it had been a sense of warmth and comfort. It was considered historic for their area, being over a hundred years old. There were only a few little family mausoleums in the cemetery, but there were stunning memorial statues, standing stones, and flat memorials surrounded by beautiful and lush trees. She loved the cemetery. But then, she loved old churches and cemeteries—truly old ones Winchester Cathedral in London, Westminster Abbey, Notre Dame, and so many in Rome and London. They'd visited so many. Her dad had said leaving donations was much cheaper than many things they might do on a European vacation.

Della had her radio playing as she drove home from work. Yet that day as she reached the southern end of the cemetery, she suddenly had nothing but dead air.

In the silence, she frowned and changed the station, but nothing happened.

She pulled off the road by the little coral wall that surrounded the place and looked in the cemetery. Jose wasn't buried far from the wall. She found herself tempted to jump over the two and a half feet of coral that comprised the barrier. But she didn't. She should bring flowers to Jose's grave, and do it by daylight when people were supposed to visit. Della had discovered the music stopped playing on her radio every time she passed by the little coral wall, a reminder that led to her stopping sometimes at night. The city lights from the street afforded her all the illumination she needed to reach Jose's grave.

Della decided to bring flowers that weekend. And it felt good to go and tell her friend she missed him, and to almost feel as if he were there with her.

She was back home for the summer after her first year of college when the killer they called the Canal Carnivore arrived in South Florida. The man had eluded police in the west, the northeast, and had struck in Biloxi, Mississippi, before heading farther to the southeast. Right before Della had returned home to take up her job as a lifeguard for the summer, he had attacked and killed a young woman in the Brickell area, a divorcee living alone in a condominium and working for a local bank. His signature was the removal of a patch of skin from his victims, usually a two-by-two square that contained the belly button. The one witness who discovered the victim near the old church cemetery in New York by Wall Street had seen a disappearing hooded figure chewing on something bloody as he'd hurried toward the Hudson River.

Thus, he'd been labeled the carnivore. He didn't bite the flesh out—that would leave marks for a dental impression. He didn't leave fingerprints or footprints anywhere. He didn't sexually assault his victims or torture them. He slit their throats and cut out his inches of flesh. He left no clues and had only been seen once calmly walking away from what would prove to be his victim. The "Canal" part of his moniker came from the fact that several victims had been found near water, though Biscayne Bay was hardly a canal and the Hudson River was, well, a river.

Naturally, Della's parents had been concerned. But she had assured them she went to work and came straight home. They were always there when she returned, along with her mother's giant sheepdog that looked like a mop but could be as fierce as any pit bull or rottweiler if he saw a member of the family threatened. They also lived in a friendly neighborhood and had automatic lights if she came home in the dark, along with a surprisingly modern alarm system. She was almost nineteen—an adult—and studying criminology! She knew how to be safe and smart. They had been studying serial killers just before the break. If anyone knew how to be careful, it was her.

She'd been home a week when her car suddenly started acting up. She kept a good eye on it. While it wasn't a new car, it wasn't old; the computer usually warned her if she needed maintenance or if anything was wrong.

It had given no warning. But the red light was suddenly blinking, screaming for maintenance.

She was about to drive by the cemetery. And the radio had already gone silent. The car was bucking strangely, and she quickly drove onto the grass at the side of the road only feet from the little coral wall.

No problem—other than she wouldn't have her car. She always had her phone and her AAA card.

She turned off the engine and reached to the passenger's seat for her bag. But digging inside, she couldn't find her phone. It had to be there. She had undressed and donned her swimsuit, left her bag in the women's locker room, worked her hours, gone back, and changed again. She hadn't taken her phone out. She had plans for the evening with friends and with her parents, and they were set. She hadn't needed her phone for anything, and she had just wanted to get home when her day had ended.

It had to be there.

But it wasn't.

She got out of the car. She was going to have to flag down someone driving along the street. She'd be careful. She wouldn't get in anyone's car. She'd just get someone to call for help for her.

Leaving the car's lights on, she walked over to the road. It wasn't rush hour anymore, but it wasn't that late, either. There were only a few cars. Most of them tended to be in the left lane, and one woman stared at her as if she were a crazy person.

She was about to give up when a car drove onto the grass near hers. It was oddly forming an L-shape that blocked part of the road, but she needed help, so she certainly wasn't going to comment on anyone's driving or parking.

But a shiver slid down her spine and a warning bell seemed to go off in her head as she approached the driver.

He got out of the car.

He was wearing a hoodie. Not black, dark blue, but a hoodie, and it was a warm night.

The L-shape he had created when he parked had cut Della off from the road. She never said a word. She knew.

It might have been a woman. But they'd been studying serial killers at school and, statistically, women serial killers preferred poison; they didn't seem to like the mess of knives or guns.

Small man...woman. Did it matter? Beneath the hoodie, they were wearing a bandanna-type mask, allowing Della to see nothing of them but the eyes.

Dusk was quickly heading to darkness, but the streetlights fell on them and their cars. Looking at the person's eyes, Della knew they were smiling and loved watching the fear that filled her as she saw a streak of light catch on the blade of an enormous carving knife.

The cars would cut her off. There was no one on the road. If she ran across it, the only thing she could reach quickly would be an office complex without a single car in the parking lot.

She turned and headed for the little coral wall just a few steps from her. She leaped over it. This killer couldn't know the cemetery.

She did. She knew it so well.

If she ran hard toward the avenue that bordered the western side of the cemetery she'd get to the caretaker's house. Her friend's family had moved to the Keys a year ago. But she'd once met the new caretaker, his wife, and his child when she'd been at the cemetery. If she could just reach the house...

The killer was after her in a flash, but she weaved through headstones and around oaks, banyans, and cypress trees.

The killer remained behind.

Close behind.

She was near the backyard of the home by one of the oldest sections of the cemetery. Both Union and Confederate soldiers who had survived the Civil War to move down to South Florida were there, perhaps friends now that the fighting was over, and the cemetery had claimed them. There was a beautiful huge statue of an eagle there because one of the Union soldiers had been with the regiment that had had a mascot, Old Abe, the battle eagle. It would be a good place to slide around to get into the yard, hopping the little fence and screaming all the while for help...

But she was suddenly struck in the head. Dazed and stunned, and with her impetus, she went down on the ground.

Instinct caused her to roll. To look up into the eyes of a killer.

"That was spectacular!" the killer said. It was a "him," a small man, maybe five feet eight inches and possibly a hundred and sixty pounds. "And you! I've been watching you the last days and the piece of skin on your midriff... Wow, kid, you're beautiful, you know."

She stared at him. She was on the ground. He was about to level his weight down on hers. She had to kick. She had to fight.

The knife... There was nothing now but moonlight, but the knife gleamed in that bit of misty light!

"Della, the rock!"

She was startled to hear the urgent whisper.

There was no one anywhere near them!

But the person who was not there kept talking. And she knew she'd been hit in the head. She was terrified. She might be going completely crazy with fear, but the person was using...

Jose's voice.

She stared at the killer and her eyes widened.

Because Jose *was* there. Something of him. She could see him, handsome in the casual suit in which he had been buried, coral shirt, gray jacket, and trousers. His dark hair was neatly combed, he looked wonderful, except...

He couldn't really be there.

"Listen to me, Della!" Jose said firmly. "He's coming down. Let him get close—despite the knife! Let him get close. Then kick him in the nuts as hard as you can and grab that rock and smash in his face. I'd do it for you, but... I can't pick anything up, I'm afraid. I'll try kicking…get it closer to you. But wait…wait…let him get down and then…"

She had to be imagining he was there, her dear friend, trying to help her, even from the grave.

She had never been so terrified in her life, watching the killer come down closer and closer to her, watching the knife gleam so strangely in the moonlight…

"Now!" Jose shouted.

She reached; she could feel the rock. Her fingers curled around it.

And she kicked. She had the leg strength of a strong swimmer, and she drew her knee up and kicked him with everything in her while slamming the rock against his head as hard as she could.

And the knife fell, dangerously close to her face, as the killer screamed in agony and clasped his bloody face and fell to her side in a fetal position.

She was up in a flash, screaming desperately for help and racing toward the caretaker's house where a door was opened for her, where the police were immediately called and then…

It seemed all hell broke loose.

They caught him that night. He still couldn't stand straight when the police arrived. He tried to say he'd just been walking down the street, and Della had attacked him. The police didn't buy it. And in the days to come, forensic science would tie him to other murders. He'd thought he'd cleaned his knife. He hadn't. Special techniques showed the knife had been used on the poor woman in the Biloxi area, and once that happened, he'd been proud to be known as the Canal Carnivore. He assured them all he was going to be immortal, one of the greatest killers ever.

An FBI agent who had been following the killer's trail of blood assured him all he had done was take some beautiful people away from those who had loved them. He wasn't famous at all. He was just Henry Worth of Los Angeles, California, and he'd be doing—at the least—life with no chance of parole.

The agent had questioned Della. A man of about forty, he was even and controlled. When they talked, Della realized just how close he'd been. He told her if it hadn't been for her, Worth might have killed again and again.

"You showed remarkable coolness in such a situation, young lady. Think about joining the Bureau. I hear you're studying criminology."

"I was thinking forensics," Della told him. "But… Well, I have three more years to go."

The agent had been kind. Her parents, of course, had been hysterical. To calm them she had reminded them she'd taken down the killer.

But in truth, Jose had done that. And when the dust had settled on it all, she returned to the cemetery just as the sun was setting in the western sky. She stood by his grave and said, "Jose! You saved my life, my friend. Please… You're here, right?"

She felt him touch her shoulders, as he had in life sometimes supporting her. She smiled and turned and he was there.

"I wasn't so sure," he told her. "I thought you might have it. Like an extra sight, the ability to see with your mind—or your heart or soul—whatever it might be. Benjamin Turner, the Yankee buried up by the house, told me about it. Some of the living have it. When I thought about the way I had seen you here at various times, I suspected you might." He grinned. "Oh, and Lieutenant Parker—he was with Lee's regiment during the Civil War, opposite side—assured me what Ben was saying was the absolute truth." He shrugged. "I enjoy the two of them. Parker is great—a man who can admit he was wrong, that a whole society was wrong… Anyway. I'm just so grateful you could see me, hear me!"

"And I'm just so grateful you saved my life," she whispered.

He smiled. "You…your folks. Always giving to others. But… I heard that FBI guy. You have what it takes, Della. I think you should consider joining the Bureau. This special thing. Whatever it is. Della, it means you have an edge. And maybe you should use that edge."

"Maybe," she whispered. "Maybe. As long as I get to keep seeing you."

Jose grinned. "We can do that! And I'll introduce you to Ben and Josiah Parker. They're great! And then… Well, talk to them, too. Then use what you've got, my dearest friend. Use what you've got!"

CHAPTER ONE

Mason Carter knew he had backup. The man now holding seventeen-year-old Melissa Wells hostage had been busy for months, and law enforcement across the country had been on his tail. Spread about in various positions outside, an FBI SWAT crew was situated along with local police who knew the area well.

Still, they were in bayou country surrounded by snake-and-alligator-infested waters and a range of high grasses, trees, and brush that might hinder any assistance.

Though he'd left a trail of carnage across the country by taking nine victims along the way, the killer's identity was unknown. He'd left behind fingerprints, but they couldn't be found in any database, and nothing else discovered by any agency across the country had given them a single clue toward discovering his identity. The truth existed somewhere; it just hadn't been found as yet.

He'd been labeled the Midnight Slasher since most of his abductions and kills had been after midnight. His note—handwritten and mailed from Las Vegas to the NYC FBI offices—had assured them he was fond of his moniker, and he'd try to make sure his murders did, indeed, occur after midnight in the future. He'd really have preferred being the Vampire, but that name had already gone to a coworker who was busy in Europe.

Coworker?

Mason knew about murders that were being called "the vampire killings" in Europe. He doubted this man and the European madman knew each other, though it appeared they were trying to outdo one another.

But then again, he didn't really know.

Maybe this killer needed the moniker because he was such an ordinary-looking man. Not exactly handsome—*cute* might be a term applied to him. He didn't appear at all insane or *creepy* as some seemed to think he must appear, not at all as people might think a maniacal killer should look.

He was about twenty-seven—the profilers had been right on his age—six feet even, perhaps a hundred and seventy pounds, with shaggy dirty blond hair, a clean-shaven face and friendly brown eyes. He smiled a lot. Mason could see how he'd managed easily enough to charm or coerce his victims out with him to a place where they might be alone.

And here they were. Mason had trailed the killer from Virginia and had suspected from the few clues he'd been told by the locals that the man would steal a boat and bring his victim far into the bayou. He'd been at the forefront of the investigation, and he called in as he made his way, seeking help from any and all law enforcement agency so they might really end the reign of the Midnight Slasher with a true force against him.

But Mason was the one who now stood alone, facing the man who held the teenaged girl, his blood-stained knife held so tightly to her throat that a trickle of blood ran down to her collarbone. Her terror-filled eyes were on Mason. She didn't want to die.

Mason didn't want her to die, either.

He was a good shot—but he'd still have to be at his fastest to hit the man before the knife could slide into the soft flesh of her throat and on to arteries and veins and…

"Okay, Midnight Slasher," he said, his Glock trained hard on the man, "do you really want to die today?"

"I've been here before, and I'm still alive!" the killer said. The girl let out a terrified whimper; the killer had jerked with his words. Another trail of blood slid down to her collarbone.

"I don't know. You're in bayou country now. With people who know it well," Mason said, shrugging.

It was truly doubtful the man would survive the day if he didn't surrender, but Mason was telling the truth. And it was true, too, that before Mason had been called in on the case, the killer had escaped a similar situation in the Shenandoah mountains.

He had killed his hostage and tossed her to his would-be captors before escaping.

Backup wasn't going to help.

Not here. Not now. While agents and officers might be all around, Mason was alone in the cabin with the man. His backup crew was holding. They all knew if the killer heard anyone trying to enter from the rear or break down any of the old wooden walls, the girl would die.

"You can do it, and there is no choice," a voice whispered to Mason.

He was alone in the cabin with the killer—and with the ghost of one Gideon Grimsby, an Englishman who had come to the new world to meet, befriend, and then serve under the legendary Jean Laffite. He had fought at the Battle of New Orleans. Gideon had survived the battle, fallen in love and changed his ways—only to be shot down in the street by a vengeful man who had once coveted the beauty who had become Gideon's wife.

Now, Gideon enjoyed the music of New Orleans, watched over his descendants and tended to haunt Frenchman Street. But having realized Mason was aware of him at a lounge one night, he'd discovered his afterlife of being a ghostly—and very helpful—investigator as well.

"Do it. Do it, Mason lad, you must!" Gideon said. "He's going to kill her. The officers and agents outside will lose patience. They'll seek entry as you know they must. And this rotten beast will die, but so will she. Dammit, man, take your shot!"

"I have to be sure!" Mason said the words aloud and cursed himself. He was accustomed to seeing the dead. And he'd learned before he was ten *not* to be seen talking to them.

But maybe this time it was good.

"Who the hell are you talking to?" the killer demanded.

Mason made a split-second decision and shrugged, saying, "I guess you can't see him. Gideon is here. You'd have liked him. He was a pirate. Well, he was, but then cleaned up his act. And sadly wound up being murdered, but he's enjoying his afterlife."

"Man, they think *I'm* crazy. You're crazy!" the killer said.

There was suddenly a gentle tap at the door to the cabin, surprising both Mason and the killer. Mason knew he frowned as the killer frowned. No one was bursting in; it was a gentle and polite tap.

The killer's young hostage let out a terrified squeak as the knife drew closer against her flesh.

"What the hell?" the killer murmured. "You—you go and see what those idiots outside want. Because I'm telling you,

you can kill me today, but she will die with me." He laughed. "Maybe the two of us can haunt you, too."

"God help me," Mason murmured. "Fine. You want me to check the door?"

"Yeah. I want to see who is trying what."

His gun still trained on the killer, Mason backed to the door.

"We don't need any disruptions here," he said loudly.

"I'm not a disruption," a female voice said. "I'm unarmed. I just wanted to offer to trade myself for Melissa Wells."

"What?" Mason demanded.

"Open the door, check her out. See if she's really unarmed," the killer said. "And don't forget—if I'm going, she's going with me!"

Mason cracked the door open. There was a woman standing there, mid-to late-twenties, about five foot eight with long light brown hair and a striking thin face. She was wearing black knit leggings and a tunic and lifted her arms to show that she carried nothing.

"I'm really a better choice," she said, looking around Mason to see and talk to the killer. "Think of it! If you don't manage to escape and get out of this or if you do, you'll have killed a special agent or used her for your escape. I'm Della Hamilton, FBI. And I know you like your victims to have long hair. My hair is long and *I'm* the right age… Come on. This kid is a teenager. So far, you've at least chosen victims who were out of high school!" She paused, shaking her head. "You have a reputation. You're a famous killer—don't sully all that by having people think you were a pedophile."

Apparently, she'd said just the right thing.

"I am not a pedophile!" the Midnight Slasher protested. "That's disgusting. I haven't gotten it down right yet, but I'm working on it, and I will be a master! I will learn to… Well, never mind! I will achieve what is necessary!"

"Whatever," Mason said dryly. "And she has one hell of a point, I mean, you want to be a master killer, get it all right… perfect it all. But you don't want to be remembered as a pedophile. That would…well, ruin your whole legacy."

"Yeah, yeah… I never touched any of them. Except to kill them. And I was going to get it all right this time, but you found a stupid boat and followed me and… Ah, screw it! But you're right. The pretty girl at the door can get me out of here, or… Well, I will be known for having killed a special agent! Yeah! Get in here, Special Agent Whoever. You come straight to me. When I can switch the knife over, this kid can go. But you need to know—if I die today, you die, too."

"I'm willing to accept that," Special Agent Della Hamilton said.

The killer laughed. "Suicidal, eh?"

"No, I just think I can talk you down," she said. "And frankly, you fascinate me! Your mind is so amazing! And I'm older, okay, and maybe this is only in my own mind, but I think I'm…well, sexier, grown-up, and just a better choice for a victim all the way around. If you want to be famous— kill an agent!"

"Talk me down? I don't think so. But I fascinate you? And you really are pretty damned gorgeous, so…hmm. Okay, lady, come on."

"I am coming—when this guy lets me!" she said, smiling and shrugging to Mason.

"Let her by!"

"She wants you to take the shot during the exchange!" the ghost of Gideon Grimsby said. The ghost's presence was near him. He all but whispered in Mason's ear, almost startling him.

But Mason was staring at Della Hamilton, and she nodded at the words. As if she had heard them.

Had she?

He'd heard there were others like him. He'd even heard there was a special "ghostbusters" unit in the Bureau with some nothing title like Special Circumstances Unit.

He inclined his head; she blinked, letting him know she had the message.

"I'm coming over…slowly, slowly, and I'll back up so you can free Melissa and get the knife right on me…"

She walked to him just as she had said she would do.

The killer moved the knife to push Melissa forward and reach out for Della Hamilton. And as he did, Della Hamilton dropped down, shouting, "Now!"

And Mason fired.

Melissa leaned to the side; Della was hunkered close to the floor.

The bullet hit the killer dead center in the forehead. While Melissa shrieked and cried with relief, the Midnight Slasher fell without a whimper.

The killer was dead. The reign of the Midnight Slasher had come to an end.

The wrap-up and the paperwork had just begun.

Naturally, there was chaos at first as other agents and police rushed in. The medical examiner and forensics arrived, and officers held the press at bay. Melissa's parents were called, but before she raced down to meet them, she fell hysterically into the arms of Della Hamilton and then Mason, telling them, "Oh, my God, thank you, thank you! Thank you, both. You saved my life!"

Mason assured her he was grateful she was alive, as did Della Hamilton.

Gideon Grimsby stood by the whole time, arms crossed over his chest, a proud look on his face. Well, the ghost did like helping.

Mason saw Della Hamilton manage a wave and a nod and mouthed the words, "Thank you," to Gideon at one point. Gideon smiled and nodded in return.

Mason turned in his firearm as necessary and was surprised to hear that a counselor was waiting to see him in the city. His Glock would be returned in the morning.

Things never happened that fast. He knew something was going on.

Mason was hailed by the waiting officers and agents, and he knew everyone was relieved a serial killer's spree had come to an end. He wished he could feel celebratory, and he knew he had carried out the only feasible action. But he didn't feel celebratory, just weary.

Of course, it had been just minutes before midnight when they'd taken down the slasher. With all the aftermath, it was the next day before anyone left the bayou country. And because of where they were, the press had finally arrived, but thankfully, by then the action was over and officers arranged to maintain the crime scene. People had a right to know what was going on but keeping details of such an event within ranks might prove to be extremely important.

He was ordered back to the city and the office before Della Hamilton finished a discussion with a member of the forensic team.

He didn't see her again until they were finishing the last of the paperwork on the case and by then everyone involved was about to keel over.

Sleep was in order. When he was finally able to return to his hotel, he had no trouble crashing down into a sound sleep—despite the fact that dawn had arrived long ago and the sun was shining brightly beyond the heavy drapes that covered his windows.

He woke in the middle of the afternoon. An evening left in NOLA, time to finish up any necessary business, and then a flight back to the DC area in the morning.

Luckily, they'd been so far back in the bayou country the media hadn't seen any of the takedown. And when asked, he assured the local powers that be he didn't want his name seen anywhere, which was the right policy as known field agents could be at risk.

A press release saying the Bureau had rescued the Slasher's latest victim and the man had been killed in the operation was just fine with Mason. He wondered if Della Hamilton was going to want more recognition.

She didn't.

Mason was out on Royal Street, trying to decide on a restaurant for dinner, when he looked into a shop front and saw a TV screen showing the news.

The takedown had been perceived just as he'd hoped—a joint effort by the FBI and local authorities.

A lot of his friends at the local FBI offices and police precincts he'd come to know in NOLA had wanted to get together that night. And while he truly enjoyed a lot of the camaraderie and understood the feelings of many that a celebration was in order, he just wanted to be on his own that night.

He felt as if he needed to shake something off.

He decided then to go over to Magazine Street for dinner and hopefully some soothing music at one of its many restaurants. He was surprised when Gideon slid into a seat beside him there; he'd been nursing a scotch and listening to some great jazz, something that helped still his mind.

"You are a strange bird," Gideon told him.

"Why?"

"That fellow stole the greatest gift from so many—the gift of life. Mason, you stopped him."

"With your help, for which I'm grateful—"

"And the help of Della Hamilton. I hung around her awhile earlier. She's something, huh? As they say in your time, that girl has balls! Wait, she can't, can she. Guts? Would that be right? She has guts!"

"She saw you in a flash," Mason said. "And by the way, I am glad I brought a killer down. I'm just tired of... I took his life. I guess I hate killing."

"But you love *saving*."

Mason shrugged. "I will always act in the best interests of the victim. Let's listen to the music, huh?"

"Sure. There's a meeting tomorrow morning. Some bigwig with the Bureau is coming down tonight. He's coming specifically to see you—"

"Why? Wait a minute. Last I heard, I run by the NOLA office, pick up another agent to drop me and bring the car back for the next guy who needs it. How did you hear that? I'll be heading back to DC tomorrow."

"Maybe not," Gideon told him. "I heard Della talking to someone on the phone when she left the offices. She was going out, but that call changed things and she didn't. She decided she'd better get some sleep. You were busy tonight," Gideon told him, grinning. "You don't interrupt a counseling session, and then it was a long day! You were supposed to have some dinner, some downtime... You'll be informed. Apparently, this is...big. A couple of people are heading down from Washington just to discuss this with you."

"And they informed another agent before me—about my assignment?" Mason asked.

"I'm guessing it involves her," Gideon said with a shrug.

"And that would be a darned good thing. You couldn't do better, from what I saw."

"She was good, yes. But—"

Mason groaned. Strange. He'd wanted this job; he'd worked hard for this job. But after his years in the military, now he was wondering why. He was good at what he did. He was a good investigator—largely because of a lot of help from the dead. But he was also good at killing.

And it just seemed to be weighing down on him lately.

"Damn you, man!" Gideon said. His accent—which he had largely lost during the many years since his death—came back strong when he was angry. "There is a seventeen-year-old girl alive and in the arms of her family because of you."

"And Special Agent Hamilton, of course—or mainly," Mason said dryly.

Gideon nodded. "I was glad to see her. I hadn't met her, but friends saw her when she worked a case here not too long ago. The bank robbery out of Baton Rouge. They say she tricked the three—it was a woman and two men. That she got them into position by pretending to be a lost tourist, crying and desperate to find her way back to the airboat they'd been on. Anyway, she has a way that makes her excellent in this kind of case. But you! Stop it. When there is no choice, there is no choice. That teenager from today is going to need therapy for the rest of her life most probably, but she'll have a life. Do you know what that man—so called Midnight Slasher—did to some of his victims?"

"Yes, yes, I do."

"No, he wasn't a pedophile. He sliced them, Mason. Slashed and sliced them! Cut off their fingers and ears *while they were still alive.*"

"I do know," he said calmly.

Mason was glad he'd paid his tab. He stood. As he'd learned

to do, he pretended he was on a phone call as he told Gideon, "I am so grateful she is alive—and our local intelligence knew where to find him before he could hurt her. Truly, I am. I just… I guess I wish I'd been a negotiator. I'd like to talk someone down for a change."

"You talk them down when you can—you save the victim when you can't," Gideon said.

Mason nodded. "Yes, I know. Guess I'm tired."

"You should be. Get some sleep."

"I'm going to."

"Finish listening to the jazz. See you in the morning," Gideon said, and then he was gone.

That was the problem sometimes befriending ghosts. Since they were excellent at slipping away through crowds and even walls, it was extremely difficult to have the last word with them.

The following morning, just as Gideon had said, Mason found himself in an office with the "bigwigs" down from Washington.

Two bigwigs.

The one was an elderly man. Mason had heard of him. His name was Adam Harrison, and he was known for both his philanthropy and the fact he'd been instrumental in forming special units of the Bureau.

He was with another man, this one in his forties, a striking fellow with Native American blood and a stature that indicated hours in the gym—and probably out in the field as well.

This man was Jackson Crow.

Mason knew who they were. Everyone in the Bureau knew about the special, separate unit that was called in for bizarre cases that included cult activity, so-called witchcraft and cases which involved "haunted" buildings, "werewolves," or any other strange manifestation. They had an amazing record for resolving cases, and while they were teasingly called "the ghostbusters," the Krewe of Hunters were also highly respected.

He had thought at times about seeking an interview with Adam Harrison or Jackson Crow. But he'd discovered he was good at working alone. He wasn't married and he didn't have children. That meant he could keep going at any time he wanted on his own—all day and into the night—when he was hot on a trail.

But now, he was intrigued.

He had been called in by them. He was sure that meant they'd been observing him from afar.

And they knew.

Just as he had known the truth about the Krewe.

That morning, the three of them were alone in the office. When the introductions were done, Jackson Crow began his speech.

"Due to recent developments, we're forming a new team, attached to our current unit. Loosely, we've been referring to our new operation as Blackbird—but officially, it will be the Euro Special Assistance Team. You'll be working with me as your immediate supervisor, and you'll still be stationed out of our Northern Virginia offices. But you'll be on the move a great deal—should you accept this, of course," Jackson Crow told him.

Mason shook his head. "Accept... I'm not sure what. I mean... Well, truthfully, I know you run a *special* unit, and you must know that I—"

"Speak to the dead. Yes, of course. Gideon didn't fill you in?" Adam Harrison asked him.

Mason's brows shot up. Then he grimaced.

He'd assumed the people who were selected for this unit

were found from across the country. Some were possibly found through the academy, and some because they stumbled into a case while working with other law enforcement or because they'd simply become involved.

Mason smiled, nodded, and leaned back. "I guess you've met Gideon."

"We started up in New Orleans," Jackson said. "We have many…friends here."

"Of course," Mason acknowledged dryly. "No, Gideon didn't tell me much. But Euro—"

"Yes, we're the Federal Bureau of Investigation, but the world has grown very small in the last several years. You are aware the Bureau has sixty legal attaché or legate offices around the world, as well as at least fifteen offices in our embassies in foreign countries?" Adam Harrison asked him.

He nodded. "Of course. I've been with the Bureau six years, ever since I got out of the service. Yes, I was aware. I admit—"

"We're federal, yes, and our focus is this country. But as Adam said, it's a small world these days, and when we have an American causing havoc abroad, conspiracies that involve Americans, felons we wish to apprehend abroad, hostage situations, and so on, we need a presence. Do we have great relationships with all countries? No. But with most of Europe and beyond, law enforcement likes to be reciprocal," Jackson said.

"Okay, so…"

"I was asked by someone as high up in the chain as you can get to begin this project, to open support on strange cases that stretch outside of the country," Jackson told him. "Someone who doesn't want to admit we have help from strange places— yet still wants to make use of our rate in solving crimes and catching killers—wants us to get a team to Norway as quickly as possible. They've now found four bodies, stretching from

France to England to Norway, completely drained of blood along with strange writing on the river embankments where the bodies have been displayed," Jackson said. "There might have been earlier victims here in the States. They are afraid the *Vampire* isn't working alone, or perhaps something even more sinister is going on. You'd work with Interpol and local police over there—"

"I don't speak Norwegian."

"Neither do I. The amazing thing is most Europeans speak English or a minimum of two languages, something I wish we were better at here," Adam said.

"You said 'a team'. So—"

"We'll be starting this with two agents and detectives from England, France, and Norway, as well as an Interpol liaison, a Frenchman named Bisset who seems able to get anything needed at the drop of a hat. And, you'll be working with support back here in anything tech or forensic. You'll be the first of a team with Special Agent Della Hamilton," Jackson told him, then nodded his head toward the door to the office.

It opened on cue.

And Della Hamilton walked into the room, wearing a pantsuit today, her long sweep of hair tied in a knot at the nape of her neck.

Very pro. When taking down the Midnight Slasher, she had made herself appear to be all casual and cute—and naive.

Today, the woman was all professional.

"Della, thanks. And Mason, you, too," Jackson Crow said. "First, we'd like you both to accept this venture. As I've explained, I hope you'll still be working with me. We have Angela—my wife and one of our first Krewe members along with a few others—and an amazing team of techs and experts in our offices to help with anything at any time. We really have a great team to deal with any evidence no matter how small. They're brilliant with video and so much more. So, here we are. We want you willing to begin this new venture, ready to accept it, and move forward. If you're hesitant, that's all right. We want you, for many reasons—"

Mason was surprised to discover he was slightly amused.

"You've been stalking me?" he asked.

"Not stalking!" Adam Harrison protested. "Heaven forbid!" Grinning, he glanced at Jackson.

"Of course," Jackson continued, amused as well, "we've done our homework. If you don't choose to accept this assignment, we'd still appreciate you accepting a transfer to the Krewe."

"I'd thought about requesting an interview with you," Mason admitted.

"Why didn't you?" Jackson asked.

"I guess I got used to working alone."

"And yet, you can't imagine the amazing abilities and teamwork that exists among our people," Jackson said. "Okay, to be blunt—no recorders in here—we know you have the ability to speak with the dead. We are a small percentage of a small percentage of the world population," he added quietly. "You've never worked with anyone who was just like you."

"No, I haven't," Mason admitted.

He was silent for a minute. He turned to look at the woman who would be his partner for the enterprise, curious as to her reaction.

She was looking at Jackson, nodding. "I've been reading about the killer they're calling the Vampire. He needs to be stopped—especially if he's gaining followers."

"We don't know that," Jackson told her. "Nor can we be certain he started this in the United States—"

"Our killer last night wasn't the Vampire killer on the move across the pond," Mason said. "He was slashing throats—not drinking blood."

"Right," Jackson said. "And he may not have known the Vampire, or wanted to emulate him."

"But...he did talk about *getting it right,*" Della said.

"Most probably not associated, but...the man you brought down was William Temple of Slidell. We've investigated his background and the profilers had it just right on him. He was bullied through school. He asked a girlfriend to marry him and she turned him down and took off—he drank heavily at several of the bars along Bourbon Street. He worked for one of the bayou tour companies until he was fired for unwanted attention toward female tourists—and calling them filthy names when they spurned his advances. He was evicted from his apartment off Esplanade."

"A killer, but hardly a brilliant one." Della nodded. "And again, nothing compared to the man leaving bodies in pristine condition and beauty, just devoid of blood."

"The display of the victims has become important now. One of our Krewe members, also a medical examiner, believes the victims discovered in the Florida Everglades and the Blue Ridge in Virginia might have been this killer's beginnings for murder—practice victims, one might say. They were also exsanguinated. While the throats on the victims were slit, because of other markings, Kat believes he was perfecting his ability to pierce blood vessels perfectly—and draw blood from the neck, leaving marks that could appear to be those left by *vampire* fangs. Right now we just know he's on a cross-country killing spree in Europe, either on his own or with an accomplice. Interpol is on it—officers from three countries are now on it. But I've been asked from on high to help, so..."

"I'm in," Della said. "Of course, you knew I would be."

"Thank you, Della," Jackson said. He stared at Mason. "Special Agent Carter?"

"I... Wow. I—I admit to being intrigued. Why us?" he asked, curious.

"Well, the obvious, of course. Della had been assigned to my office already when this came up. And, yes, we have watched your work."

"Someone else knows your record for finding resolutions to cases. Remember, I told you voices on high in the government wanted this, and they were adamant you were the man for the job, Mason," Adam Harrison told him. "But you're hesitating."

Mason shrugged and grimaced. "No, not really. Maybe I'm afraid of failure. This is important to many people, naturally, and I am hoping I am capable to stop—"

"You may be afraid. We're not," Jackson told him. He leaned forward. "Should you choose to accept this assignment—not *mission*, assignment," he added dryly, "you'll be leaving this evening."

Mason lifted his hands. "I've been chasing the Midnight Slasher for months now. I guess I thought I'd be getting a few weeks of vacation."

"You get this *Vampire*," Jackson said, "and I'll see to it you get a month's vacation after, if you wish."

"I..." Mason lifted his hands again. "Honestly, it's not that I need or expect so much time off, I just..."

"You may refuse," Jackson assured him. "This isn't for everyone."

"But should you?"

He turned to see Della Hamilton had spoken quietly and was staring at him, again, as if she read something in him, as if she knew more than he did about himself.

"I..."

He didn't know what it was about the way she was looking at him. Challenging him? Or seeing something in him he really wasn't sure of himself.

He looked from her to Adam Harrison and then to Jackson Crow.

"So," he said with resolve, "we're leaving tonight. I take it we'll be briefed—"

"Every file from every country will be sent to your inboxes immediately. Along with connections here in the home office for any help you need, and bios on the members of European law enforcement you'll be involved with. We will be planning a larger team, of course, but this came up suddenly. And they need our help. Also, one of the officials in Norway has a suspicion the Vampire might well be an American."

"American?" Mason said, surprised. "I understand there were similar killings here that *might* have been this killer's start-up. But now, the *display* of the killings has apparently stretched from country to county. Maybe he's gotten it all right where he wants it to be, but these killings have been in Europe—"

"I think, in the killer's mind, the killings have been perfected in Europe," Jackson said. "I believe the killer's *practices* were here in America. I have been involved in this for a long time, and I consider it an educated theory. You'll find everything you need will be sent to you, every piece of information or even supposition that we have. I've done all the reading on this and, trust me, there's plenty of reading material for a long flight."

Mason nodded.

"All right. So, tonight. When and how do we leave?"

"Private jet, Krewe jet," Adam told him. The older man shrugged. "I've been lucky in life. The plane is my gift to special agents who are…special."

"I'm packed and ready," Della said. She looked at Mason.

"I've been living out of a suitcase here in New Orleans. I'll get my things from the hotel."

"We'll meet up at Louis Armstrong International," Della said, rising. She nodded to Jackson and Adam. "I know we'll have cooperation, and I truly hope we'll do the Bureau proud."

"I know you will," Jackson said.

It took Mason less than fifteen minutes to collect his belongings from the hotel. The drive to the airport where he returned his rental car took another forty-five. He met up with Della Hamilton at the coffee bar in the terminal.

"You're here," she said.

"Of course, I'm here. I said I would be."

"But you don't seem pleased with the assignment."

"Oh, you're wrong," he said. "I'm just enthralled."

"You're just enthralled," Della murmured. "Strange choice of words."

"I was obviously being sarcastic," Mason told her dryly.

"I didn't miss your tone," she assured him. "It's just that we're headed for Norway. The word *enthralled* comes from *thrall*—which is what the Norse called the human beings they enslaved. People tend to think the Vikings were after gold and jewels—and they were, but they were also slave traders. They needed slaves to build their ships and sew their sails and work the land when it was workable, but they also found great wealth in the slave trade." She paused, shaking her head. "Humanity hasn't changed. Of course, it wasn't just the Vikings. The Romans were big on enslaving conquered people, and so on throughout history. And still, though we try to stop it, there are still some places today that enslave others. Anyway, the conquerors could be cruel. Some of the sagas that were written in Iceland in the fourteenth century portray the invaders as great heroes—and the thralls as dull and stupid creatures who needed owners since they were fit for little more than slavery. They've found iron collars and chains in archaeological digs, proof of man's treatment of man, or in slavery, more of woman. But anyway, being *enthralled* means you're basically enslaved by someone or something."

"Woah!" Mason said. "Woah, so, I'm traveling with a walking encyclopedia! But, hmm, you are hard on those people. Are you sure *you* should be going to Norway?"

She shook her head impatiently. "I hardly blame anyone today for the Viking age. It ended a long, long time ago. We call the Dark Ages the Dark Ages because that's what they were—dark. Torture chambers abounded! Oh, and I love Norway and the Norwegian people. My maternal grandparents were born there."

"Ah, that's why they're sending you," he said. "You know the terrain?"

"Hopefully, they're sending me because I'm a competent agent, capable of rolling with whatever comes up. And yes, I know some of the terrain, of course. We traveled fairly frequently when I was a kid."

"Rich kid?"

She shook her head. "My parents just knew how to make travel with the family into both a fun and profitable event. My mother was an artist and my father was a great marketer—he found buyers for her work all over in ad campaigns and the like. So yes, I know and love Norway."

"And the Bureau?" he asked.

She shrugged. "I was majoring in criminology when an old friend suggested I use everything I have to get bad guys. I went into the academy straight from college."

"A dead friend?" he asked quietly.

"Yes, a dead friend. You?"

"College, the military, more college, the academy. Oh, and on the enthralled—maybe I said it just right. I get the feeling you're something like me."

"Oh, I doubt that! And why—"

"Because work became your life at some point. Basically, we're slaves to it."

Della shook her head. "Not true. Or I don't see it that way. I'm still dedicated. I believe in what we're doing, and the fact we can get help sometimes from those who are gone—that not everyone can—is amazing. Don't you believe in what we're doing?"

Mason hesitated. "Yes, of course. Okay, honestly? I just... I don't want to kill anymore. Maybe what I thought I needed was a breather. Not that I would have preferred to have been killed myself, I mean..." He paused. He barely knew Della Hamilton, and he wasn't really ready to pour his heart out to her. But...

"Seeing so much death," he continued, "I've gained a marked appreciation for life. I have never killed in any circumstance in which I wasn't being shot at myself or in a situation in which it was necessary to protect another—an innocent, someone stunned and terrified to suddenly find themselves the target of a killer, or in the middle of a crime, war, or violence. But I wish I was better at...negotiating! Getting people to surrender. I... No matter what, it still takes something out of you when you take a human life."

"Yes, I agree," she said, "and everyone hopes to bring a suspect in alive because our job is to uphold the law while judges and juries do the rest. I understand how you feel. I was told you were a good guy. You are. No one wants to kill, Mason. But sometimes, negotiation doesn't work, and we must care about the victim first. Negotiation is great, but when there is no choice... Well. And honestly, I guess you haven't had much chance to read about this *Vampire* yet, but... Mason, he's a truly terrifying figure. And if he has others joining his ranks... Mason, you do know there are groups of people across the world, I believe—I know of a few in the States—who call themselves vampires, right? Some just meet and drink one another's blood. Some say they are spiritual vampires, and claim it's in a good way—they can gain kindness from others and all that. But...if this guy really thinks he's a vampire, we may be looking at worse things to come. At one time, people believed in blood-sucking vampires—diseases that destroyed the blood caused that kind of theory. In the 1800s, even in the United States, people dug up their loved ones to stake them through the heart or burn their hearts, afraid they were coming back to drink their blood when in truth, the disease was just spreading. But—"

"I don't think this killer believes he's a vampire, though if he is seeking followers, he'll want to convince them he is a supernatural creature. I believe he'll be like the guy we just got—probably handsome or charming enough to lure victims. Somewhere in his twenties or thirties. Thirties, I think, old enough to have gotten clever enough to clean up a crime scene and have the finances to pull off what he's doing. He'll be making sure he gets a lot of press all over Europe. He wants the fame or the infamy."

"You spent time with profilers?"

"I did," he said. "And we all know a profile can be wrong—but most of the time, it turns out to be right on. Let's hope we have good help once we get there."

"We will. And we have tons and tons of time to study all the files on the plane. Mason, we can make this work. And I know you're a loner. This is the first time you've worked with a partner and a team in a long time. But I swear, I've got your back."

He nodded. "I've uh… I'm sorry if I'm…difficult. You're right. I've been on my own for a few years now. And—I swear—I've got your back, too."

She smiled. "Hey, I've gotten to see you do that already. And I'm so sorry. I heard. I heard your last partner was killed in the line of duty," she said.

He nodded, looking away, and not sure why he didn't want to look at her.

Yes, Stan Kier had been killed. Mason had been nearby when it happened, and seeing Stan, he had felt a burning fury. Perhaps there had been no choice, but the searing sensation of anger and hatred he'd felt when he brought down the killer had been horrible.

There were things an agent had to do. Times when he had to kill.

But the amount of hatred he'd felt then…

It had scared the hell out of him.

It was just something he didn't want to ever feel again. Though he had to admit, it didn't come close to the pain of seeing Stan die. Stan had been a great guy, a family man, a friend.

He started, feeling her hand on his knee. He looked her way. In truth, he knew nothing about her.

"Like I said. Not to worry. I've seen you in action," she said.

"Yeah, thanks. And I'm sorry. I'm not sure if I ever said anything to you after the events in the bayou. You were amazing. For what you did in that cabin. That was…"

"Unorthodox?" she asked, wincing.

"I was going to say it was very brave. Coming in unarmed."

"I had a little Beretta hidden in my waistband," she said. "I also read up on you and I knew you were a crack shot. The SWAT director there was getting edgy. And while you are such a good shot and you'd have been fine without me, I figured a little help couldn't hurt. It can be hard to get a guaranteed clean shot. I had talked to Melissa's parents and... We just couldn't let him take out another victim."

"Well, then, thanks. You threw me. I had heard things about the Krewe of Hunters, but I didn't know you were with them—"

"Newbie," she reminded him. "Not quite a year. The Krewe was formed over a decade ago. In New Orleans, as a matter of fact. There were originally just six, and now we have dozens of agents, and it's good—we're all always out, all over the country."

"So you were down in this area with the Krewe before?"

"Right before I joined the Krewe I was on assignment as a field agent down here. In fact, it was almost right after the case I was on here that I had my interview—and found out they were real. I promise you, it's like...sanity in the insane world we've chosen to work in."

"And I think I still doubted in my way—since we're taught by our parents and families not to let other people think we're crazy—that what I'd heard could be real, that the Bureau *really* had a unit in truth that was composed of..."

"Weird people like us?" she asked, grinning.

He nodded.

"As I told you, I'm still fairly new to the Krewe. Well, not that new, almost a year. I went to the academy, started in the field, and then my supervisor told me I had an interview with a special unit," she told him. "I believe sometimes the head players at the Krewe know from our records or cases... Well, they have it themselves so they recognize it in others. They seek people from other law enforcement agencies as well. I believe Adam Harrison and Jackson Crow are pretty amazing at studying situations." She paused, smiling. "It's a wonderful place to be, with others like us, and they just have that talent for determining who the *weird* people are. And instead of hiding and feeling weird, we get to see that it is amazing, this ability we have, because it's like so many things with DNA, just a fraction of a fraction of the population has it, so..."

"Hmm."

"Hmm?" she asked.

He smiled. "I wonder if Norwegian ghosts will speak any English."

She smiled in return for a minute, and then she was dead serious. Her eyes were a true green he realized—like emerald lasers the way she was staring at him. "We're going to make this work," she told him.

"All right. We're going to make this work. Partner."

Her phone was ringing and she answered it quickly and told him, "Our plane is ready and the pilot is aboard. I understand the plane is great. So..."

"On to hours of reading in the air," he said.

"We are going to work well together," she vowed.

He forced himself to nod. He had been so uncertain; and then again, as Gideon had said, she had balls. And she was *unorthodox.*

He might even like her. He imagined she was an excellent agent, able to use her natural beauty and abilities in her investigations and takedowns.

Yeah, he liked her. But he was going to be careful.

He vowed he wasn't going to like her too much.

Because nothing changed the fact there were kill-or-be-killed situations.

It wasn't a good thing to become too involved with a partner—not in their line of business. He'd learned that the hard way. And he'd worked on his own—with plenty of backup, of course—for several years now. Working as a loner had its advantages.

He would have her back. And he'd try to be a team player.

He just couldn't lose another partner.

CHAPTER TWO

Crime scene pictures tended to be horrific.

And as far as that went, Della had seen far worse: bodies shredded and covered with blood, bodies broken and rotting with bones protruding.

And these were perhaps more horrible because of the very fact the dead appeared to be doing no more than sleeping.

The victims had been left like angels, laid out as if with loving care. But there was no loving care involved in the murders, and the angelic display of the bodies was a mockery.

Della closed her eyes and leaned back for a minute.

Leaning back was comfortable.

As far as travel went, Della decided, being with the Krewe of Hunters was proving—beyond the obvious simple ability to be honest about her "sources"—to be a very nice thing.

The jet had a small galley, desks, comfortable reclining chairs as well as couches, and could easily fit eight to twelve people if necessary. There was availability for agents to sleep on long flights, and she just might take a nice long nap while they traveled.

After she had set all the information available to them in her mind, she could do whatever she wanted to do—something new for her.

On this flight, it was just her and Special Agent Mason Carter.

She remained curious—and a little uncertain—about her partner. He was professional and cordial. And while she had refrained from saying anything to either Adam Harrison or Jackson Crow, she was just a wee bit afraid he was going through a bit of a mental crisis. But she had seen him in action. He was an excellent marksman. Whatever he was going through, he wasn't letting it affect his reasoning. Even though they had never worked together before, had never even met, her ploy had gone off brilliantly. She didn't disagree—talking the man down would have been a good thing—but saving another life had been their prime objective.

They couldn't let the "Midnight Slasher" kill again.

Of course, they'd had help in the little shack—Gideon Grimsby, pirate, revolutionary, and all-around intriguing man, even if he was a ghost.

She'd had a few interesting conversations with Gideon Grimsby, who apparently knew Mason Carter well. Gideon had assured her she'd seldom find a more professional or ethical man. And if and when it was necessary, he would have her back. She knew that; he'd read her signals clearly in the little shack. If she'd had doubts, she'd have never played it as she had.

There wasn't an *if* for them in the field; there was only a *when*.

Yes. She didn't know if she would have attempted what she had if she hadn't heard he could *hit a fly's eye at a thousand feet*. It was a wild exaggeration for anyone, but he excelled with firearms. Experience. He'd been in the military.

Yes, of course. She believed he would always have her back. Or…

She hoped.

No, she was certain—or else she *would* have spoken. Cops and agents and other law enforcement often waged wars within their own minds.

And if she ever met anyone who found it easy to kill—even in self-defense—that would be when she needed to worry. Then again, there were times when a person's crimes had been so cruel, brutal, or atrocious that when a shootout occurred, it was difficult to feel more than relief when such a heinous human being went down.

Mason Carter was seated across from her, heavily involved in reading on his tablet. She returned her own focus to the matter at hand. It was going to be important to know every little detail regarding the killer they were seeking.

The "Vampire" had begun his European killings in France, according to the briefs they had been given to read. His victim, Colleen Denton, an American tourist, had been left on the bank of the Seine, not in the water but rather displayed on her back, hair spread out around her, hands folded in prayer on her chest.

Death had been by exsanguination. Pinpricks at her throat appeared like the movie version of a vampire bite. She had displayed no defense wounds, but at autopsy it was revealed that she had been given a sedative. And there had been something odder. The "pinpricks" had been caused by human teeth.

They had DNA.

The killer had grown bolder in London, England. His victim, Isabelle Ainsley, a local girl, had been found on the banks of the Thames. Written in the dirt in the embankment had been the words *Dracula lives!* Cause of death, again, exsanguination. She had also been drugged.

And in death, she'd been laid out with her hair spread around her, hands folded in prayer on her chest. The killer had somehow eluded traffic cams, security cams, and any business or personal cameras.

Both victims had last been seen at local bars. Both bars had cameras, but the girls had walked out alone beyond their range. Their cars had been found parked where they'd left them when they arrived.

Each had been gone for three days before their bodies had been discovered.

It had not been so with the killer's third victim; she had also been left on the embankment of the Thames, but Leslie Bracken, another American tourist, had been found the morning after she disappeared. Police had searched every known business and residence for miles, seeking some help from a security camera. They had put out a call to locals and tourists alike.

Nothing.

Written in the earth by her side had been the message, *They who sacrifice their blood live on forever, for life-giving red harbors and extends the beauty of the soul to the ages.*

"Sick," she murmured.

"Pardon?"

She looked over at her new partner. All in all, she decided, he was, at the least, a formidable-looking companion. She thought he was six-four or six-five, straight as a poker when he stood, leanly muscled and broad-shouldered. His hair was so dark it was almost black, and his eyes were so deep of a blue they could appear to be black as well. He was an enigma. Well, that was a given, of course—she had only met him in the little shack where he had taken down the Midnight Slasher before the man could kill again—or so much as scratch her flesh as she made her strange exchange.

Surely somewhere along the line, they would talk. Or he would talk—she felt as if she had talked a lot.

She smiled. He was staring at her and frowning. She realized she had spoken the word *sick* out loud.

"The killer," she said quietly. "I—I'm sorry. This is an organized, but sadly deranged person. Sick. I was reading what he wrote—"

"Want to know what I think?" he asked.

"Sure."

"I think it's all a con. I don't think this bastard believes he's doing anything for anyone. He has some kind of an endgame. He's seeking all the would-be vampires out there. Which is as scary as he is—we don't need anyone else picking up on his game."

"Right, but... Mason, this guy must have had dental work to sharpen his canine teeth enough to allow him to puncture his victims' arteries."

"Yes. And our intelligence agencies and others have been seeking information from dentists. Semi-crazy people have been known to do such things before, but never that I'm aware of with this kind of—as you eloquently put it—*sick*. Trust me, there are people out there who think they are vampires. There are cults where they share blood."

"I know that—but they share *each other's* blood."

He nodded. "As far as those we know about—who admit to it—yes, they do. And there are those who claim to be psychological *vampires* who feed off the spirits of others, seeking only to give and take goodness." He shook his head. "This killer doesn't fit into any of those categories."

"What are you thinking?" Della asked.

"I'm thinking this person *isn't* crazy."

It was Della's turn to frown. "But if he's walking around with vampire fangs, I would think he's a little crazy. He probably doesn't have a lot of rational or normal friends. Or family."

"Ah, but define friends and family. Otherwise, if he's walking around with vampire fangs, I keep thinking someone would notice eventually."

"But…" Della began. She paused, shaking her head. "I'm not sure what you're saying. The MEs in all cases have said the teeth that made the puncture wounds were human. And they left DNA. How would you do that—and not have the teeth attached to a human body?"

"I'm not sure. I do have an idea. He does have human teeth, and he gets human saliva on them, but they aren't his teeth."

"Ah, now there's a theory."

"And this killer is organized. He obviously moves easily throughout Europe—through countries that are and aren't in the European Union. Norway is part of NATO, but not part of the European Union. He needs good ID to be doing what he's doing, real or false. And hopping that many flights— with what social media is today—someone would have noted something about a man walking around with vampire fangs."

"So, he somehow hides the teeth—or slips them over something? That is a better idea than trying to figure out how he does his globe-trotting while keeping his mouth shut."

Mason shrugged, gazing out the window. He shook his head. "I don't want to make any assumptions yet. Maybe I will make just one—and we agree on that one—he is organized. I believe he's also intelligent—"

"I'm not sure how organized and intelligent yet. And I don't get it. Why the DNA left behind?"

"It's done on purpose. It's DNA that doesn't connect in any system or with a suspect since we don't have one. He's gotten away with several bizarre murders, obviously committed by the same man or, at least, the same method. Look at history.

The Golden State Killer got away with rape and murder for decades before he was caught—"

"Ah, but DNA did him in. Now, we have DNA. But this DNA—"

"As I said, DNA is only good when you have a suspect with whom to compare it. So, we need to hit the ground running and find suspects. We are better equipped today than in the past, but I don't know. Something about the teeth is really bothering me. I told you my theory—which means this guy could be getting the saliva or DNA to put on the teeth. When you have no prints and DNA that's part of his game, there's little to go on. And finding this guy could be ridiculously difficult because it seems as if he's watched too many crime documentaries. Depends on how he's playing all his globe-trotting. The BTK murderer had a family—and got away with heinous crimes for a very long time. This *vampire* has given himself his own name, much like several who came before him. Something about it just… I don't know. Something isn't right. This killer plans on getting away with his crimes while creating a media sensation. The notes on the embankment… the whole thing with the teeth…he wants to taunt law enforcement and he is outrageously confident."

"I don't care how confident he is. We can't let him get away with this!"

"I'm just saying he might be someone walking around as rationally and normally as anyone else. Don't forget, Ted Bundy was considered charming."

Della nodded thoughtfully. "Charming. And he was under arrest in Salt Lake City, escaped, and committed three more murders."

"You weren't even born when he was executed," Mason said, watching her. "Ah," he murmured, "you studied serial killers."

"Right. I wasn't born. So? What were you then? Five?" she asked him.

He grimaced. "Yeah, well, something like that. Yes. We've both studied the past. Something important to do." He grinned. "I'm a big believer in the philosopher George Santayana. 'Those who cannot remember the past are condemned to repeat it.'"

She nodded. "Of course. We both went to academy. But I'm also from Florida. My mother… Well, I guess even those who were against the death penalty wanted to see him gone. There's a song called 'Windy' by a group, The Association. People in the state were singing it with changed lyrics. 'And Windy has stormy eyes' was changed to 'Ted Bundy, you're going to die.' There was also a line in the changed lyrics that went 'who's gonna fry like microwave pizza, everyone knows it's Bundy!'"

Mason looked out the window again. Della surprised even herself when she leaned across the space that separated them, setting a hand on his knee. He looked at her, startled, but she was surprised by the emotion she felt as she told him, "I talked to Gideon. I know you're feeling badly about—about killing people. But sometimes, there's no choice. I don't mean to be beating a dead horse here, but…this is a truly monstrous killer. You wanted to get the Midnight Slasher to surrender. He didn't. You had no choice. And if he had eluded us, he would have killed again. And this killer…you know he will kill again, and again, and again. And it's truly frightening he might have followers."

"Right. I know. And…"

"What?"

He shook his head, indicating the files they had on the killer known throughout Europe as the Vampire.

"He has his display—his way of taunting police and media.

But I don't believe he thinks he must follow his protocol if someone is in his way. I believe this person will kill thoughtlessly at any given moment. I believe the person we're looking for is a true psychopath in every sense of the word. The death of an innocent human being means absolutely nothing to him at all. Anyone is expendable."

"So, what do you make of the writing in the dirt on the river embankment?" Della asked.

"It's a game. It's all a game. Like I said, he's taunting us."

"So, we've determined he's not just a sick killer?"

"We don't know yet. There are several theories we could go by. Any idea we have right now could be wrong. We're going to have to find suspects and more evidence."

"All right. The cause of death is exsanguination. Method—human teeth. He doesn't leave behind a drop of blood. Then he displays his victims as if they are images of Snow White ready to be awakened. Of course, there are several theories. But I think we both believe he's an organized psychopath."

"Hopefully, we'll find out the truth—or at least something that will lead us to the truth—once we get to Norway."

"I haven't found the reason they suspect this killer is American."

He smiled at her. "Harbor."

"Pardon?"

"His spelling. He wrote in English. But he didn't write *harbour*, he wrote *harbor*."

"Hm. If this guy has an endgame and he's so smart, wouldn't he have thought of that? Maybe it was just to throw us all off."

"Maybe. Anything is possible. You looked at the cases Jackson researched that might have been the killer's *practice* killings?" Mason asked.

She nodded, then shook her head. "Again, we just don't know. Mary Salazar, killed three years ago, found in the Everglades, throat slashed with an incision that would control the flow of blood—and no blood found at the crime scene, so she was killed elsewhere. But no teeth marks. She was, however, lain out as if she were asleep. Local law enforcement found her before she became a meal for any local scavengers."

"And Andrea Milton, found in the mountains of Virginia, same details. Both cases unsolved. Both bled dry. But knives used, perhaps even scalpels. Nothing left behind, though the bodies were found within twenty-four hours. Killer had to have worn gloves—and if there was anything at all, well, nature took care of getting rid of it before forensics had a chance. Both cases remain open. Families were checked, obviously, boyfriends checked out, alibis solid… The police were left with nothing."

"Our Midnight Slasher seemed to think the Vampire had fans or perhaps…others who were cohorts with him. Of course, he could have been talking out of his—" Della began.

"I don't think the Midnight Slasher knew the Vampire or anything about him," Mason said, wincing. "I think he wanted…well, that kind of mythical fame. I hope there isn't more than one person killing at this rate with this method. Let's also hope you and I can find something solid. Something others have missed. Again, travel like this takes money."

"The young women found in the US might have been the first victims for our killer. We may need to start looking at CEOs."

"Possibly," Mason agreed. "And that's the word of the hour. We possibly have two American victims—starters as he learned how he wanted to kill. We have a victim in France and two in England. All three with puncture wounds from canine teeth. We do have DNA—but it matches nothing in any system. Norway now. We know he moves about easily.

There might be more than one person on this crime spree, but I think it unlikely."

"We have to get this guy," Della said with decisiveness.

"We will get him," Mason assured her. "Because we won't stop. And we're not alone. The murders in the states were handled by the local police without a connection to other events that might have been pertinent. It's different now. No one is saying exactly who wanted us in on this, but someone at the Krewe brilliantly put all this together. We will have what others didn't until now—a team, law enforcement from the countries involved and from Interpol and the investigative brilliance of the Krewe offices back home. We can't stop— because he won't. We will get this guy."

Della nodded gravely. Maybe, deep in her heart or mind, she hadn't been sure about Mason Carter.

Now she was. And she realized they would stop the man so proud to steal the lives of others as the Vampire even if it killed them both—literally.

From their landing in Norway, the small but beautiful town of Lillehammer was a two-hour ride. They were picked up at the airport by Jon Wilhelm, chief on the investigation from the National Police Directorate.

Mason quickly found the man to be direct, competent, and ready to work with assistance from afar. He also spoke English perfectly and even with an American accent, that from having headed to Yale for his college years. He was a man of about fifty, Mason thought, one who had handled the most serious cases throughout Norway, and who seemed to believe the killer was indeed an American.

"It is possible, of course," Wilhelm said, glancing quickly at Mason through the rearview mirror, "that he wrote as he did to throw everyone off."

"We've thought of that," Mason said. "For all we know, the killer could be from any continent."

"Web translator will get you far," Della murmured, watching the terrain as they drove.

"When you've rested, we'll get you to the site where the bodies were discovered," Wilhelm said.

"We don't need to rest—we slept on the plane," Mason assured him.

"Enough sleep?" Wilhelm asked skeptically. "Hopefully, you'll enjoy Lillehammer as a base, at least. The town is truly charming, surrounded by mountains, filled with immaculately kept homes and businesses that are several hundred years old. The city and municipality came to prominence during the winter Olympics back in 1994. And the winter Youth Olympics in 2016."

"It's a beautiful place," Della said, glancing to the back seat and smiling.

"You've been here before?" Wilhelm asked her.

"My grandparents were from Oslo. I visited a lot as a kid," she said, turning to face Wilhelm.

"Ah, well, great. You'll know the lay of the land."

"Some," Della said. She hesitated. "I know the area is beautiful."

Wilhelm nodded. "Beautiful and often remote." He shook his head and stared straight ahead as he drove, seeing the road and more. "I was born here, but I'm now stationed in Oslo. Lillehammer...is not that big, and the murder rate is extremely low. We have had a specialist medical examiner here out of Oslo as well, Dr. Andersen. Things happen, yes, but..."

"The Lillehammer Affair," Mason murmured.

Wilhelm glanced back at him. "Yes, of course. There hasn't been a murder here in over thirty years when Mossad agents arrived in Operation Wrath of God, hunting down the man responsible for the massacre of Israeli athletes, among others, at the 1972 winter Olympics—and killed the wrong person. Disaster for all involved, an innocent man paid the price. And the world trembled because… Munich was a horrible affair, but the death of an innocent man is a tragedy as well—and hatred creates more hatred. We learn, of course. We seek justice not retribution, but I imagine it was hard for many not to want dead a man who caused the deaths of so many. That was long ago. Lillehammer is a beautiful and generally peaceful place." The police chief paused, as if remembering the grim cause for their being in Norway. "Asta Dahl was found by hikers—they tried to wake her up at first. I was called out to take the case. They had moved the body, but just to try and wake her up. She looked like a princess out of a fairy tale—just needing a kiss to be awakened." He let out a long breath. "And we were back at the crime scene with our forensics people, trying to find anything that was a clue or a lead, when we found Brenna Arud." He paused a minute.

"This killer has struck in France, England—and now here. Once in France, twice in England, and here…two," Mason murmured.

Wilhelm looked back quickly in the rearview mirror at Mason. "Do you think he'll move on again already? Or that he has already done so?"

Mason shrugged. "I do believe he's traveling with an American or European Union passport—probably forged, or perhaps he has several. He's traveled easily between countries. But he's gotten away with his killing spree thus far—perhaps he will decide to strike again here. He may be feeling extremely confident."

"We *really* must stop this killer before he strikes again," Della murmured.

"Okay, you're sure you don't want to settle into your rooms in Lillehammer?" Wilhelm asked.

"No, thank you," Mason told him.

"Right," Della agreed.

"Then we'll pass by and head to the base of the mountains. It's on foot from there. After, we will meet with Dr. Andersen and our Interpol liaison, François Bisset, at the morgue."

"That sounds like an excellent plan," Mason said. He looked out the window at the land they passed.

The landscape was beautiful. Rolling hills, lush foliage, the mountains a creative beauty in the background.

Mason had been in Norway before, but like many foreigners, he'd gotten to Oslo and then up to Bodø, a spectacular trip in which he'd seen the midnight sun. But if there was one thing he'd learned in years of law enforcement, most people were the same everywhere. Most people sought lives in which there was a home and a desire for love, be that from a spouse, children, family, or friends. Most people sought happiness without violence or bloodshed.

Goodness came with every nationality, ethnicity, gender, and sexual orientation.

Just as human evil might be found anywhere as well.

As they drove, Mason could see the town across the river. It appeared charming with its many late-nineteenth-century wooden buildings rising only a few stories, not like towers to the sky. It was a setting for a fairy tale, he thought, and then remembered the victims had been left like sleeping princesses just awaiting true love's kiss. The mountains rose with nature's beauty on this side of the water, and Wilhelm took a turn that led up a winding path. He parked the car, saying, "This way."

Mason and Della exited the car and followed where he led. Jon Wilhelm paused before starting up a trail to tell them,

"Hikers come here, or just nature lovers, not climbing too far. You are likely to see a lot of trees—"

"Noted," Mason told him, grinning as he swept out a hand to indicate the heavy growth of trees to each side of the trail they were about to take. "I'm not an expert, but..." he paused to point "...there. Birch...then a group of gray alder trees. And..."

"Downy birch, and over there, aspen, and rowan," Wilhelm said. "You do spend some time in forests at home, I take it?"

"I like forests," Mason assured him.

"And you, Special Agent Hamilton?" he asked Della.

"Who doesn't like a good forest?" Della said. "My natural habitat is a bit different. Very wet. I grew up near the Everglades."

"Ah! Well, no alligators here. But we do have wolves, bears, and other carnivores. But you're most likely to see some squirrels, maybe a few bats...possibly red deer or elk. So, while we're here under horrific circumstances, I hope you like the land."

"I'm beyond impressed already," Mason assured him. "The drive was beautiful, though, yes, the circumstances are horrific."

"Well then, follow me. There are clearings up here. Sometimes, folks bring picnics. Norway is a beautiful country from our glacier mountains on down to the valleys—and as I've said, our crime, our violent crime, is low, and this..."

"I'm sure this is beyond horrific to everyone here," Della said. "We're both good hikers, so let's head on!"

Wilhelm nodded and started off. The walk was a steep incline, but while the path was earth and scattered rock, it was solid and the walk was good. Even as summer neared, the mountain air was crisp and clean, sweet to breathe in and out.

At last, Wilhelm stopped.

Forensic markings remained to show them where the body had been.

"This is the site where we found the first victim," Wilhelm said. His voice was grim as he stared down at an evidence marker showing where the young woman had lain. "I believe you've been given the information we have on Asta. She was a bank officer in Oslo, visiting the woods with a friend from America, showing her Lillehammer and the natural beauty all around. We found her body three days ago—her friend has been asked not to leave, so you may interview her later. The friend is Marlene Rogers from New York City. She cries when we talk—but we've ascertained so far that Asta was heading for the mountains and Marlene was just too weary to take the trek. They'd been out doing some drinking the night before."

Mason looked at Della who was already glancing at him.

"Easy enough path. She wasn't killed here—she was carried here," Della said.

"Correct. We have not found the place where this human monster carries out his crimes," Wilhelm said.

"Where is Marlene Rogers staying?" Mason asked.

"A hotel in town. But she'll be brought to the station tomorrow afternoon." Wilhelm paused again. "Asta had just turned thirty. Marlene Rogers is twenty-nine. Her parents arrived to be with her. They are all anxious to help, but naturally, the parents are defensive and protective of their daughter. They are anxious for her to come home, since…well, since obviously. She hasn't dragged herself out of bed since Asta was taken."

"Curious. She was coming here. She wasn't killed here—but she was found here," Mason said.

"As was Brenna Arud." He shook his head vehemently. "Two days after Asta was found, Brenna was found! We have forest personnel, we have police, but…things like this do not happen here. In the past years—in all of Norway—we've averaged thirty murders or less. Our population is not quite five and a half million, but still. American cities with similar populations are often looking at hundreds of murders per year. We are good, and we are competent, and we're either friendlier, more stable people or we are dealing with laws better. That said…we don't have massive units to deal with violent crimes because we so seldom have violent crimes. Still! We had personnel on alert, and yet this monster killed again— and brought the body so near to where he had left the first! Brenna was also here from Oslo, her original home, where she was visiting with her grandparents. Her parents immigrated to the United States when Brenna was ten. She disappeared from Oslo but was found here. That site is just ahead."

When Wilhelm turned, obviously distraught, Mason set a hand on his shoulder. "Trust me, sir. We have cases in the United States in which dozens of law enforcement officers and agents run around wildly trying to catch monsters. Sadly, there are monsters out there who love to take risks and taunt law enforcement. But they do make mistakes. This man— monster, as you say—will make his."

Wilhelm nodded and let out a long breath. "As I told you, I was here for Asta—when Brenna was found. I can't help but…"

"You arrived when she was found," Della said. "There was nothing you could have done."

He nodded and shrugged. "Thank you. Thank you both. I am the man most frequently called when murders do occur. This just… Well, thank you."

He hurried on, walking uphill at a slant, and taking a slim path to the right, which brought them to another clearing. Again, evidence markers indicated where a body once lay.

Mason thought of the crime scene photos, of seeing the

beautiful young woman as she'd been lying here with her hands folded in prayer.

"There are many of these clearings along the trails?" Mason asked.

Wilhelm nodded. "We have personnel moving through in numbers now—but as you can see, the landscape is rich, beautiful, and can seem endless."

"We need a few surveillance cameras," Mason murmured dryly. "Though… Della, we need to call and get any tech footage based on the info we have from Lillehammer and Oslo. With Wilhelm's help, we can pull from banks and the like. Tourists can often help, too."

"I believe François Bisset, with Interpol, has been combing through all he can find from Paris and London," Wilhelm said. "I have had local police put out a call, but as I said, we are grateful for help."

"Trust me, we're grateful for help when we get it," Mason assured him.

"Really? There isn't a terrible rivalry between the Feds and the locals?" Wilhelm asked, grinning.

"For some, maybe. Not the agents and cops I know," Mason said. "Della?"

"Pretty much so, we just want to stop the crime," Della said cheerfully, looking up. She had hunkered down by the evidence markers, studying the exact position where the body had lain, the trees surrounding the area, and the path they had taken. "Wilhelm, only one way up here, right?"

"One path. I suppose you could climb through the trees and brush if you chose, but that would be difficult carrying a body," Wilhelm said.

"Difficult," she murmured.

Mason wondered if she might be on to something—if their killer might be taking a route through the trees and brush.

"Any bracken found on the bodies?" he asked Wilhelm.

"I suppose a few leaves attached to the clothing. Dirt, of course, they were left lying in these clearings, dirt beneath them, trees around them," Wilhelm said.

They would see the medical examiner soon enough, and there were questions he might answer for them as well. But Mason found it hard to imagine—even in a place as small as Lillehammer—that a man might have taken known hiking trails and not be seen by anyone at all.

Then again, they hadn't passed another soul today.

"I guess people are avoiding the area right now," Della murmured, her thoughts following his. She stood, looking over at him. "Thinking of a direction?"

Mason looked over at Wilhelm. "If you were trying to come up here without being seen, and you thought there might be others about, hiking, enjoying the air...from which direction would you try to reach this spot?"

Wilhelm cast his head at an angle, frowning. "I know the path, so I wouldn't be coming up another way. But if I was an organized murderer—who I believe would easily kill any-one in his way but might not want to because it would de-stroy his plan on displaying his victims—I would have started where we did. But I would have taken a direct route up. No gentle curving, but a real climb through thick foliage where one might encounter some angry rodents or other creatures. Maybe even a resting predator. But if one did come that way, they would arrive over there to your left."

Mason quickly strode over to the foliage, inspecting the trees. He had never been a forest ranger, but it didn't take sheer brilliance to study trees and bushes and determine if they'd been disturbed.

"Here, Mason," Della said.

She was about fifteen feet to his side and he joined her quickly. Wilhelm came behind him.

"As you Americans say, I'll be damned," he murmured.

A broken branch on an aspen tree gave way to thick brush with much of it disturbed. Della anxiously started to push ahead, heedless of the branches and brush that pulled at her clothing as she forged ahead.

At one point, a branch snapped back at Mason, and she paused and turned quickly.

"I'm so sorry—"

"Not to worry. Let's move on."

She pushed ahead. Then stopped suddenly. He almost plowed into her.

Wilhelm did plow into him and apologized quickly.

"No problem, we're on a mission," Mason said lightly. Della still hadn't moved.

"Della?" he said.

"There is a break here...as if there's another path leading... somewhere," Della said. "Look. It's narrow...but a path, I think?"

"I guess there are those who do choose to push on through bushes," Wilhelm said. "I am not sure if this will take us anywhere, but let's see."

Della remained in the lead, pushing forward. But as she said, it was something of a path although very narrow—and probably created by enough people cutting through the brush.

She suddenly came to a dead stop. Mason and Wilhelm right behind her.

"Oh, my God!" Della breathed.

He set his hands on her shoulders to step around her to see what she was seeing.

A woman.

The clearing here was small, almost half the size of the

other two they had seen. But it offered a circle within the trees, and at the base of a towering aspen, she had been laid out.

Mason thought he had never seen flesh so devoid of color. She had long blond hair, and it was splayed out as if her head were surrounded by rays of the sun.

Her eyes were closed, making it look like she slept peacefully.

Her hands were folded on her chest. A bouquet of wildflowers had been set within them.

She'd been wearing a long-sleeved velvet dress and the skirt of it had been stretched out around her so that she appeared to be a fairy-tale princess, indeed.

She had been young. Twentysomething, Mason thought, perhaps thirty.

He was startled when Wilhelm, at his side by then, suddenly cried out and fell to his knees, choking on a sob.

He looked up at Mason with his face knit in grief. "She was one of ours! My God, my dear God! This time, he's murdered an officer of the law!"

CHAPTER THREE

They didn't go to the morgue under the circumstances, but rather the medical examiner they were due to meet, Dr. Dag Andersen, came to them. It was important to get him to the scene as soon as possible. He would be the first to touch the dead girl in situ, offering his preliminary investigation. He arrived along with his assistants and a forensic crew. In minutes, another two new arrivals included Jeanne Lapierre and Edmund Taylor, detectives from Paris and London respectively.

They met and spoke only briefly and grimly. Dr. Andersen, his concentration on the corpse, did the talking. He believed the girl had been dead about twenty-four hours, exsanguinated like the others. In his estimation, someone adept with a needle and phlebotomy had killed her at another location, draining her blood in the same way anyone might take a blood sample—though not usually through the throat—except taking the drainage all the way. In his opinion, the *fang* marks had been added after death.

Della glanced at Mason.

His theory was probably correct. The *fangs* were sharp-

ened teeth the killer had gotten from somewhere. He probably used different saliva, but none of it was found in a DNA
sample in any database.

Della and Mason, just as Wilhelm, Lapierre, and Taylor,
were quiet as they listened to Andersen's preliminary findings.

But she observed the men. Lapierre was tall and straight,
white-haired, and probably in his mid-to late-fifties. He had
the look of a man who had been on the job a long time
and, while saddened, was no longer shocked by anything one
human being might do to another. She didn't think he'd be
where he was in French law enforcement if he wasn't capable
and accomplished.

Taylor was younger than Lapierre, either in his late-twenties
or early thirties. The Englishman was tall and broad-shouldered, serious and intense as he stood, listening. He was an
imposing man with dark eyes that matched his neatly clipped
hair, but younger though he might be, he had the same look
in his eyes. He was silent, grim, and thoughtful, and Della believed he'd be the kind of man to put his nose to the ground
and work a case with absolute purpose.

He had probably seen a lot in his years.

Detective Wilhelm stood as silently as the others, but she
could see he was hurting. He had known the young woman;
she had been a friend, and he had cared about her. Della
wanted to suggest he didn't need to be there, but she heard
Edmund quietly say he didn't need to suffer, and Wilhelm tell
him no because he needed to be there to know everything.

Edmund fell silent. Best to let Wilhelm deal with the death
in his own way as any of them might.

Sometimes it was just best to work a case.

Della stood in silence, observing Dr. Andersen, listened to
his assessments, and studied the members of their team they
were just meeting. Then Dr. Andersen finished his prelimi-

nary work and called his assistants. They'd be winding their way down a path carefully with the body to get it to the morgue vehicle. She saw something moving in the bushes.

She almost spoke out, but then she looked slightly uphill through a bank of trees and realized *someone* seemed to be moving, but not rustling the bushes at all, not causing the least bit of sound or motion.

A Norwegian ghost?

Forensic crews were working the area; she carefully stepped broadly around them and walked a narrow trail that led deeper into the woods.

"Della?"

Mason was calling her.

"Just taking a peek in a different direction," she called back. She hoped he would take on the necessary conversation with the French and English detectives and Wilhelm.

Maybe he would have trust in her, enough to let her follow this strange lead without coming after her and bringing the others along with him.

A Norwegian ghost. She winced. Because, of course, the question was there—would he speak English? She did know some words. As kids, they'd learned you always made a point of knowing the sentence, *Excuse me please, do you speak English?* in the language of any country they traveled to. And it was true she had seldom met people in the Scandinavian countries who didn't speak English, and often another language besides their own as well.

But a ghost…

She came upon him at last. He knew she was there, but his attention was on the proceedings.

Her fears might well be justified. This ghost had not died anytime recently, not unless he'd been buried in costume. He was clad in trousers, a linen shift, over-tunic, and a cape that was secured around his shoulders with a handsome brooch. His belt held a knife and an axe. And whatever his burial method, she was certain he'd been so clad when he'd been given his final send-off.

He'd been a mature man at death, but not an old one by current-day standards at any rate. He'd been about six feet tall, and extremely well-muscled. He'd shaved his facial hair while a massive sweep of blond hair was held up in a knot at the top of his head.

"Who are you, sir?" she asked softly, mentally trying to remember the words in Norwegian. But in his day, Vikings had spoken Old Norse or…various dialects of the same accrued in the different areas of the world where they'd roamed.

He looked at her, frowning, not certain she was speaking to him. But there was no one else around, so she was addressing either him or a tree.

"*Unnskyld meg, snakker du Engelsk?*" she said hopefully, hoping she'd retained some grasp of the language she had learned in bits and pieces from her grandparents.

"You are speaking to me," he said. "You see me, that I am here?"

She smiled. "That's why I'm speaking to you. But your English is excellent—"

"Madam, I died over a thousand years ago. In that time, I assure you, I've kept up. I am also fluent in the language of the French and Italians as well."

"How commendable. Well, then, how do you do, sir? My name is Della Hamilton—"

"American," he said, and she thought it wasn't without something of a weary sigh.

"Yes, American. I'm with—"

"The CIA?"

"No, sir. I'm with the FBI, and we're trying to stop these horrible killings—"

"If only you could," he said quietly. He shook his head. "In my day, I was a warrior. But I never slaughtered the innocent nor did my men. I was a warrior, and killed in war. And the concept of bleeding out an innocent maiden, well...far beyond what a warrior would do, far beneath any concept of honor!"

"Yes, sir, far beneath. That's why... Are you often here? Did you see who brought this young lady here and laid her out so? Or perhaps did you see the victim before?"

He shook his head slowly. "I spend my time with what friends I might be lucky enough to meet—not many stay behind, you know—in town. I am glad to roam such a beautiful place, but..." He stopped speaking, frowning and reflecting. "I do believe I saw that lovely young woman. There is a bar in town called Brager's. It's a charming place with screens for football games, as we call them, good food, fine drinks. I was there, watching tryouts...and I believe I saw her with a friend."

"Male or female?"

"She was with a girlfriend, and many men looked at the two pretty girls.

"Sir! You've given us something! I can't thank you enough."

"It may be nothing."

"It's far better than the nothing we have now," she assured him.

"I hope to see you again. In different circumstances," he said. "I haven't encountered a living seer in years and years now. Oh, I am Orm. Orm Olafson."

"Orm, thank you," she said, and she smiled. "I'm here with a partner. He is also a living seer. I know he will want to meet you when..."

"You are with a second seer?" he asked, pleased and amused.

"Yes. Um, in truth, I work with many living seers. There is a man who seeks us out among those who work in law enforcement, but...you will meet Mason Carter, I'm sure. And he will be so grateful for any help you give us, too."

Orm nodded solemnly. He indicated the little break in the trees that allowed him to look down on the medical team, the forensic team, and the detectives. "He is the exceptionally tall man. He rises over me. Time, of course, has allowed more people to grow to greater heights. I was a tall man for my age."

"I'm sure you were." She smiled and assured him, "A very handsome one."

He inclined his head as he smiled. Then he grew serious. "I will help in any way. Warriors go to battle against their equals. They do not do this to women and children."

She arched a brow to him. "You were a good Viking? Olm, I'm glad to hear that and curious as well. History shows Vikings often massacred anyone they found during a raid."

"We were warriors, yes. Plunderers. We invaded—we slaughtered. But we weren't one *we*. To go a-Viking, a man might come from anywhere in Scandinavia. Different leaders behaved in different manners. Oh, we were also settlers. Iceland, Greenland—and for a time, your America. We traded. Did I do my share of killing? Yes. But never a woman or a child. And sometimes, such a thing was not a matter of ethics—the slave trade was great in my day. Women and children dead were worth nothing. Alive, they might garner quite a price. And the..." He paused, shrugging. "The Norse founded Dublin, Ireland, you know. Admittedly, it was a large slave market among other things, but... I fell in love with a lady who might have been for sale to the highest bidder. Rather than chance the disapproval of those who thought I should marry elsewhere, I escaped with her to what is now Iceland.

Later, when Sven One-Eye was among the dead, we returned home—and my beautiful wife bore me eleven beautiful children. Of course, I will not lie. It has taken me a thousand years to know the error of my ways in my youth, but I watch the world now, and it never changes. In all nations, there are kind men and women with learned minds. In all nations, there are human monsters. We never learn that war and conquest bring nothing but tears and death."

Della was deeply touched by his words and the passion in them. "I would have loved to have known you in life!" she said.

He laughed. Her Viking had learned English well, and he also had quite a sense of humor.

"Trust me! Oh, no, no, no! You would not have liked me much in life. Of those I meet, some stay to right a wrong, to help descendants, or for a reason they discover at some point. I believe I stayed to learn, and it has been a journey that has given me great wisdom, so I am grateful. Oh! Not to mention all the languages I speak—or could speak with people were they to hear me—and at least understand."

"Well, sir, you are a most admirable ghost," she assured him.

He shook his head. "But I haven't seen who is doing this!" He frowned suddenly. "Maybe…"

"What is it?"

"Well, as I was telling you, I was in town. I do quite enjoy the modern sports bar—watching games and pretending I am imbibing fine ale. I was at Brager's a night or so ago and there was one of those fellows who watched pretty girls there and he was quite deep in his cups at the bar. He kept ordering *Bloody Marys*. Each time the barkeep would serve him, the fellow complimented him, but told him that sadly, no matter how good, they were never as good as the real thing. A

Bloody Mary, I understand, is vodka and tomato juice and whatever else hot stuff someone may like...but the real thing? A woman named Mary—who is bloody?"

"Drinking the blood of a *Mary*, or a woman, perhaps," Della said. "Orm, could you describe this man for me?"

"He may have been nothing but a blithering drunk!" Orm warned.

"But it's all we've got," she told him. "All we have now. Our technical departments from several countries are researching the DNA they've found—but so far, we have no hits. And we have nothing but bodies in the woods. If you could describe this man..."

"Once, I could draw!" Orm said. "Now...well, I can muss the dirt up a bit."

"If you tell me, I can do something of a sketch. I'm not much of an artist, but if you tell me everything you remember, I can tell a sketch artist. The sketch artist can do something with whatever I can come up with."

Orm nodded gravely. "Lean, but wiry, and not skinny, just lean, and solid. His face...no hair, no whiskers. Eyes...light. Perhaps blue or green. Shaggy brown hair. I believe that he appeared to be in his mid-twenties—thirty, tops. Silly fellow. Ah, yes! He talked about *the dig*. I believe archaeologists are here, researching and digging up an old settlement not far from town. He was an Englishman, I believe. The dig is made up of scientists from many countries, but this fellow... I believe his accent was English. Straight nose, slightly pointed chin, quick, good smile. I think he appeared fine to the women who were about."

Della had drawn out a pen and pad and done her best to sketch a face. She also wrote down what Orm told her.

She smiled at him. "Well, we may just question a drunk,

but then again…we have no other leads, and I am grateful for this."

He looked at her sketch. "Hmm. You're right. You're not an artist."

"But I am a good agent and investigator," she assured him.

He grinned and indicated the break in the trees. "I have no doubt. But now, I believe your very tall man, Special Agent Mason Carter, is looking for you, perhaps growing a bit concerned."

"Yes, I'm anxious for him to meet you, but…"

"The others down there—they wouldn't see me. They'd want you sent back to the United States immediately for psychiatric care."

Della laughed. "Something like that. But thank you. And I do hope to see you again. We will need and be grateful for your help."

He nodded somberly then. "To help is sweetness for my soul," he assured her. "If you are seeking me and do not find me, don't worry. I will find you."

He disappeared into the trees, and Della hurried on down to join the others.

"Anything?" Mason asked.

She gave him a smile, indicating she had something—but just for him.

"Where are we here?" she asked quietly, looking at the others. Then she apologized quickly in French for assuming they all spoke English. Lapierre laughed and assured her he was quite adept at English.

"My English friend speaks French, just as I speak English. We are but a hop across the channel from each other and have worked together before," Lapierre told her.

"Oh, well, that's…excellent," Mason said. He grimaced. "I can order coffee, a beer, and find the men's room in a few languages. Oh, and ask if others happen to speak English, say good morning, please, and thank-you."

"All appreciated!" Lapierre said.

"And," Wilhelm said, trying to offer a weak smile, "my English and French friends, do not mock our American friends. They speak a bit of my language, which is not at all common!"

They all grinned briefly, but their smiles faded as they watched the morgue attendants packing up to leave. Then Wilhelm cleared his throat and said, "We should get to head-quarters. Our Interpol agent will meet us there. And...now we have another dead woman, as I said, one of our own, Ingrid McDonald."

"We are so very sorry," Della told him. "If you need time—"

"No. I don't need time. I need to work. We have been given the ground floor space of a building on the block with the police, and they have kindly set us up with desks and screens and all else we might need. For Lillehammer... Well, it is known as a beautiful and peaceful place where people love all that surrounds them. We must solve this and soon."

"Agreed by all," Mason said. Della thought he'd had a good conversation with their French and English counterparts, and they would work together well as a team.

She fell back with Mason, letting the others lead the way. She didn't want to rudely whisper, but she needed to let him know about Orm and the man at the bar who had been drinking Bloody Marys. She did so, indicating the woods as if she were discussing something everyone already knew.

"He said something about a dig?" Mason asked her.

"An archaeological dig," she said.

"We need to ask Angela to get information on all the archaeologists and workers who are involved with the dig," he said.

"And maybe have a Bloody Mary," she said.

He winced. "Maybe a beer."

She grinned. "I have a sketch of a man we should be looking for. He apparently talked wildly. But how do I explain we have a possible lead?"

"Someone you met briefly on the street?" he suggested.

"They'll want to know—"

"We'll deal somehow. Now, let's get to our headquarters. Get the lay of the land. Oh, find out where we're sleeping… and reach home. Then we'll get on to the nightlife. Also, these fellows have some interesting information to give us."

"Oh?" she asked.

He looked at her. "English techs managed to get a hit on the DNA found in the bite marks of one woman."

"Oh?"

"I guess that someone is really trying to perpetuate the vampire myth," Mason told her. "The DNA matched a murder suspect—"

"Well, that's something! Who? We have a name?"

"Oh, we have a name," Mason told her.

"And?"

"The DNA belonged to a man named Judson Burns."

"Any clues on where to find him?"

"Oh, yeah. The man was a suspect in another murder in the States. He can be found six feet under, buried at potter's field on Hart Island in New York. He was murdered two months ago."

"So…"

"I believe we'll discover the DNA at other sites where the *fangs* were used at the throat will turn out to belong to dead men as well. How else do you perpetuate the image of a vampire—the dead who are the undead?"

The headquarters that had been set up for them was just about as perfect as it could be in a place where crime was rare and seldom violent, and investigators from different countries had determined to stop a heinous killer who might appear anywhere around the globe.

What had probably been executive office spaces at one time had been turned into interrogation rooms with doors that could be securely locked. There was individual space with desks and laptops for the agents and the detectives. A large computer offered standing space for their group with a massive screen. Every conceivable research program was available through the computer. And while Mason had found that facial recognition programs were certainly better than nothing, not even the best program could recognize the back of a person's head or the details of a face beneath a mask or disguise.

That was all right. Mason had been assured a call back to Angela Hawkins Crow could provide them with just about anything. She was so good that seeking information from her was almost as fast as a speeding bullet.

His concern was growing rapidly. Because he feared this killer was going to move quickly. It was wonderful to have this setup in Lillehammer, but the killer had already struck in London and Paris. There was no reason to think he wouldn't move on.

If it was a *he*, of course. Or a *she*. It might be a *they*.

The space they had been given offered a large whiteboard. From the time they arrived and surveyed the space, Della was at work—after having asked their colleague if they minded—marking out what they knew on the board in one section, what they were speculating about in another, and the information they had on the victims in yet another column. While she worked, the others chose spaces at the desks supplied in the room and discussed what they had so far and what the day had brought.

"My fear is we have a *head* vampire, if you will," Mason told the others. "And he is attracting a following. But I don't believe it's a case where he would just rile people up. They must do things his way and do them right. If I am correct, I believe our *head* vampire is responsible for *practice* murders in the United States and for the first murders—but we might discover he has taken on, trained, or allowed a recruit here in Norway."

Lapierre nodded gravely. "Yes, he will be very careful as far as allowing followers—he is pursuing a myth, or…"

"Or there's an agenda," Della said, turning around to look at them all. "But what the hell it can be, I sure can't figure yet."

Edmund nodded. "There have been cases in history in which a killer struck at random victims as a *serial* killer so the intended victim would be chalked up to someone who will never be caught. A bit like *Strangers on a Train*. If you have a solid alibi for a killing, you go free. And the first people we look at in a murder investigation are those closest to or rebuffed in some way by the victim."

As they spoke, Wilhelm glanced at his phone and then headed toward the door.

François Bisset, their Interpol agent, had arrived. They all rose to meet him, and Della left her board to walk over and join them.

Bisset was of medium height, a pleasant-looking man with soft blue eyes but a solid handshake. He quickly assured them they were the investigators. His job was to see they all accessed whatever they needed from local law enforcement wherever they might be, and to mediate with any difficulties they might have. As they spoke, Mason's phone rang.

It was Angela, and Mason excused himself to take the call.

"Anything new?" he asked her.

"We've been collecting information, of course, from all the law departments involved. We'll be the central point, getting all information to you at your European headquarters as soon as we gather it—that way none of you are tied to a desk. But I'm afraid it's as you feared. The DNA has been resolved on the cases in Paris and London. The first, as you know, was the suspected hitman, Judson Burns. That was the same on the first young lady discovered in London. But on the second, the DNA belonged to another man who was the suspect in the murder of a business executive killed on Baker Street. That suspect was Ned Romano—who died mysteriously in a London jail while awaiting trial."

"Mysteriously?"

"Poisoned."

"Ah. So, dead men are turning into vampires."

He could hear Angela sighing over the wire. "It doesn't matter that it's ridiculous. Sane minds will immediately eschew the idea these criminals are walking the world again as vampires now. The media will run riot if they get a hold of any of the details."

"What about this archaeological dig that's going on here. Can you compile—"

"I'm on it. There are at least forty professionals involved with it from eight countries: USA, Norway, of course, Denmark, Sweden, England, France, Italy, and Romania. As I'm sure you're aware, it's not as easy gathering all that's needed when our pool of people is from so many places. And not only do you have the professional archaeologists, including forensic archaeologists, historians, and so on, you also have paid workers who are catering food, digging in the dirt, and supplying support. It's a nightmare."

"Thankfully, I hear you're great with nightmares."

"Oh, yeah. This nightmare might just take a night," she said dryly. "Or more. But we're looking into everyone involved, hoping for something."

"All right. Thank you. Well, we have a lead that may or may not pan out. A new friend suggested to Della we should find a fellow who frequents a local bar and tells the bartender his Bloody Marys are good but don't compare to the real thing. We'll head over there soon."

"Keep me apprised," Angela told him. "And I'll report frequently, even if we have nothing to report."

"Ah, but you will have something to report. You're investigating those involved with the dig."

"Who may have nothing to do with it. The dig started up a few months ago. If this is one killer, they'll have had to have been in Paris, London, and then Lillehammer at the right dates—and if they've been working—"

"It's not that hard to move around Europe. Put a bunch of countries together and you're still not talking the full size of the US."

"There's still movement," Angela reminded him. "The techs and I will get all the information we need, but there's no guarantee—"

"Gut?" he asked.

"Pardon?"

"Gut feeling," he told her. "And while that's not scientific—"

"Sometimes, it's everything," she said.

"Thanks."

"Back to you later," she promised.

"Thank you again."

Mason ended the call, reflecting on Angela Hawkins Crow, Jackson Crow, Adam, and the Krewe of Hunters.

It was good to be where he was. Della was a charming human being—something that surely helped when they needed assistance from others. She was gifted at her ability to manipulate a situation. And after his phone call, he was glad to realize the Krewe had faith in their agents, and there was no argument with a *gut* feeling.

He returned to the others and reported on what Angela had told them.

"I'll speak with her myself," François Bisset said seriously. "You are field agents—I'm Interpol, here to facilitate whatever you need. I can keep the communication chain going while you work the streets."

"All right, then," Mason said. "So, Wilhelm, check at the morgue, please—"

"It has gotten late. The doctor won't start on the autopsy until the morning."

"Right, but please see if anything in the preliminary report positively identifies the same killer—or suggests more than one man is at work." He looked at Wilhelm. "Detective," he said, addressing Wilhelm, "you knew her."

"Ingrid," Wilhelm said quietly. "Ingrid McDonald, father a Scot, mom from Trondheim, good people, and not in the country right now, but…"

"Can you find a way to locate them?" Mason asked. "Before any information gets out. We don't want them seeing information about their daughter's murder on a newscast."

"I'll find them," Wilhelm promised. "I advised her superior already, so yes, I must reach her family."

"Then, I think you'd be best at looking over her last cases, finding out if she was on to the killer in any way, if she left any information…or if she kept a diary and just met a charming man at a bar and was looking forward to seeing him again."

"Yes," Wilhelm said again. Angrily, he shook his head. "Now they strike at the heart of us! He, they—the killer or killers—we must end this reign of ridiculous mythic terror."

"And we will," Della promised him gently. "We have a solid team here—we will discover this killer, whether he is truly crazy or leading a team for an agenda."

"I think we should hit the streets," Edmund said, nodding toward Lapierre.

"Agreed," Lapierre said.

"Exactly what I was about to ask you to do," Mason said. "Cruise the area, especially looking into coffee shops, eateries, and so on. Keep eyes and ears open for anything you might see or hear."

Both men nodded. "Where will you be headed?" Wilhelm asked him.

"A bar," Mason said.

They all stared back at him—including Della—and he grimaced, nodding her way. "Angela had a report on someone speaking wildly at a place called Brager's—"

"Great sports bar," Wilhelm said knowingly. "And here I was thinking Americans couldn't stomach a few hours without a drink!"

"We're going to go and see about a Bloody Mary–drinking fellow who talks about the drink not being as good as the real thing," Mason said.

"You're going to go to a bar and not drink?" Lapierre asked politely.

"Let me suggest a Lervig—there are several different varieties—and if you stick with beer or ale, you can have one or two and not want to belt your wild Bloody Mary–drinking suspect," Wilhelm said. "If you want to get this man talking, I believe you'll want to blend in."

"Good point, well-taken," Della assured him. "It will be great to sample a Norwegian beer."

Wilhelm grinned at her. "Partial to Heinekens myself," he said.

"Whatever!" she teased in turn, smiling.

"So, let's move," Mason said.

"One second, *s'il vous plait!*" François Bisset said. "That desk—anyone claim it yet?"

"Yep, you," Mason assured him.

Then, finally, they were back out the door. Wilhelm pointed out the pub, a place within easy walking distance. The building itself was a charming Victorian as much of Lillehammer, wooden, offering porches with benches and tables as well as an inside eating area. The bar itself was crafted of mahogany, handsome and well-polished. Della headed straight for the bar, took a seat, and he followed.

They were lucky to find seats. The hour was growing late, and more and more people were out for the evening. Two old codgers were arguing in a friendly manner at the end of the bar, while two couples were to their left and another couple was to their right.

Looking out at the tables, he wondered if a group that included two women and four men might be with the dig outside the city.

The bartender, a fellow who looked like he could have chosen a career as a linebacker, approached them with a friendly smile.

Della greeted him with her bit of knowledge regarding the Norwegian language, and Mason thought he had learned enough to believe she also asked him if he spoke English.

"Americans!" the man said. "Yes, I speak English. The Queen's English, not the president's, I'm afraid, but..."

"You have a great accent!" Della assured him. "Americans love accents. A British accent on a Norseman is great."

The man grinned. "Well, typical Norse name, too. I'm Sven."

"Sven, hi. I'm Della, this is Mason."

"Nice to meet you. What can I get you?" Sven said, nodding politely to Mason and then to Della.

"Something Norwegian," Mason said pleasantly.

"Like a mojito?" Sven teased.

"Norwegian beer," Della said.

"Gotcha! That's American, I think!" Sven said.

He turned to the taps and poured them each a drink, sliding the glasses expertly before them. They thanked him as he went on down the bar to check on his other patrons.

"We're going to have to ask him," Mason told Della.

"Ah, but our Bloody Mary drinker might just come in tonight, too."

"And we may just sit here and drink beer."

"Worse things can and will happen," she assured him.

"Right."

Their drafts were good but a single swallow reminded Mason they hadn't eaten in hours and hours. When he saw Sven was standing back, he called the man over and asked about food. If they liked salmon, Sven assured them he could recommend a great plate.

They ordered the salmon.

He and Della spoke softly between themselves, listening to the conversations around them—many of which were in English. Naturally, people were talking about the *vampire* killings.

"Horrible! So horrible!" a woman, speaking English, teased the man at her side. "I'm so happy I'm married right now!"

"Great!" her husband said, grimacing. "You're glad you're married to me—so a vampire doesn't get you!"

"Hey, not a good time to be dating," she returned. "I can promise you, if we hadn't been married for a decade, I wouldn't be hanging out with you."

Sven stopped in front of Mason and Della to produce their meals. He was glancing at the couple. He shook his head and spoke quietly.

"I don't think they realize just how horrible this is for us. We are a peaceful country and a more peaceful area. These days, and since the Dark Ages, just about. Yeah, yeah. Vikings. Long ago. These murders...so painful for so many."

"I am sorry. Maybe...maybe that's their way of relief," Della suggested. "We've heard, though, that others at the bar—"

"Right. This wacko—appropriate English word?—the other night was going on and on about Bloody Marys and the real thing. Can you imagine that? I'm surprised someone didn't freak out and nervously attack the fellow. People are talking, of course. But..."

He stopped speaking, frowning, looking at the two of them. "I understand," he continued, "we're getting investigators in from Paris, London, and the United States."

"Yes," Mason said quietly. "We are two of those investigators. We aren't here to offend in any way, but we are curious about your Bloody Mary patron. Do you know him? Is he a local?"

"No, he's not local. But he is in now and then. He's with the dig that's going on. They think they've discovered a gravesite circa 1000 to 1250. I guess you know, the *Viking Age* basically began with the attack and massacre at Lindisfarne Abbey, Northumberland, and most agree, ended at the Battle of Largs in 1263. Yes, at death, Vikings were sometimes sent out to sea with their ships ablaze, but sometimes they were buried as well. One of our premier scholars, Eric Lindstrom, found sagas suggesting the site and then… Well, I'm not sure, but it aroused a fascinated colony of archaeologists."

"You think your Bloody Mary guy is an archaeologist?" Della asked.

"He didn't happen to pay with a credit card, did he?" Mason put in.

"The man isn't stupid. He's just a drunk, and he was teasing a girl at the bar next to him when he was going on and on. He'd say something and her eyes would widen, and he'd laugh and be charming and, well… I guess I was just offended. We have young women who have died."

"It is offensive," Della agreed, touching his hand. "We understand, believe me."

"Of course, you do," Sven murmured. "I guess you see too much." He frowned, looking out at the tables. A pretty blonde waitress was moving effortlessly through the room as it grew more and more crowded. As Mason turned to see what was causing Sven to stare, he saw the waitress was moving back from a man.

He was young, mid-twenties. He had shaggy soft brown hair, straight nose, good features, and a ready smile.

He had all the features described to Della by the ghost.

And Sven was frowning.

"Don't look now…" he murmured.

But, of course, they were all looking.

And the young man looked at them. At first, he appeared puzzled. Then frightened. And then he turned and bolted out of the pub and raced into the street.

"Argh! Had to be a runner!" Della cried.

But she was already up and racing for the door. With all speed, Mason leaped to his feet and followed her.

They needed to catch Mr. Bloody Mary.

CHAPTER FOUR

Della was thankful she had spent her young years growing up with two brothers who played soccer and spent hours a week just running through their local park.

One thing she could do, no problem, was run. In college, she had managed to come in first in marathons that took place in New York and New England.

"Stop! Agents, stop!" she shouted.

As she had expected, the man ignored her.

She was on him, and he didn't get more than a block before he was just a foot or two ahead with Mason Carter running neck and neck with her.

Their suspect hopped over a dividing wall. Without hesitation, Mason gave her a boost and she was over the wall and landing down hard on their suspect. Naturally, he struggled, but she kept him down. Mason was right there, having skimmed his own way up the wall. He hunkered down at her side and drew their suspect's arms behind his back, got hold of his wrists, and cuffed him.

"Police brutality!" the man shouted.

"I don't think so," Mason said, standing and drawing the man to his feet.

"She jumped on me!"

"You were running," Mason told him. "Why were you running?"

"Because I didn't do anything!" he swore.

He was young, mid-twenties, Della thought. Her Viking ghost had given her an excellent description of the man, shaggy hair, casual appearance.

And now he was upset and spouting out threats.

"I'm going to sue you! I'll sue the Norwegians, and I'll sue you in America, too!"

He was an American, Della decided. His accent was neutral, as if he'd come from the center of the country, or at least there was no Southern drawl to his speech nor did he have the sound of a New Yorker or a man from New England.

"Okay, well, do what you must," Mason said. "But—"

"Get me out of these ridiculous handcuffs and let me go this instant, and I'll consider forgetting about the incident!" he raged.

"Oh, I don't think so," Della said.

"You can't just hold me!"

"Oh, we wouldn't just hold you. You're under arrest," Mason said casually.

"Under arrest! For being at a bar?" the man responded indignantly.

"No," Della murmured.

"Oh, no, no, no," Mason agreed. "You're under arrest for murder."

"Murder!" the young man shouted.

Della had to admit, if his astonishment was an act, he was damned good at acting.

"Yes, I'm afraid it's a very grave charge. A victim—seen with you—was law enforcement," Mason told him.

"You—you—you can't! I didn't, I swear to you, I didn't… Oh, man!"

He stared at them both with wide eyes. When they didn't speak, he repeated himself.

"I'm not a perfect human being—but I swear to you, I never killed anyone, I never would kill anyone! Oh, wow, please, don't arrest me!"

"Well, we're going to walk a few blocks to our headquarters and have a discussion," Della said. "Maybe you can talk us out of arresting you."

He nodded, swallowing painfully. "I'll come, I'll talk to you, but…please. Please! I swear on my mom's life, let me out of the handcuffs. Let me just walk with you. I don't want anyone to see… I don't want to lose my job."

"You're working at the dig?" Della asked him.

He frowned and nodded. "Please! We had to be invited. My father managed to get a friend of a friend to get me an invitation. I majored in history and archaeology and this is…so important to me! I don't want to get sent home. I mean, before God! I didn't kill anyone. And I swear that I will not run!"

Della looked at Mason. She was still surprised that it seemed they could look at one another and make the same decision.

"All right. We'll get the cuffs off you. And you can walk right along with us. May I have your wallet?"

"Are you shaking me down for money?" the man asked.

"No, I need your name, and I'd like to see your passport," Mason told him.

"Scott Harrington," he said quickly. "And here's my passport. I'm from Denver, Colorado."

Mason looked at the passport and nodded to Della.

"Not British," Mason murmured.

"No, but I…"

"You like to pretend you're British?" Della asked pleasantly.

"Sometimes in Europe, it's better, more fun. Hey, I like to say I'm Canadian, too. Most people like Canadians! They're nice."

Mason removed the cuffs.

And he indicated the path they needed to take.

The three of them walked the few blocks back to their *headquarters*. François Bisset, busy at the desk he had chosen, looked up.

"We have a few questions for Mr. Harrington," Della told him.

"Ah, yes. Shall I get water or coffee?" Bisset asked.

"Mr. Harrington?" Della asked.

"I, uh, was about to go for a Bloody Mary, but…hey, yeah. Coffee." He hesitated a minute, looked at Bisset, and said, "Thanks."

Bisset nodded.

Della and Mason led Harrington back to the interrogation room, indicating he should take a seat on one side of the table while they took chairs on the other.

"Let's talk about Bloody Marys," Della said.

"What?" Harrington demanded.

"Bloody Marys. Not as good as the real thing," Mason said.

Harrington blinked and stared back at them. He didn't have to answer right away because Bisset arrived with a tray with coffee cups, creamer, and sugar.

Della thanked him. Bisset nodded and said, "I'll leave you to it."

Once he left the room, Harrington leaned toward them, his elbows on the table, his eyes filling with tears. "I didn't! Yes, I like Bloody Marys. And I like to tease girls, and hey!

I'm young. I like the opposite sex. I would never ever hurt anyone—"

"But you have enjoyed the *real* thing, right?" Mason asked him quietly.

"I don't... I mean... I don't... I like the bar. I mean, Norse women are...well, like all women, but many are so pretty! I..."

Della cleared her throat and interrupted him. "They are pretty, and you're a flirt. But the thing is, you have had the *real* thing. And we need to know how, where—and who gave it to you."

He sat back, blinking.

Della glanced at Mason and she knew they were both certain he was thinking of a good lie.

"New Orleans!" Harrington said.

"New Orleans? Louisiana?" Mason asked politely.

"Yes. There's a group there. They believe we give all good things and energy to one another by drinking one another's blood. I've...uh, been with the group."

"Oh, good!" Della said. "You can give us names of people involved. We can talk to them and verify your story."

"Oh, no, no," Harrington said, shaking his head. "You don't understand. These people don't allow one another to give out names. In fact, we don't know one another's names— not real names or surnames. I mean, they don't want to be on the radar of the local police. They aren't doing anything wrong or illegal, but other people don't understand their desire to gain energy and insight and so much more from one another."

"Oh, well. Hmm." Della murmured.

"That's a problem," Mason agreed.

"Well, what's the problem?" Harrington asked.

"That's not enough. I'm afraid we'll have to arrest you," Mason said regretfully.

"No, no, you can't! I'll lose my job. My father will kill me."

Della leaned closer to him across the table. "Beautiful young people have lost their lives. I'm afraid there's no coming back from that."

He was silent for a minute.

"You really don't understand," he said.

"What don't we understand?" Della asked.

"I could lose my life, too," he whispered.

She and Mason glanced at each other once again, then both sat back and watched Scott Harrington.

"So, you drank blood here. You didn't kill anyone. We believe you," Della said.

"But someone gave you human blood to drink," Mason said. "And you thought it might be like one of those groups you came across in New Orleans. And you probably had a few drinks—maybe not Bloody Marys—before that."

"So," Della continued, "you met this person who gave you human blood to drink. You weren't even sure it was the real thing, but it sounded cool—so you talked about it when you ordered Bloody Marys at the bar."

Harrington remained silent for a minute, looking downward.

Then he nodded slowly.

"Who?" Mason asked.

Harrington shook his head.

"We need a name."

"I don't have a name!" Harrington said, looking at them at last. He winced. "Okay, I met this man just outside Bruger's. He was with a really pretty girl and he said, hey, and then asked me if I was with the dig. I told him yes. Then he said it was really cool to meet me and they were local and knew where to have a real party. I asked him where and he said in the woods. So, we went to the woods, and when we were there, I realized we were the party. The guy told me it was a special party, and he had learned how to receive the power and the strength of the Vikings. He said we were drinking blood—real blood. And I guess I looked surprised and maybe worried because the girl said I shouldn't worry, the blood was hers. They came and did this thing once a month, drinking a bit of each other's blood. He had it in some kind of a vial. I said the next time we could drink my blood, and they were both really friendly and I thought they were…well, the really cool locals."

"For drinking blood," Mason murmured.

Della looked at him. "When you left, this girl was alive and well?"

"Yes! And we came back into town together. She was a pretty blonde."

"Have you seen either of them since?" Mason asked.

"No, but that was just about a week ago. They wouldn't be looking for me yet."

"Did they give you names?"

Harrington shook his head. "Well, they called one another *honey* and *darling*. And *darling* laughed and said he was Vlad Dracul and we all laughed at that."

"So, did this man work at the dig?" Mason asked.

Harrington looked away.

"Well?" Della prodded.

"I… I don't know."

"But he and the woman spoke Norwegian?" Mason asked.

"I think." He shrugged. "I, uh, don't speak any myself, but I would have recognized one of the romance languages."

"Okay, what we're going to need you to do is give us a description of these people, and I'm going to have Detective

Wilhelm get a sketch artist in here and do up likenesses for us," Mason said.

"Oh, I… Of course. But please, it's getting late, and… I don't want anyone to know I've been stopped by the police, except—" He paused, frowning. "You can't be Norwegian police!"

"We're FBI," Della said.

"What? Then you have no jurisdiction and—"

"Yes, there is an FBI presence in other countries, I'm afraid. We were especially asked here by the Norwegian police, so…" Mason said.

"You can't arrest me!" Harrington said.

"Oh, not to worry. We have Detective Wilhelm for that. And all his force, so—"

"Okay, okay. Honestly, I want to help, anyway, I just… I just don't want to get fired off the dig!"

"We'll get you out of here in a few hours," Della promised. "Hey, don't worry—we flew in and haven't even seen our rooms yet. We're anxious to get to sleep. In fact…"

She turned to Mason and oddly enough, once again, they seemed to be thinking the same thing. It was six hours earlier in Washington, DC.

Krewe headquarters was always open, 24/7, with a skeleton crew at night, but that meant little because agents worked whatever hours were required wherever they happened to be. And Angela would still be in the office ready to call up one of their best sketch artists.

"I'll get a computer," Mason said. "Make the call and tell Angela what we need."

"Right," Della said.

Mason exited to get the laptop from his desk and Della made the call. Angela assured her she'd be ready in five minutes, getting a conference call through with Maisie, one of their best, and she'd create an image and get it out to them immediately.

She finished the call and found Harrington staring at her, confused.

"We're going to get you out of here quickly—we're going to have you work with the artist online, okay?" she asked.

"Oh, yes, great, I can get out of here!" Harrington said.

"Yes." She smiled sweetly. "We know where to find you if we need you again."

"Yeah, you do," he said dryly.

Mason reappeared with a laptop and they quickly made a secure connection. They introduced Harrington to Maisie. She was a people person as well as a wonderful and intuitive artist and she quickly had Harrington at ease. He gave her a description of the woman first.

She'd been about five feet five inches, which, of course, didn't matter in the sketch, but would be included in the description that would go with the sketch. She'd been stunningly attractive, with wavy blond hair that curled long around her shoulders, blue-green eyes, and a perfect slim face, small nose, defined lips, arched brows, delicate chin. She'd been wearing a blue maxi-dress with a V-neckline, lace at the wrists.

Maisie sketched, then scanned her work into the computer and asked him to tell her where she might have gone wrong.

"Nowhere!" Harrington said with surprise. "That's—that's her!"

"The man now," Mason said.

As Harrington began to talk, Della and Mason stared at one another, frowning.

"Height, let's see, six or six-one. Hair, just about pitch-black. Very powerful dark eyes, strong, squared chin, high-boned cheeks, dark brows... Oh, and he was wearing a cape, you know, like the kind you'd wear in a vampire movie."

"Mr. Harrington, you're describing a movie vampire," Della said gently.

"I know. That's exactly what he looked like," Harrington said. "Seriously, vest, tie, cape…and his eyes, well, they were as black as his hair."

No one had truly black eyes—unless they were wearing contacts. But this man's entire dress seemed to be costume, just as his name— Vlad Dracul—was all play-acting.

They finished. Della and Mason both thanked Maisie and Angela, who had stayed online with them. They ended the call.

Harrington looked at them.

"Yes, you get to leave now," Mason told him. "But someone out there is killing people, Mr. Harrington. So far, the killer targets women. But he's dangerous. Be careful."

"I'll be careful, I'll be careful!" he promised. "I mean, I'd heard about some guy who was calling himself a vampire and killing—"

"You heard about him, but you went to the woods with a man claiming to be Vlad Dracul?" Della asked him, shaking her head.

"Well, he was with the blonde! If she was with him, I figured he was just a kook—and they were playing off what was going on and…it was stupid."

"Yes, it was stupid," Mason said.

"And I was drunk," Harrington admitted. "I mean… Oh, man. I won't be stupid again. I room with a guy who is more serious than I am and doesn't go out often, and I just might be hanging around the room arguing over the remote control with him more often. I… Wow. So…they might really have been the people who killed these women?"

"We don't know. But I do suggest you take greater care.

Maybe have a drink or two, but don't get drunk and run off to drink blood with a so-called vampire?" Della suggested.

Harrington nodded and rose slowly. "Um… I don't think anyone who knows me saw you two attack me—"

"We asked you to stop," Mason reminded him.

"Okay, that you two handcuffed me, and I'd just as soon…"

"What?" Della asked.

"Well, can you pretend you don't know me and I'll pretend I don't know you?"

"That will work," Della assured him. "Unless we need you," she added softly. "But, don't worry. We're going to find our vampire. We'll have to have evidence to get him, so I believe you'll be in the clear."

"I am fine with it. You don't know us, we don't know you," Mason said.

"We'll see you out," Della told him, rising as well along with Mason. They walked back through the main office area where it seemed François Bisset had been waiting for them by the door. He smiled and bid Harrington good-night and opened the door for him. Once he had stepped out, Bisset turned to Della and Mason.

"I took the liberty of asking for a police officer to keep a protective eye on the gentleman, since you brought him in for questioning, and I didn't believe you'd be holding him," he said.

"Perceptive and great, Monsieur Bisset," Mason said. "He could be in trouble—or he could be approached again, and then again…"

"He wasn't our vampire," Bisset said.

"No, but he might be contacted again by someone who might be," Della said. "He works at the dig—that's not a bad place to have an officer positioned to keep an eye on things."

Bisset nodded. "By the way, please just call me François. We will be working together for... Well, it could be a while."

"François. Della, Mason, please," Della told him.

Bisset nodded pleasantly. "Did you get anything helpful from the man?"

"Yes, we're looking for Vlad Dracul from the movies—not the old creepy Vlad Dracul like Max Schreck from the old, old 1922 *Nosferatu*. Say the vampire from the times he was played by heartthrob actors, Gerard Butler, Jonathan Rhys Meyers, or a young George Hamilton," Mason told him.

"What?"

"A man in costume, from what we've gotten, but we're getting the images from our headquarters that were done over the Internet with a Krewe artist. As soon as she sends her finished product, we'll get it to our group and the police. Our *Dracula* is styled after the good-looking seducers in certain films, and he is spending time with a stunning blonde woman," Della told him.

"Well...this man you just interviewed knew something about them?" François asked.

"Yes. They drink blood they claim to be their own," Mason said. "Anyway—"

"The others have finished their tasks and headed in for the evening," Bisset said. "Nothing earth-shattering. Dr. Andersen informed Wilhelm he wouldn't know more until he had performed a full autopsy, and that will be in the morning. Wilhelm plans to attend, leaving you free to pursue any leads you may have."

"I wonder if Wilhelm should be the attending," Della said softly.

"He will be all right. Yes, he knew the poor woman. And because of that, I believe he feels he owes it to her to be at her side," Bisset said.

"All right," Mason said. "I can understand that."

"So, we've done all we can right now. And we're grateful you're taking precautions for Scott Harrington."

"Yes, yes, of course. Now, it's extremely late. And you've flown and worked for hours upon hours. Oh, Wilhelm let me know he delivered your bags to your lodgings. I think you'll be happy. We've gotten you a townhome with two bedrooms and a kitchen, two short blocks from here, with parking, and we've arranged for a car tomorrow. An SUV for easy trips to the crime scenes."

"Great," Della said. "If you'll point us in the right direction?"

Bisset gave them keys to the residence and walked outside with them, coming to the corner where he pointed up the street. "Two blocks. The little corner place with the charming balcony. We supplied some basics in the kitchen, water, coffee, tea, bread, and so on."

"We'll see you back here in the morning," Mason told him. "Thank you."

Bisset said good-night. The two of them started walking.

"Strange. I'm not even tired and we've been up forever."

He nodded. "But I have a feeling we'll hit our beds and be out in a matter of seconds."

"Possibly. And…"

"And?"

"Well, I think we have to find our vampire, and you know the thing about vampires?"

"They roam at night," Mason said. He shrugged. "What is your feeling on archaeology?"

"Love it! And history. You want to go to the dig in the morning?"

"Might as well. We'll need the lights to go low to troll for our vampire. I know they'll coordinate with us if they dis-

cover anything via the autopsy." He shrugged. "She looked...
the same as those women we saw in the crime scene photos.
But if our vampire has followers, they will be obeying the
proper commands. And there still might be some small difference that a medical examiner will find."

"The dig. Are we going as tourists or as ourselves?"

"They may have a media person—someone who deals with
the public. I think we should go as tourists or, better yet, as
journalists. They'll want to show us everything good then.
I'll shoot a text off to Angela. She'll find a friend to say we've
worked freelance for them in case someone chooses to check
our credentials. Hey, we can write something up so we're
not complete liars."

"Like an arrest report?"

He grinned. "Well, no matter what we say, we technically
detain people—and Wilhelm arrests them. And nice. Here
we are!" he said.

Della had just been following in step with him and might
have been far more tired than she had imagined. They had
walked the two blocks and were standing in front of a small
but charming townhome. They headed up the walk to the
two steps leading to the porch and front door. Mason had his
key out and quickly turned it in the lock.

Lights had been left on for them on the porch and in the
hallway, but Della hit the overhead so they could get a good
look at their lodgings.

"It's great," Mason said, surveying the stairs that led up to
the second floor, the parlor to the right and dining area to
the left. "I take it the kitchen is through there and maybe a
family room, entertainment area or even an office behind the
parlor. I'll go right, you go left."

"Okay, but sleep is going to be up."

"Yeah, but I like to know about windows, doors, exits—and entrances—when I'm someplace new," Mason said.

"Good thought. You go right. I'll go left."

Della walked through the dining room, set with pleasant Victorian-era furniture. But behind the dining room, the kitchen was modern, offering a large refrigerator, oven and stove, microwave, center preparation board, and a small table.

And a back door. She checked it, glad the place wasn't equipped with *code* locks.

She'd seen far too many *safe* houses or rooms with codes that had been easily broken.

This back door had two solid bolts and a twist knob. She made sure that all were secured.

There was a door in the kitchen and she opened it, finding stairs to the basement as she had expected. She flicked on a light. The basement was filled with shelves and storage, and also a pool table and a few comfortable chairs. She imagined that this house was popular among travelers and was usually on a rental site. She guessed someone in power had really wanted help from the Krewe, because they had gone out of their way to see that she and Mason were accommodated.

She turned off the light and headed back to the entry and checked the windows for locks as she went. All seemed in order.

"The back is an office," he told her.

"Well, that's nice. And hey, if we run out of work, there's a pool table in the basement. Doors secured and windows locked as well. I think we'd have to hear it if someone tried to break in on us."

"Right. But curious, no alarm system."

"It's Lillehammer, Norway," she reminded him. "And their crime is much lower than ours—other than the stray vampire here and there."

"Right," he agreed. "Well, hmm. Let's see the rest. After you."

Della nodded and headed up the stairs. She looked in the left bedroom. It had a four-poster bed, two dressers, and a stand with a television. There was luggage at the foot of the bed.

Not hers.

"This is you," she told Mason.

"Yeah, your stuff is in here."

They brushed by one another, changing places.

"Ah, good night!" Della said awkwardly.

"Good night. I'll have the alarm set for seven, and that will get us out of here by seven thirty, if that works for you."

"Like a charm," she assured him, smiling, stepping into her room and closing the door.

She heard his door close as she looked around the room. It was small, but she thought that at some time in the last years, the owners had installed bathrooms in both the bedrooms, necessarily having to take space from what was there. But the room also had a four-poster bed, dressers, and a television with a cable box. All the comforts of home.

She brought her toiletries into the bathroom and arranged them, thinking she'd shower in the morning.

But then the length of the day seemed to wear at her, and she opted to shower then. She'd move faster in the morning.

And it was good. The water, sweetly hot, poured over her, cleansing away travel, her crawl through the woods, and her nearness to death.

But just as she turned off the water, she heard the slamming of a door below. The front door.

Stepping out, she snatched a towel, wrapped it quickly around her and grabbed her Glock—thankfully set behind the commode. She never went anywhere on assignment without it near her.

She ran out of the bathroom and then her bedroom, checked Mason's room and saw he wasn't there, and went racing downstairs, Glock ready and barely aware she was wearing nothing but a towel.

They'd left a night-light on, but once she left her room, the house was filled with shadows. She held her Glock at the ready and approached the front door—which stood ajar. She carefully approached in a manner to use the open door as protection.

The door pushed inward.

Della lowered her weapon. It was Mason. He was breathing hard, as if he'd just had the run of the century.

"Whoever the hell it was, he got away!" Mason said angrily. "I was on him like a flash, but there was a car waiting. I don't think we're looking for just one vampire. I think our worst fears are being realized. Someone has others convinced they need to be vampires to achieve immortal life or something of the like."

"I… What happened?" Della asked.

He was silent, frowning, apparently realizing he was staring at a woman wearing a towel and carrying a Glock.

"I saw our so-called vampire, or one of the so-called vampires, out there," Mason said. "He was down in the street, staring up at the house. I slipped away from the window and out the door—but he was already heading down the street, and there was a car waiting for him—a dark SUV. And, of course, I couldn't get a license plate number because it was covered with mud. I called the local people and thankfully they understood me, so they'll have their eyes open."

"Maybe we need to sleep in shifts," Della said.

"And be useless. I wake up at a whisper," he said. "I was

already in bed, just about out, and I heard a noise—just a rustle—from the street. And there he was, standing to the side of the house, staring up."

"And he looked like a vampire."

"The vampire our friend Scott Harrington described today."

"So, somehow, he knows us."

"Maybe. But it's known that this place is rented to tourists. Maybe he was just checking out whoever might be here. Some sweet innocent young things here to enjoy Lillehammer."

"But maybe we need to move," she said.

"When I talked to the police, they planned on having someone watch here, too."

"We are going to stretch the resources here to a breaking point," Della murmured.

"No. We call Jackson. We have agents in Europe already who can come and cover some of the guard duty. But it's interesting that a *vampire* was here."

"That means we have to play it a little differently."

"Or maybe not. Let him think we didn't see anything, and I was chasing a ghost. What was your plan?"

"Chatting him up. Getting to know him."

"You wanted to pretend you were being charmed—seduced?" Mason asked skeptically.

"Well, I'd learn about him. With you at my back, of course."

"I don't know. I don't like it. But we can talk about it in the morning. For now, the plan has to be—"

"Well, for me, it's going to be to finish drying off and getting clothes on," Della said.

"Good plan. I guess... Well, hell, I thought I could sleep. But it will take me a bit now. Guess I'll take a shower."

"I might have used all the hot water."

"Well, you know, that's okay. I think a cold shower might be in order."

He swept past her and hurried up the stairs. She heard his door close.

She checked the front door. But even in his anger and frustration, he had remembered to relock it. Adjusting her towel, she headed back upstairs, set the Glock on the bedside table, found one of the big soft, comfortable T's she used as pajamas, and quickly dressed.

She laid down, exhausted, yet with her eyes open.

It had been an impossibly long day and night, or night, day, and night. She was tired and she needed to sleep, but her mind was racing.

A policewoman was among the dead. The killer might well have been in the street. Or one of several killers might have been in the street.

She still barely knew her partner. Yet, she felt as if she had known him for years, as if there was a strange kind of connection you had with some people. No matter how often or how sporadic you saw them, the connection was always there.

She'd been wary of him.

No more.

And...

She remembered standing on the stairway. In a towel. And realized he was standing there, watching her, stunned that she was in a towel.

There'd been...something.

A spark?

No doubt the man was extremely attractive. But many agents were tall, young and, perhaps just because of their youth and the fact of their work, fit and attractive. But she'd never...

Never what?

Been drawn in? She felt their minds had clicked, and after that...

Maybe she'd noticed him physically to a greater extent?

Groaning, she tossed on the bed and punched her pillow. Then she smiled, unable to resist the concept that maybe he was equally intrigued by her.

After all, he had said a *cold* shower was going to be just fine.

That made her smile as she finally slept.

CHAPTER FIVE

"It's amazing how many people believe *all* Vikings were laid out on their ships, and the ships were sent out to sea ablaze! Some were, yes. There was a belief that by doing such a thing, those left behind were helping their leader on to the great rewards in the next world. But many great Viking leaders were buried—some in burial chambers—and some with their ships and other goods as well. We used the same high-resolution geo-radar they used at Halden, and we've had much the same luck," Lars Vander explained as he welcomed Mason and Della at the dig site.

Lars was a man of about forty, the dig liaison for media, sponsors, and all curiosity seekers. He was made for the job, being a dignified man who still managed a quick smile and had an easy personality. He might be called a *people person*. He was a little over six feet, wiry strong with muscles from the physical work he also engaged in—he'd told them right away that while he didn't have to assist in any of the physical labor, he loved history, especially Viking history, and was thrilled when discoveries were made. He had a contoured face with eyes so light of a brown they were almost yellow, and neatly styled light brown hair.

Angela had set up their meeting from the main office. And while the dig site had been cordoned off, he had been at the entry to meet them when they arrived.

"This is a massive venture, I see," Mason said. "You have people working here from around the world, right? That's what we've been told."

Lars smiled and nodded. "The largest majority are from Norway, the USA, and Great Britain. We also have two Frenchmen, an Italian, an Australian—and his friend, a Kiwi, a New Zealander. Also, three from Sweden, two from Switzerland and three from Denmark." He grinned. "For Scandinavians, working conditions are easy. I'm not sure how long you've been here, but our main meal is in the middle of the day while you people have dinner. And for your dinner, we often have teatime with little open-faced sandwiches. Unless you're in one of the big cities, you won't find any giant-sized American hoagies. And beef! You are big on beef. Here we eat salmon, trout, and yes, we have lots of pigs, so pork."

"We haven't been here that long," Della said, "but I'm accustomed to a lot that is Norwegian. I have a set of grandparents from Oslo."

"Ah!" he said, beaming. "And you?" he asked Mason.

"Maybe someone somewhere along the line," Mason told him. "I think I'm a mix of just about everything. But tell me, how do you keep control on something this big and this international? Do people come and go?"

"Yes, of course! Take Mr. Dean Oswald. He finished his task with a remarkable piece of jewelry that was discovered, and then had to return to Britain and head up to the Orkney Islands. They were Norse until 1472 when a dowry wasn't paid to James III, and the Scottish Parliament annexed them.

Wonderful place, the archipelago of the Orkney Islands…but I digress! Yes, people come and go. Even the workers, the diggers. This is massive, and we have muscle to dig when it's deep—but when it gets to the fine line, the experts want to go in themselves."

"Fascinating—how do you keep track?" Della asked him.

He was suddenly silent.

"I thought the article you were working on had to do with the incredible wonder of this site! We are inland, but Magnus Fairbeard—the jarl buried here circa the late 1200s—owned the land here. His family kept it and worked it when he went a-Viking. This is a rare and incredible find, and I was led to believe—I mean, you are journalists, right?"

"Freelancers," Mason said. "Della does a video blog. I'm going to film her somewhere, but wanted to make sure wherever we filmed, you were okay. I see tons of people by that huge pile of dirt over there, so I was hoping that wasn't an area you're trying to protect until you have all your findings."

"That's the ship! We're unearthing it carefully, and the big dig has been done now. The ship was barely four feet down. Anyway, you'll note that before the piles, people are now working with smaller trowels and brushes. But if you wish, you can film there," he said. "Just keep your distance from the workers. I have sheets for you with the information we have on Magnus Fairbeard. He was admired and feared. He never fell in battle, but rather did something rare for his kind of ruler. He lived to be a ripe old age and died of natural causes."

"Fascinating!" Della said, smiling at him. "And thank you, thank you! This must be the hardest job here, fending off everyone curious about what's going on. Especially with…"

"With?" Lars asked.

"Nothing, nothing."

"No, no, please," Lars pressed.

"I'm sorry. Just...well, all this going on, bringing up the past, bringing up history, and now...well, the vampire killings that have happened here," she finished in a whisper.

He stared at her with deep consternation. "What would that have to do with us? Vikings and vampires have nothing in common. Vikings were very much alive. Deadly, yes. But this isn't Transylvania. The killings have not had anything to do with the so-called real Count Dracula or the historical ruler he was based on, Vlad the Impaler. The man impaled his enemies! He didn't lay them out in beauty. There are no vampire legends around here. They suspect the killer is an American you know. No offense."

"And none taken," Mason assured him quickly.

"We're just thinking history, I guess," Della said. "And the women are laid out in beauty!" She whispered the last again.

Lars sighed deeply. "The concept of the vampire or the zombie has been around forever in almost every society known to man. The plagues that killed so many in the Dark Ages and medieval times caused more and more people around the world to believe. There were so many dead some had to be moved. And digging up a partially decomposed corpse, well, you had gases that made them move and people believed. Seriously, people all over had superstition and fear, but this Viking burial has nothing to do with a Bram Stoker vampire at all in any way!"

"I'm so sorry! I didn't mean to imply... I just wondered if... I am so sorry!" Della said sweetly.

"She just wondered if you lost people because they were frightened about what has happened," Mason said. "No offense intended toward you or the dig."

"Of course not. I overreacted," Lars said. "Anyway, go over there. If you don't mind, talk about how special it is. Because while burials like this might have happened often enough over the Viking age, it's still rare to find such a magnificent ship that is nearly intact along with so many artifacts. Talk about the fact it has been an amazing international effort on behalf of the scientific community, historians, and so many others."

"Oh, naturally! Absolutely!" Della said.

Lars extended a hand, indicating where she should speak. Mason hadn't told her she was going to be doing a video blog. The idea had occurred to him when he had seen how many people were working the dig.

How many potential suspects he might catch on video.

She quickly caught on to his plan.

Once they were out of earshot, she told him, "I'll keep moving—if you follow me, we'll get the entire scene. Of course, there are people working in the tents they've set up as workshops for the artifacts they discover, but we can still get a lot."

She smiled and pointed as if she were talking about the wonder and scope of it all.

"Great. I'll follow you—wherever you go."

She smiled and stepped out before him. And because Lars might come near or someone else might pass, she kept up the ruse, moving about and pointing as she did so. And as Mason had expected, Lars came as they were finishing.

Della gave him a brilliant smile. "And here we have—"

"No, no, no!" Lars said quickly. "I just walked over to make sure you were doing all right."

He waved a hand at Mason, indicating he needed to stop taping.

That was all right.

Mason already had a good shot of him.

"Sorry," Lars said. "I don't want to be on video. It will draw out every nut from here to the moon. Forgive me, I know I should be the face of the dig, but I keep my face out of things. The right people called about you, and that's why I've seen you and allowed you your blog."

"Well then, thank you, thank you so much," Della said.

Lars was suddenly frowning. Mason looked in his direction.

He saw their suspect from the night before, Scott Harrington, was on the site carrying a set of tools toward the mound where the ancient ship lay.

"Well, that one is late," Lars murmured. "For some, it's just easy money. A way to keep traveling. For others, this is a dream. All right, then. I'm sorry. I need to escort you back off this site."

"Of course," Della murmured, glancing at Mason.

Since they had decided to come to the dig as journalists, it was a good thing Scott Harrington had begged them not to let on they all knew each other.

He had surely seen them there. But he hadn't blinked or shown a reaction.

"Thank you again," Mason told him. "We'll get out of your hair now."

In a minute, they had bid goodbye to the dig's liaison.

"Well?" Della asked.

"I don't like him," Mason said.

"Now, he tried," Della said. "He just got aggravated when we asked about people coming and going—and suggested someone involved might be a vampire."

"He was anxious to make us understand Vikings never had anything to do with a vampire legend from any part of the world."

"They had their own gods, goddesses, and demons," Della said. "As did all cultures. But he's right about one thing—there was certainly nothing in Viking culture similar to movie vampires. I'm not sure he's read *Dracula*—Bram Stoker's creature did not look like a handsome dark-haired seducer. But Stoker definitely created an immortal legend."

"The legends have been out there. Lamia was an ancient Greek child-eating monster and a demon. Norse mythology was the religion of the Vikings. Yes, they had powerful gods. But they had all manner of creatures as well. Such as draugar!"

"And they would be?"

"Norse undead!"

"Somewhat handsome like young Lugosi, young Hamilton, or Luke Evans?"

"No! Oh, no, no, no. Super strong, maybe magical, but undead and gross and rotting."

"Well, then, I guess he had his point."

Della sighed softly. "He has his point in that the poor women this vampire has attacked—or these vampires have attacked—are left as if they're in a modern movie. And there is nothing similar that I know of in Norse mythology. Though, seriously, the way the women are being left, we are talking Hollywood movies. In almost every culture, the undead were rotting, putrid, and terrifying. Yes, they existed all around the world. And all around the world, people believed they might be real. Burial sites have been discovered in which the corpses had their chests ripped open and their hearts torn out. While some had knives left on their throats to slice them or decapitate them should they try to rise. It happened all over. Of course, as Lars was saying, plagues caused so much death that corpses had to be moved sometimes, and gases accumulated, and they moved, so..." She broke off, shrugging.

Mason listened to her and shook his head. "We need to see what Wilhelm learned at autopsy. And I'd like to interview Marlene Rogers, the friend of Asta Dahl, the first victim discovered here. I want to know where they were before...well, before Asta disappeared. Friends don't usually leave friends."

"Maybe Marlene had jet lag. Maybe she drank too much. No, friends don't usually leave friends. But there are logical reasons she might have done so."

They headed for the car. As they did so, Mason saw a man sitting in a small car, leaning back, as if just resting before moving on.

But he opened his eyes, leaning up as he saw them, then nodded and leaned back again.

Mason nodded in return.

He was with the police and here to watch over Scott Harrington.

It might not have been a bad idea at all for the young man to receive protection. He could hope no one he knew had seen what had happened. Just as they could hope the people at the dig believed they were journalists.

In Mason's experience, a lie only lasted so long.

And if someone knew Scott Harrington had spilled everything he knew, his life could well be in danger.

Too bad he hadn't really known anything! Well, he had helped. And they now knew someone was walking around Lillehammer in a movie-Dracula cape.

Mason had seen the man who had been watching the house. Did he know they were law enforcement? He shouldn't—unless he somehow had connections with the local police department.

"Cop or the equivalent thereof?" Della murmured, referring to the man *resting* in his vehicle. Mason glanced over at her and nodded.

"Okay, here's the thing. We need to speak with Marlene Rogers."

"And Wilhelm, and find out if there is anything different in this autopsy," Della said. "Then as evening falls, we can troll the streets for a vampire in a cape."

Mason shook his head.

"He won't wear the cape anymore."

"You know that how?"

"He knows I saw him in a cape last night. Whether he knows who we are or not, we need to go with the possibility he does. So—"

"We still need to play it as if we have no idea who he is."

"That's dangerous—because you intend to flirt with him and see where he leads you."

"I still do."

"Della—"

"You'll have my back at every turn," she said quietly.

He found himself thinking of the night before, of the fierce and beautiful way she looked—standing on the stairs. In a towel. Her Glock aimed and ready.

"Trust me, I intend to have your back. But you don't know where this guy might lead. And we don't know if he'll be on his own or with a girl. He could be a master of disguise—he could be anyone."

"It doesn't matter. I think we'll know. But, Mason, we must find a way to stop this. We'll have to take risks. We can't let more innocent women become his victims."

He nodded. "We'll play it as it comes. I'm going to give François a call and have him get Marlene Rogers down to our little headquarters."

"Great. I'll give Wilhelm a call and see how it went at autopsy."

He nodded. They both made their calls.

He spoke quickly with François who assured him he'd get Marlene Rogers in.

When he ended the call, Della was still listening to Wilhelm. She appeared grave, thanked him, and ended her call.

"What?" Mason asked her.

"Andersen said he couldn't be sure. Maybe our killer was a little anxious. The marks weren't quite as clear and defined as they were on the other victims. Of course, she was a cop. She would have known how to fight, and maybe she gave her killer more trouble than the other victims. But Andersen just couldn't say for sure if he believed the murder was committed by the same killer or not," Della told him. She shook her head. "Everything in this case just seems to lead to more puzzles and riddles. He's American, he isn't American. It's one killer, it's a killer with copycat fans… I just feel we're not getting anywhere at all."

"But we are. We met a Viking who led us to Sven at the bar and then Scott Harrington."

"Who turned out to be a young fun-loving idiot."

"But, we know we might be looking for a man who is scouring for other victims with a woman."

"They took him to drink their blood."

"Maybe they needed to appear to be nothing more than a little crazy themselves. Or perhaps, they were trying to draw him into their realm."

"Ah, well, let's see what Marlene has to say. And what about our French and English counterparts?" she asked.

"Out on the town to find anyone they can to speak with."

"Okay, so…" Della stopped speaking with a deep sigh. "Now we get to speak with someone brokenhearted about the loss of a friend."

"At least we don't have to tell her what happened. She already knows," he said quietly.

"I know. That is the worst. All right, wait! What did you think about Lars?"

"Cagey!"

She laughed. "Well, we did offend him. But he has no idea who is coming or going from the dig most of the time."

"Call Angela. Give her a report. She has acquired names. She'll be on it."

"She will be. She's magic."

"Or a computer genius. And a field agent."

Della turned to him. "I'm glad you accepted this. I realize the plan isn't for us to be at the home office often, but I've never been with a better group of professionals. Or... well, you know. People I can tell I got my information from a dead Viking."

He smiled. "Yeah. You're right. I didn't get much of a chance to meet other agents with the unit—but from what we've gotten so far, well, you're right. It's the place for me."

They returned to headquarters, but due to the narrow streets, Mason opted to leave Della in front of their temporary offices and park by their townhome.

Walking the two blocks to the headquarters, he found himself pausing to look down the street.

Lillehammer was small, easily maneuvered on foot in the central area by anyone who didn't mind walking. Of course, moving toward the outskirts of town was better accomplished in a vehicle, but...

The streets were narrow. Most of the people in the country owned smaller cars than those in the United States. He had learned there were also tunnels that had been dug in the earth for navigation around the country with large circular spaces here and there should a turnaround be necessary. Instead of white light, they utilized blues and greens, changing colors to keep drivers awake and aware in the underground.

Here...the street was quiet. But restaurants and shops were not far away. The man could have come from anywhere.

Then he was swept up by a car, and he could have gone anywhere.

Mason gave himself a mental shake and hurried to the

offices. François Bisset greeted him and told him Marlene Rogers had arrived with her parents. They were in the back with Della.

He hurried on to the back and entered quietly.

Marlene Rogers was an attractive young woman, a slim girl with long dark hair and at twenty-nine somewhat younger than Asta. Her head was bowed and she was crying softly. Della sat with her, an arm gently around her shoulders as she tried to tell her she couldn't have changed anything. The heinous, criminal behavior of another person wasn't her fault.

The young woman's parents sat on the other side of the table holding hands, distressed as they watched their daughter.

"Marlene, Mr. and Mrs. Rogers, this is my partner, Special Agent Mason Carter. We will find who did this. We're not alone. We have Norwegian law enforcement in full swing and detectives from other countries as well. You are not responsible!" she said softly but passionately.

"But I left her!" Marlene cried. "I was tired, I couldn't stay awake, and I had to go back to the hotel. And she was having fun, and I didn't want to make her come with me."

Mason walked around to the girl and hunkered down to her level. "Marlene, Della is right. The person who did this is a predator, and we need to be thankful he didn't take you, too. I think it will be helpful," he said, glancing at her parents, "if you find a therapist when you get home. What you're feeling is natural. They call it survivor's guilt. But please know you couldn't have changed anything. You might have been lost, too. What you can do is try and tell us everything that was going on when you left. You said she was having fun. With who?"

"We were at the bar," Marlene said. "There were several people there around our age. There was a blonde woman who was flirting with a few guys. The guys were laughing and then everyone was talking and… I wish I could have stayed. But I was up all day and then I took a night bus to get to Oslo and then drove out and…when I was there, I wished I'd had the energy to stay. But I had one beer, and I was afraid I was going to pass out on the bar. So…"

"You walked back to the hotel by yourself?"

She nodded glumly.

"Marlene, where was the bar?"

"In the center of town, not far from here. Bruger's."

Mason glanced at Della. The bar seemed to be a prime location for their killer—or killers.

"I told the police. I told them everything."

"Of course. Can you tell us more about the people who were there? Was the blonde woman alone, or was she with one of the men?"

"I… I thought she was alone. There were two other girls there, together, and three guys. They were all cute, but two were more…young cute. The third—"

"Did he have dark hair?" Mason asked.

Marlene shook her head. "No, he had sandy-colored hair. He was tall, really good-looking, like movie-quality good-looking."

Mr. Rogers, a balding man with a gentle demeanor, cleared his throat.

"We'd like to take Marlene home. Yes, we'll make sure she has a therapist."

"Please!" his wife, an older heavier version of her daughter, whispered the word.

"Of course, of course," Mason said. "But we'd like to ask you to do one thing for us, please. We want you to do a video chat with our office in the States. Describe the people who were there when you left the bar. Do you think you could do that for us?"

"We almost had her not crying!" Mrs. Rogers said. "Please!"

"No, Mom, no, I need to do this," Marlene said. "If there's anything I can do to help them get the horrible person or people doing this… I have to help. Mom, I have to!"

Marlene's parents were silent. Mason excused himself and headed out to his desk. He glanced at the clock. Angela would be home now—working hours were long over in the United States. But someone would answer at the offices, and there would be someone there who could do sketches for them.

As it turned out, Maisie was there. She told him she'd had a feeling she'd be hearing from him, and she'd planned to sleep in one of the small rooms offered at headquarters for any agent staying long hours.

He was grateful she had stayed, and he was able to set her up with Marlene. Della glanced at him, smiling as he told them Marlene would be working via video with Maisie; in his opinion, she was about the best to be found anywhere.

They all waited patiently as Marlene spoke, closing her eyes now and then, doing her best to describe everyone who had been there when she'd left the bar.

As Maisie showed her drawings, entered them into the computer, and enhanced them with directions from Marlene, Mason glanced at Della.

The blonde was the woman Scott Harrington had described.

And only one other person appeared to be familiar. It was the man Marlene had described as *really good-looking, movie-quality good-looking.*

He was the man Scott Harrington had described.

Except now he had light hair.

No cape, no look of a Hollywood vampire.

When the work was finished, Mason and Della thanked Marlene and her parents. They were grateful to leave at last.

When they did, Marlene was no longer crying. She clung to Della for a minute at the door, saying, "I hope I've helped. I want to believe I did something for Asta!"

"You were wonderful. And I promise you, we will do everything in our power to see Asta's killer is brought to justice."

The mild manner Mr. Rogers had previously displayed slipped away, and he looked at Mason and said, "Justice! Shoot the bastard. If you find him, shoot the bastard!"

Neither Mason nor Della replied. They thanked the trio again for coming, and then the Rogers family was gone.

François Bisset had been standing quietly off to the side, but when the door closed on the three, he walked over to Mason and Della.

"Well?"

"She described the same man—and the woman—who shared what was supposedly their own blood with Scott Harrington," Mason told him. "Maisie is sending her sketches of the bar patrons. We'll get them to all members of our team and Norwegian law enforcement."

"So, we do have a suspect," François said.

"A chameleon," Della told him. "Everyone will need to know he changes his appearance easily, but he still has the same face. Hair color doesn't matter, eye color doesn't matter. He probably has a dozen wigs and can change his eye color with contacts."

"I will make sure all are advised. And," he added, "Wilhelm called while you were in with the Rogers family. He has begged that you forgive him—he is with the family and friends of Ingrid McDonald. He does need this afternoon."

"Of course," Mason said.

"Also, Detectives Taylor and Lapierre checked in—they

are returning to the woods with a forensic team seeking any kind of a clue."

Mason nodded his approval. He looked at Della. "We'll check in with Angela and head out. We have a good concept of what this man may look like, no matter his disguise."

"And the blonde woman he travels with," Della agreed.

"Yes, of course, you must keep moving," Bisset said. "But I took the liberty of ordering food to be brought. Here, the main meal is the midday meal. There are many specialties, but they include sheep heads and pickled herring and deer meat and… I wasn't sure about your American sensibilities, so I opted for a salmon meal. We don't do many salads here, but I have greens and delicious bread arriving, so…"

"Kind of you to think of us," Mason replied. "And I'm quite fond of salmon. Della?"

"Salmon will be great, and thank you," she assured Bisset.

Bisset told them the food would arrive any minute. It did even before he finished speaking. They ate quickly, but the salmon was probably the best he had ever had, and Mason told Bisset that it was. Their Interpol liaison was pleased, but leaned forward to tell them, "Quite good, yes. But even Americans know that French food is the best in the world!"

Neither of them chose to argue the point.

When they had finished eating, they thanked Bisset for his thoughtfulness and he reminded them he was there for whatever they needed. He'd continue communicating with the teams throughout the day and convey the images Maisie would send to every possible law enforcement officer in the country and beyond.

They left headquarters, walking down the street in silence.

"Maybe we should have a public argument," Della said. "I mean, nothing obnoxious. Something quiet—and then I walk away from you."

"Pardon?"

"Well, if I'm with you, I'm hardly a good target." She smiled at him wryly. "You do realize even here where people are tall, you stand out and you look as if you could take down half a football team at once. We need this person to come after me."

"Della, I'm not sure—"

"What? If we see him, we just stare at him? We can't hold him for just walking down the street or ordering a drink in a bar."

She had a point.

But he had lost one partner.

And while they'd barely known each other a few days, they had been intense ones. And whether he wanted to accept it or not, he was attracted to her.

And he knew what it was to lose a partner.

She sensed something in him, and he feared she might realize just how much he was attracted to her.

But that wasn't it.

"You know, what you said to Marlene is true. You blame yourself for your partner's death, and I read the file. It wasn't your fault in any way. Mason, when we get into this line of work, we know our lives will be in danger. He wouldn't want you blaming yourself. You did nothing wrong. You have to accept that—and accept the fact that I am an agent—a Krewe agent at that—and trust in me and let me do my job."

He smiled and nodded slowly.

"You may be too good a target," he murmured.

She frowned.

"Okay, right. I'm tall. I've got that. But you're stunning—and this guy likes attractive women. And one of the dead was with the National Police Directorate."

"But she was probably just out with friends—not expecting

anything. I am well aware now of what this man and his ac-complice are after. More than that—I have you at my back."

"All right," he said. "We'll play it your way."

They headed on into Bruger's bar. Sven was there. They sat at the bar and he came over to speak with them. "Anything?"

"We think you might have served a man truly responsible for some of this," Della told him, leaning close across the bar, and smiling. "Hey, play along with us. We're just a couple. An American couple enjoying the sights of Lillehammer."

"You got it," Sven assured her. "Anything I can do!"

She laughed and playing her part, turned to Mason, draw-ing a hand down his arm, coming close as if they were a cou-ple just as she had said.

He laughed in turn, stroking her chin, lifting her face to his.

He hadn't lied. She was stunning. And she could play a part brilliantly. A little too brilliantly for his—

They were professionals, he reminded himself.

People came in and out. It was still a bit early for the real nightlife to start. But then...

People began to arrive. It was a beautiful time in Lilleham-mer, and tourists were in abundance.

Despite the vampire murders.

The bar grew crowded. And leaning close against him, Della whispered, "I think that's him. To our left, alone right now, watching the brunette and her friend at the other end of the bar. Tonight, his hair looks almost platinum. But his face..."

Mason took a long sip of beer, carefully studying the man Della had seen.

Yes. It was him. The man described by both Scott Har-rington and Marlene Rogers.

Della set her glass down a little too hard, creating a noise.

She didn't turn; she stared at Mason as if he'd just said the worst thing in the world.

She shook her head and stood up. He set a hand on her arm, but she shook her head again, took her drink, and moved down to the other end of the bar.

He turned away, shaking his own head. There was a mirror above the bar. In it, he could see their suspect.

And he was studying Della.

He didn't walk over to her immediately.

He watched. He waited.

Mason pretended to ignore Della. But he was watching when she set her beer down, waved to Sven, thanked him, and walked out.

Their suspect waited barely a minute.

Then he, too, left the bar.

He was going after Della.

Mason let him get out of the bar. Then carefully, he followed, holding in the doorway to watch for a minute.

Yes. She had set herself up as bait.

And she had been great bait.

Because their vampire suspect was talking to her already, smiling, the tone of his voice as charming as his smile as he offered to walk with her, show her another establishment or anything else she'd like to see in Lillehammer.

They started to walk together.

And Mason knew he had to find a way to follow them, to have her back…

She'd been right about something else.

He was tall.

Blending into the night to be her shadow wasn't going to be easy. But if he had to disappear, he could ping her phone and get her location.

And yet…she was walking with a killer and he had to be close!
No, he would not lose another partner!

He would not lose her.

CHAPTER SIX

Mason had seen someone outside the house the other night.

Did that mean someone knew who they were and why they were in Norway?

Or did someone know the house was on the vacation rental sites and were they just checking to see if the newest arrivals happened to be attractive young women filled with beautiful life-giving blood to make them immortal?

Or was it all a sham for another agenda?

Well, whether this man knew who and what she was or not, Della was determined to play the game. She did not have a death wish. She did not feel she was being reckless. She had learned her new partner, no matter what demons haunted his mind, was spot-on. He would have her back. And he also had access to her phone. If she kept that on her, he could track her. Of course, this man could take her phone before attempting anything...

Nope. He wasn't getting her phone.

Generally, police officers in Norway did not carry firearms, but they did keep weapons in their patrol cars. Luckily, specialized units were allowed to carry, and Jackson had seen to it she and Mason were under the *specialized* category when they arrived. She had an FN Baby Browning pistol, small but lethal, tucked into the side of one heeled boot. Mason, she knew, was carrying in the small holster stuck into his waistband at his back.

Neither one of them wanted to shoot anyone. They desperately needed any suspect alive in order to get to the bottom of things. Although she wondered how Wilhelm was feeling. It was difficult when a killer had taken down someone close. No matter how enlightened a law enforcement officer might be, it could be difficult to separate revenge from justice.

But Wilhelm wasn't with them. It was just Mason at her back.

And the killer...or one of the killers.

Just as she had expected, their suspect came upon her in the street, calling to her politely.

"Excuse me!"

She stopped and turned and waited, a brow arched.

"Miss, I'm sorry to bother you, but I couldn't help but see you were upset and I—"

"I'm fine, but thank you," she said.

He was a good-looking man, just as she had seen in the artist renderings of him. Today, his hair color was very light and wavy and fell slightly over one side of his forehead. His eyes were blue, and his physique was nicely displayed in casual jeans, T-shirt, and jean jacket.

She didn't think English was his first language, but she wasn't sure where he was from.

"I'm Tom," he offered. "Okay, Tomaso, but I go by Tom. Tom Romero. And honestly, I'd just like... Well, I can tell you're American."

"I'm that obvious?"

He smiled. A charming smile. The kind of charming smile and slightly humble attitude that had helped killers like Bundy seduce victims with kind hearts into helping him.

"In the best way. I just happened along and… Well. I am sorry, I don't mean to be a bother, and I will leave you alone at any time, but…let me show you a bit more of the main area. There are other great hangouts. I can get you a drink and walk you back to your hotel." He winced. "There's a vampire running around, so they say. Let me escort you, at least. And forgive me, it may just have been a lover's spat, but that man had no right to treat you that way. Let me improve your evening just a shade."

She hesitated as if she were truly torn.

"No strings attached. I promise."

She smiled. "One drink. And… Well, yes, that would be nice. I seem to attract the wrong… Well, never mind. You do seem to be nice and courteous and… Sure. One drink."

She could see Mason was behind them, leaning now against a whitewashed pillar that supported one of the few new build-ings on the street.

"Come along, beautiful. Oh, I didn't get your name yet!" he said.

He had lied about his name, she thought. "Serena," she told him. She'd always liked the name. If she ever had a daughter, she was going to name her Serena.

"Serena, beautiful, like you," he said. He offered her his arm. She took it.

They walked another block and took a slight turn toward the north. As he had promised, there was another pub with cocktail tables inside and out. She opted for a drink. When he suggested she take a seat and he go retrieve their cocktails, she smiled and said, "Oh, no, please, let me come! I love see-ing the bar areas in Lillehammer. They're so pretty here!"

She might have frustrated him. He might have intended to spike her drink before it ever reached her. But he smiled. "Sure. Come with me!"

She did so. When he ordered, she told him she'd have whatever he was having. He bought two stouts and then suggested they sit outside where they could feel the ambience of the town and do some people watching.

They sat. She sipped her stout and asked him, "So, where are you from? Your English is so perfect, and yet there is a hint of something there!"

"Ah, because I'm a child of the world!" he told her. "Italian father, French mother, but a Spanish grandparent—and a Norwegian grandparent on the other side. We moved all over Europe when I was young. And I opted for college in the US. And you? Where in the US are you from?"

"The Sunshine State," she told him.

"Florida! Raised on sunshine," he said. "A water baby?"

"Something like that. So. What are you doing in Lillehammer?" she asked him. "Where is home now?"

"Well, you see, that's one answer in two. I'm trying to decide where to live. I love the world, and it's not easy making choices!"

"Right!"

He looked down the street. She followed his gaze. "Places can be so different!" he told her. "Look, look, over there. You see a row of tiny cars. Now, in the United States, you'd see a row of SUVs and vans. Big cars. Big country! And in the US, something is old if it's from the 1800s! Here, and throughout Europe, you'll find that history stretches back hundreds and hundreds of years, or over a thousand like Viking history!"

He kept his eyes on the tiny cars, urging her to do so as well, one hand on her shoulder. She looked in the direction he had indicated, smiling.

He was good. Very good. Out of the corner of her eye, she could see he was manipulating a tiny capsule, emptying the contents into her beer with an amazing sleight of hand. She wasn't at all surprised. She had been expecting him to drug her.

"Ah, well, Americans can get a bad name, huh? I try, of course, to undo all the negative aspects some people put forward. However, you're saying you're a child of the world. Well, then you know that everywhere, people are people. Some are kind and caring for others. Some are not."

"Oh, how true!" he agreed.

She stood up suddenly, frowning.

He looked up and then followed suit, asking her, "What is wrong?"

"Nothing, nothing, I just thought I saw a girlfriend over there. But it's not her." She pointed across the crowded street, and after she had done so, she played his game again, subtly, swiftly, switching their stout glasses.

Tom was none the wiser.

"Ah, too bad, I'd have loved to have met any friend of yours!" he assured her.

She sat and he joined her. "So," he said softly, "tell me. Did you have a lover's tiff? Or can I hope I might see you again."

He had leaned close to her. She leaned closer to him.

"I just met him a couple of days ago," she said. That much was true. "And...well, he wasn't the man he appeared to be at first. So, yes, I'd love to see you again. I think, though, I'm a little tired tonight." She picked up her drink and took a long swallow. "I mean, let's finish our drinks—but then, I'd love you to walk me back to my place. Then, well, what did you have in mind for our next encounter?"

He reached out, touching her hair. She didn't allow herself to flinch.

"Hmm. Let me consider the best place ever! Maybe the woods."

"The woods!" she said excitedly.

"Yeah, you'll love it! Beautiful hiking. We'll start bright and early!"

She watched him gulp down his beer, his eyes on hers with excitement. "Oh, yes, you'll just love all I have planned for you!"

She managed a very sweet smile and sipped her beer and then drained it. He did the same. "Come on. I'll walk you home. I'll know where to pick you up tomorrow."

"Wonderful!"

He stood, reaching out to her. She stood and took his hand. As they walked to the street, she saw the blonde companion he'd been with before. She had been waiting in a small sedan just down the street. She knew he was going to lead her to the car.

He was expecting her to pass out. And then...

Mason was there. He had probably seen the blonde waiting in the car by then, too.

She hoped he had, at least. But she had her little—but powerful—gun. Something he wouldn't expect. And he'd be passed out, she assumed. That left the blonde.

"Oh, look! There's Mandy. She's a friend of mine. Come on, she'll give us a lift."

"But it's just a few blocks..." Della said, but then she pretended to stumble.

He caught her.

She looked into his eyes. "I am so sorry. I swear, I'm not drunk or anything. I guess jet lag is catching up to me."

"Then it's a good thing we have a car, if only for a few blocks."

She nodded and they headed to the street.

"Hi!" Tom Romero called to the blonde driver. He held onto Della as they approached the driver's seat and he introduced her to the blonde. "This is Mandy. Mandy, meet Serena! She's just a few blocks from here, but if you want to drive us, that's great."

"Sure," the blonde—Mandy, it was today—said. "Hop on in. Serena, you look so tired!"

"Just all of a sudden," Della said. "Jet lag. So, thank you!"

"Crawl on in," the woman offered.

"I'll get her in the back," Tom said.

He opened the door to the back seat, ushering Della in, and then crawling in beside her.

"Oh, thank you," she murmured, and then she pretended to rest drowsily against his shoulder.

He had consumed his own drug. He should be going soon.

The blonde drove. Della weakly protested she was going the wrong way.

"Oh, I just have to make a quick stop first!" the blonde explained.

Della glanced at the man calling himself Tom Romano. His eyes were closing. It was time to see where they were going.

Mason had seen the blonde driving the car, and he saw Della was being helped in by their suspect.

They hadn't driven, but he couldn't let the car out of his sight. It would be a long shot for the speed he needed, but he called François Bisset.

"I need a car, about two seconds ago," he said. "There's probably a cop car somewhere, but I can't let them realize we're on to them. I'm on the street, about four shops down from Bruger's—"

"I will run right out," Bisset promised.

Mason kept his eye on Della, her would-be abductors, and

the car. She was making a great play of being drowsy, but he knew she hadn't allowed herself to be drugged.

Thankfully, their suspect hadn't seen her switch the glasses. But he had.

Fear almost caused him to step up to the car, but they would have nothing if he had done so. There was nothing illegal about a man stopping a friend on the street for a ride. And he knew Della was playing at being woozy, and her abductor would pass out soon. But hopefully, the blonde would drive to somewhere that would give them what they needed to bring the pair in.

And Della was armed, he knew.

Still, he had to follow the car. The blonde was probably as lethal as the man.

But as the suspect and Della crawled into the car, and the blonde started into the street, Mason heard Bisset calling out to him.

Mason was impressed with Bisset's quickness.

He drove up next to Mason and hopped out of the car, allowing Mason the driver's seat.

"Go!"

Mason didn't argue, didn't ask if Bisset wanted to join in the mission, he just headed after the blonde woman's car.

As he had suspected, they were going toward the mountains and the forest away from civilization.

He had to be careful he wasn't seen. As they traveled away from the center of Lillehammer, traffic grew sparse. He allowed several car lengths between.

But he guessed they weren't expecting company.

They came to a small road that skirted around an area of dense trees. The ground was beginning to rise, but they weren't at any great height.

When the car turned off onto another road that was barely

wide enough for the blonde woman's vehicle, he drew to the side of the road himself, slipped out, nodding to Bisset to do the same, and started jogging carefully after the other vehicle. Taking great care, he hid within the trees.

The blonde woman stopped the car in an area of heavily thicketed forest.

Mason watched and waited.

The good thing was with these two possible killers, they weren't talking about a pair of Harvard scholars with deep knowledge regarding criminology.

The blonde had glanced back while driving, and Della had pretended to be asleep.

They had reached the small highway leading away from Lillehammer when "Tom" went out like a light. But Della leaned against him, and her assumption that he was left to care for their unconscious victim must have been accurate.

The blonde didn't try to speak to him. And the way Della had maneuvered things, it looked as if his head was just bent— the better for him to watch her.

And when she parked the car, "Mandy" stepped out of it immediately, coming around to Della's side of the passenger seats, and opened the door.

Della pretended to half slide and half fall out the door.

The woman swore, stepping over Della and looking into the car.

"Tomaso!" she snapped.

Of course, he didn't respond.

"Men!" she snapped in English. "Ass drank some of the beer. Well, he is an ass. Leave it to me. And if you want it done right, do it yourself. The Master is a fool, too! Male, and... Damn, I'm better than this idiot, but...argh! But I will prove myself! I will sit beside Him through all the sweet years of our immortality!"

The blonde was apparently American—one who believed whatever she'd been fed. Incredible! Then again, throughout the years, people did often believe the most bizarre lies that could be told. Maybe people just believed what they wanted to believe.

"I will do it!" the blonde snapped.

Of course, Della still had no idea of what *doing it* meant, so she lay still, eyes slit, and tried to see what the woman was up to.

She opened the car's tiny trunk, taking out what looked to be a physician's medical bag. She set it down near Della and opened it.

There was a small pole for an IV drip that the woman set up, and then an apparatus with needles, what someone might see in a hospital to deliver life-saving fluids and medications intravenously.

Or the same type of apparatus that might be used in a traveling blood bank, where donors gave in the almost-comfort of a large van or bus.

And Della knew then, of course, what was about to happen. The woman meant to assure herself Della was out—and then insert those needles into her neck and bleed her dry.

She'd waited; she'd needed to be sure.

But when the woman started toward her to lay her out in a better position for the operation, Della struck, rising to a seated position and head-slamming the woman while reaching for her Baby Browning.

The blonde jumped back, a startled scream escaping her, and then a barrage of curses.

"Drop it all," Della said. "Hands behind your back."

"Maybe not!"

Della was startled herself when Tom or Tomaso suddenly appeared on the other side of the car, still the worse for wear, but brandishing what appeared to be a high-powered German gun.

"Drop it. Now!" he ordered her.

"Oh, no, no," Della said. "You are not going to bleed me dry for *the Master.* You'll have to shoot me—but by then, I'll have shot her."

"Do what you must. You're dying today."

"You'd let her shoot me?" the woman shrilled furiously.

"You know the Master! You are lucky he lets you live on with us!" Tom said.

They were at a hell of a standstill, and Della feared she might die that day. It was obvious that whatever vampire cult they'd become entangled in, it didn't value the lives of women. He really didn't care if he needed to kill his companion.

She held her Baby Browning firm, and Tomaso raised his gun higher. Then a shot rang out, an explosion that seemed to rip through the forest.

Della hadn't seen him fire… She hadn't fired…

But Tomaso screamed in agony. His gun went flying from his hand. He dropped down and fell behind the car.

Mason Carter came striding out from the bushes and trees, followed by Bisset. "Whoever the hell you are," Mason said, "we're taking you in. They'll be charging you both with murder. Hands behind your backs, please," he said, producing cuffs from his jacket pocket as Bisset, staring at the couple with narrowed, furious eyes, remained straight and silent.

"No!" the woman screamed. "No! He made me do this! He made me do all of this. I'm innocent, I never did anything—"

"I'm bleeding! Brutality! You've destroyed my wrist!" the man cried.

"Be grateful that's all," Bisset said quietly.

The woman started to make a mad rush for Mason, now that his gun was lowered as he handled the cuffs.

He would have been all right. But Della stepped forward swiftly, an arm straight out, hard. "Mandy" ran into it and went flat on her back instead.

Mason glanced her way.

"Nice move."

"Thanks. And good timing, too."

He smiled. "I have it all recorded."

He hunkered down and rolled "Mandy" over and cuffed her wrists. Della drew her to her feet while Mason went for "Tom."

"You can't! You can't! You've shattered my wrist!" the man screamed. "I... No, no, and she's a liar. She's the most vicious human being I've ever met. She loves it when the victims wake up. She loves to see their faces when they know they are dying. She's the monster. She's horrible, horrible. I... I was nothing but her servant. She's the killer, not me!"

"How are we taking them—" Della began.

"We're not. Wilhelm is on his way with local police. They'll see to it this man receives medical care for his wound, and that they're both incarcerated until we're ready to talk with them."

The pair were at the car, staring at each other now as if they'd truly like to murder one another in the most brutal way possible.

"You will pay! This is brutality. You shot me!" Tom said scathingly. "You will pay for this—"

"Well, as my friend noted, I think you're lucky I shot you in the wrist," Mason told him. "You killed a friend of a detective who is coming now to take you in. He's a good officer, so I imagine you'll arrive alive—but I wouldn't argue with him—he spent the day at her autopsy and with her family."

The woman suddenly started sobbing, great wet tears, gasps that shook her shoulders.

"I will never reach it now! Reach that level of immortality! Never...never. Unless!" She suddenly looked up at Mason and Della, venom in her eyes. "The Master will come for you. This last kill was for the life-giving blood! I would have earned my place, I would have...found another recruit among the men and taken another woman for her blood. But you will die! It may take time, but you see nothing, nothing. The Master is all-powerful, and he will save me and take your lives! He prefers the blood of women, but he will allow his followers to indulge in yours!" she told Mason.

"We'll see, won't we! Ah, listen. I hear a car. Yes, here are the fine men and women of Norway's law enforcement! And there's Wilhelm."

The man went silent, holding his injured arm. Two cars arrived, and Wilhelm got out of the driver's seat of the first.

He walked over and nodded to Della, Mason, and Bisset.

"We'll take them from here," he assured them.

He wasn't alone. Three uniformed officers had arrived as well.

"Wilhelm, the arrest is yours. But we'll need to interrogate them," Mason said.

"And I believe we need a forensic team," Della said, indicating the medical bag and the strewn contents.

"Of course," Wilhelm said. "The station will provide the room we need for these two."

"We'll all head in," Mason said.

"They must be processed, but you will be able to interrogate, of course, when it's done. But take your time. I believe Forensics is right behind us," Wilhelm said. "Jensen, one of our officers, will watch over the scene until they arrive, if you wish to speak with them first, but…" He paused, shrugging. "We'll keep them separate, wondering, waiting."

"I will head with back Wilhelm," Bisset said.

Mason nodded and looked at Della. She walked around to him, and he told her he had a car back on the dirt road before the turn.

The forensic team arrived before Mason, Della, and Wilhelm left. Wilhelm paused to speak with the head of the team. Then Della quickly explained she'd set herself up purposely—and the pair had been about to take her blood. She told them about the bag.

She suggested there might be a fair amount of DNA to be found on the various instruments, linking them to the murders.

Wilhelm drove the unmarked car and headed out just in front of Mason and Della.

They left the scene and drove back toward Lillehammer.

"You took a hell of a chance," Mason told Della.

"I knew you were behind me. And your timing was impeccable," she said.

Mason smiled, his eyes on the road. "Well, I saw you switch the glasses."

"You did? And I thought I was so subtle and crafty."

"You were. I was watching—and I knew what you were planning. Of course, I knew you were carrying your little Baby Browning. Still, when the car came, I had a bad moment. Interpol may be the liaison agency, but Bisset was right on. He had a car to me before you were down the street. Now that was lucky. I was afraid once you were in a car, I'd lose you."

"But you didn't. And, as I said, your timing was impeccable. Like your aim."

He was silent for a minute and then let out a long breath.

She thought they were maybe having a moment that might break down the strange barrier he seemed to keep erected against her and perhaps everyone else.

"Seriously, you did the absolute right thing, perfect snap decision-making," she told him sincerely.

"Della, I admit there was something in me shaking me up, and I didn't want to take any more lives. But...part of that had to do with the fury I felt when my partner was killed. I didn't want to shoot the guy who did it—I wanted to skin him alive. Obviously, I didn't act on the feeling, but it was so intense it scared the hell out of me. Anyway, I know how Wilhelm is feeling right now. Though we haven't known him long, it's been long enough for me to know how he feels— but he's too good of a law enforcement officer to act on it."

"It's difficult," she agreed. "I wasn't with the Krewe long before I met you in the bayou, and I was just with the Bureau about a year before that. One of the first cases I worked had to do with a man who killed nurses. We brought him in, and I know he was recently sentenced to seven consecutive life sentences—he'll never get out. But I also know some of the loved ones of those he killed felt the same thing—they didn't really want us to bring him in. They wanted him to die. Because loss is painful. I had to convince one husband the kind of prison sentence the man was receiving would make him pay for years and years. Death would have ended any earthly pain too quickly."

"And did he believe you?"

She shrugged. "I don't know. But at the very least, we could give the victims justice—and keep him from killing anyone else. And today... Well, if shooting one of them point-blank would have saved my life, I'd have expected you to do so. In case, however—"

"We need them alive."

"Yes, we need to find the Master."

"The Master. A master vampire. Here's where I'm curious. They haven't killed any men—that we know of. They took Scott Harrington out—probably very near where they took you today—and shared blood with him. Blood they claimed to be their own. I'm assuming they had taken the first step to bring him into their fold. But is there really a master vampire? And if so, just how many people has he convinced that killing is just and right, and drinking blood will give them eternal life?"

"There are cultists who believe the world is flat," Della reminded him. "Tell a lie often enough and it becomes a truth—at least to some."

"Apparently. Okay, here's another. The men are supposed to kill young beautiful women. But the blonde—"

"Called herself Mandy today," Della added.

"Whoever she is, she is in on it. What? Do you think they needed one woman to lure others? Or as a second? But as far as we know, she is the only female involved."

"She was talking about this kill being the one that put her in some special place," Della said. "I'm trying to remember exactly what she said. So many kills would put her on the path to immortality."

"And they turned on each other like rabid dogs when they were caught," Mason noted. "Well, hopefully, that will make them willing to throw one another under the bus, so to speak."

He was quiet.

"What's bothering you?"

"They never used a name. They just talked about the Master. 'The Master will come for you. This last kill was for the life-giving blood.' And so on. Whoever the Master is, he's created a rite or a religion. So many successful kills, and you're supposedly on the way to immortal life. Like any strange cult or religion, a leader preys on those who are vulnerable. Or in this case, maybe just people he believes will be easy because they might have the desire to kill in them already. Maybe he strikes at people who believe the world has treated them badly. But… I think we've stopped something. You've stopped something. But I don't think we're near the end of this."

"You think they don't even know who they were really serving?"

"Maybe not."

"These two are guilty of murder. Of how many, I don't know."

"And they will rot in prison. I know Wilhelm will see to that."

Della shook her head. "Norway doesn't have the death penalty, nor do they have what we consider to be life sentences. They are all about reforming prisoners. And they do have one of the lowest crime rates in the world."

"I don't think they've seen events like this often. But our killers may be wanted in other countries. Including the United States."

"But they may have only been the pair to kill here, in Norway."

He nodded. "We're going to need to find out just where they've been lately."

They arrived near the police headquarters and Mason parked. He glanced over at Della.

"Wilhelm wanted to get them processed—and then alone in interrogation rooms for a bit. Give them time to stew awhile, so—"

"Time to stew or think up some good stories," Della said.

"He asked us for a little time. And it's getting late again.

Let's do the tea thing they do here. We'll slide into that café and have tea and open-faced sandwiches. Sound good?"

"Sure."

It might be teatime, but Della opted for coffee. They were putting in long hours, and she wanted to be awake and aware for any discussions they were going to have. Mason went with coffee, too, and they ordered a sharable plate of little open-faced sandwiches with all kinds of toppings.

They chose a small table out on the walkway, and Della thought again that Lillehammer was truly a beautiful place.

Mason must have been thinking the same. "Strange," he said.

"What's that?"

"We're in the land of *Northmen*. Once upon a time, Vikings were the savage rage of the seas. 'From the fury of the Northmen, deliver us, oh, God!' And it's one of the most beautiful and peaceful places I've ever been."

"Well, remember, Vikings came from all over what we now call Scandinavia, and they collected warriors sometimes wherever they went."

"And slaves."

"Right. Well, the world was brutal. It can still be brutal, we know that. But it is kind of cool that things could change so much, right? This is beautiful. Crime is low. Norway is amazing."

He nodded. "Agreed. And the Viking era was long, long ago." He shrugged. "We still have despots in the world, though. And I tend to love being in Germany—great people. Yet it wasn't that long ago Hitler practiced genocide. And I'm sure a good majority of the people didn't believe in killing. They were just terrified for their own lives if they spoke out. Anyway..." He paused, looking at his watch. "We can head over soon, I think."

"Okay. This was nice," Della said. She hesitated. "And thank you. I mean, thanks for telling me about your feelings. It's bizarre to think we only met a few days ago because…"

"Yeah. Feels like we've been together forever."

"Sorry," Della murmured.

He smiled, moving closer to her. "I meant that in the best way," he told her.

"Oh, well, cool. I guess you're growing on me, too."

His grin widened as he stood. "Guess it's time we get over there."

She stood, too. "How are we doing this?"

"One and one and switch?" he suggested.

"You want to start with our blonde, Mandy? And I'll tackle our vampire."

"It's a plan."

When they walked across the street and entered the police station, Wilhelm was waiting for them. "We've drawn IDs off the fingerprints. The man is Tomaso Rodriguez, dual citizenship, Spain and the United States. Rap sheets in both countries, one a serious felony, assault and battery, in New York City about five years ago. He served a year but was then paroled for model prisoner behavior. He's railed against his companion in several languages since they've been in custody. The fingerprints on our blonde woman also gave us an identity. Maryanne Green, again, dual citizenship, the UK and the US. She has decided to clam up since they've been here. Just sits in the room, sobbing."

"Thanks, Wilhelm. Della will start with Tom, and I'll take on Maryanne," Mason told him.

Wilhelm nodded somberly and showed them down a hallway. He indicated a door to Della and she thanked him and headed in.

It might be a peaceful country, but the police here were taking no chances.

Of course, they had lost one of their own.

But Tomaso Rodriguez was still wearing cuffs, and the cuffs were attached to strong steel bars on the table he sat behind. His right hand and wrist were heavily bandaged—he had probably received expert medical attention—but the police still managed to see he was cuffed and secured.

He looked at Della as she walked in, bitter hatred rising to his eyes.

"You," he said. He shook his head. "You could have been in the place for heroes, but…now we are all lost. You were perfect, a beautiful sacrifice, and I… What a fool!"

"Well, Tom, I'm afraid you've been sold a very bad story— a book of lies. Killing is never a good thing to do."

He smirked at her. "Ah, you have never killed, right?"

"Only to save another."

"And I haven't killed. It was her—always her."

"Really. She committed all of the murders? I guess your so-called Master would be highly disappointed in you."

"In me?" He started to laugh. "I could draw them, I could draw them all. I secured the women for the blood we needed—"

"That is called conspiracy, you know. You're just as guilty."

"I'll be out in no time," he told her. He smiled pleasantly. "This is Norway."

"Ah, the Norwegians do hope for the best. But I think you'll discover you're mistaken if you think they're fools. They won't release you just because you might be as charming as you think."

"I will be out, I promise."

"You committed murders here, in England, in France—"

"Oh, no, no, no. My work has been here. Rather, that vicious Maryanne has kept her work right here, in Norway."

"You claim you didn't kill women in England and France?"

He smiled, appearing truly happy for a minute. "You are such a fool. They should lock you up. You don't begin to understand. And now, when it is your turn, you will truly twist and turn in agony in all the blazes of the Master's fire, far worse than any hell you might have imagined. You don't see the truth at all. You don't understand. The Master is... the greatest god. We serve him. And for our service, we are rewarded. But...now, I am not rewarded. So, I promise you, when I am free, I will find you. Wherever you may be."

"I'm not terribly worried," Della told him with a shrug. She leaned forward, smiling. "I switched glasses with you at the bar. My partner and I took you down easily enough...but here is something. If you help us, we'll help you. Now, when the forensic department goes through your bag of tricks along with all your paraphernalia for bloodletting, they're going to find fangs. Human teeth, sharpened to appear to be vampire fangs. And they'll find saliva and DNA that doesn't belong to you or to Maryanne. It will probably belong to another dead man, a prisoner who died while incarcerated. So let me help you. You help me. How did you get it?"

"The Master, of course."

"The Master. So, the Master was here, in Norway?"

He shrugged. "The Master is like the mist that falls at night. He comes and goes—he is wherever he pleases to be."

"So, um, hmm. He can turn into a bat? He can be invisible? Wait, I'm not even sure what the real specs are on a vampire. Though, honestly, it sounds as if someone read Bram Stoker's book just a few times too many." She dropped her pleasant tone. "A name—we need a name."

She was surprised when he stared at her with real confusion. "His name is… Master. Some like to call him Dracula, but he will be the first to explain that Vlad Dracul was born in 1431 in the town of Sighişoara, which was in Hungary, if I remember right, at the time. He was Vlad the Impaler. He was inspiration for many rulers. He was strong—he saved his people. But the Master doesn't have to go by a name, he is simply Master. And he wasn't born, he was created—a burst of life and energy, a being of blood and eternity."

"Fine. But you did see him here? We have your passports. We'll know where you've been."

He started to laugh. "Good for you. You have our passports."

"We will find where you've been staying and search through everything you own. We'll find all your passports and aliases," Della assured him. "You can answer me, or I'll figure it out. The more I have to figure out, the less I'll suggest any kind of clemency for you—no matter what country winds up with you."

"I stay here!" he said, lunging forward. "I didn't kill—Maryanne didn't kill—anyone in any other country. I will stay here!"

"We will see about that, won't we? Because I believe we'll discover you were both in England and France—where murders just like yours took place."

"No! Don't you understand! We are a family in blood! Bitch!" He swore at her.

"Where did you meet with your Master?" she demanded again.

He leaned back. "Here, right here, right on the street. I met with the Master here. But he is gone, gone like the mist. We were about to be eternal!" She thought he was going to cry. Instead, he flew into a rage. "You! You are the destroyer! And you will bleed and bleed, and I will see to it you die the most brutal death, and your flesh is seared, and you are broken and beaten in torture forever!"

She smiled pleasantly and stood. "Good luck with that," she told him. "And goodbye."

She hadn't expected he would give her what they really needed.

She believed he didn't know his Master's name.

But he had given her far more than she had expected—and what Mason had theorized. The "Vampire Master" was creating a family, a clan, convincing the vulnerable they could achieve immortal life. Most importantly, they now knew the so-called Master was providing the saliva DNA for the teeth. Angela could check prison visitation records.

And that meant he could be found.

As she stepped out of the room, she saw the British detective Taylor was standing in the hall, waiting for her.

"They committed the murders here," she said. "He confessed but claims he didn't murder anyone in another country."

"I know," Edmund said quietly.

She frowned and he continued, "I just received a call from my superiors. There's been another *vampire* murder in England. Elizabeth MacDougall. Drained of blood, laid out like a sleeping princess. This time, in the Orkneys."

CHAPTER SEVEN

"An archipelago of seventy islands, settled about eight thousand five hundred years ago by Mesolithic and Neolithic tribes, and then by the Picts," Mason murmured.

The Orkney Islands. It seemed strange they were already moving on.

Necessary, when the killings kept moving on.

"Mainland is the largest island and Kirkwall is the center of government and administration, and that's where we'll be," Della told him.

"We're on our way to Kirkwall Airport," Mason said. "On Mainland, yes? And you've been there, of course," he added dryly.

They were back on the Krewe jet, moving from country to country. Only they weren't alone this time. François Bisset and Detectives Edmund Taylor and Jeanne Lapierre were with them. The three men were napping in the back.

He and Della had dozed off along the way, though they'd had time to return to their lodging, pack and catch a few hours of sleep.

It had been a long night.

And they had boarded the plane just after seven o'clock. Della had fallen asleep. On his shoulder. He had nodded off as well and awakened to find her head resting against him. Something a little bit too powerful and frightening had stirred within him. But she'd woken up and quickly apologized, and he'd assured her it was fine.

Strange. And maybe all right. As a killer had once said, she would have been a great sacrifice for their ridiculous *Master*. She was a beautiful woman, but many women her age were beautiful. Hers was something greater; it was in the energy she exuded in her longing to right what wrongs in the world she could while still being able to laugh and tease and smile. He had, naturally, felt an attraction to her from the start. Now, when she touched him, it soared.

But in life, the one thing he had learned to do was control his feelings. He couldn't get over the anger he had felt when his partner was killed, and how he'd forced himself to tamp it to go forward—to remember always he was seeking justice and not revenge.

He dared to care for her. And as for attraction...

He had learned the hard way to control his emotions. And his libido, and still...

Yes, having her sleep with her head on his shoulder and her body against his had been a little too...nice.

But even that was beginning to seem okay. The days they had known one another had been the longest and most intense he had ever known.

And they were onward with part of the case solved, but it seemed the hard-core part of it was just beginning. He'd been right about there being more than one killer. And he wasn't happy about being right.

But while the liaison and detectives were with them sleeping on the plane, Jon Wilhelm was elsewhere.

He'd be working with the Norwegian legal system, handling the murders that had taken place there.

And the murderers who had both confessed their guilt.

He noticed Della shrug, bringing him back from his tirade of thoughts. "I told you, my father thought the world was incredible, that we all needed to appreciate one another, and he knew how to travel." She grinned. "There were a few times, when I was young, that we slipped onto a train at night in one country, closed the compartment doors, and pretended it was full, and used the train as our hotel for the night. But as for the Orkneys…they brought me to Scotland for my twenty-first birthday. I'd fallen in love with some of the great ghost stories regarding the underground in Edinburgh."

"And? Do your parents know about your ability with the dead?"

She nodded. "Yeah." She shrugged thoughtfully. "They were great. At first, I don't think they believed me. They were worried that my having survived a killer had fractured my mind. They wanted me to go to therapy."

"That's kind of the way it goes," he said. He waited for her to say more, but she went on about the therapist. She'd say more when she was ready, he thought.

She smiled. "So, I acted completely normal with the therapist—a nice woman. I didn't mind spending time with her, and I went to work and I went to school, and then…"

"Then?"

"A friend of my dad's passed away. I saw him at his funeral. He told me it was important I get to his wife. He'd left papers and policies behind, but they weren't in the regular vault. He'd gotten a new one not expecting a heart attack. So, I told the widow, and she told my folks everything I said

was true. She thought it was exceptional and wonderful. And
my folks talked to me again—I should say they listened to
me and accepted it all. Then I had to explain it wasn't like I
could call anyone up on a cell phone. Some stayed, some for
years, some just until something was solved, and some not at
all. But now…now they're just glad it helps in my work. The
good thing, though, was that they had faith in me. I know
my work scares them, but they don't try to stop me. So, give.
Who, um, was *your* first?"

"What? My first? Now that's a really personal question!"
he teased.

She looked away, grinning, and groaned softly. "Not talking sex. Your first ghost? I know Krewe members who talked
to the dead from the time they were little kids. That must have
been difficult to explain and to understand and…to exist in a
world where most people don't talk to the dead."

"I think we all talk to the dead in our hearts," he said, smiling ruefully. She was far more of an open book than he was,
Mason knew. And she was just right for him at this point of
his life—and definitely just right for the case they were working together. Each day he was more amazed by their ability
to read one another.

"Let's spill. I told you my story—it's your turn."

"Oh, so risqué!" he said. He couldn't help himself.

She groaned. "Ghosts! Not risqué. So? You tend to be Mr.
Keep-it-all-in. But please! You need to share a little bit. We're
strange team members, part of an even stranger team."

"Okay. I'll talk! But, hmm, still hurts a bit," he admitted.
"When I was a kid, we had a neighbor. Nicest man you'd
ever want to meet. You lost a ball in his yard, no problem.
Halloween? He was out with all kinds of candy and gifts—
dressed up, always, to entertain whatever kids came by. I
found out later in life that his pregnant wife had been broad-

sided in a horrible car accident. The baby was lost. His wife was in a coma. He never socialized much, just went to the hospital every day. But he didn't become bitter—he just tried to make life better for others. Anyway, there was some gang activity in the area, and he was out one night and was caught in a drive-by shooting. I didn't see him at his funeral, but a few weeks later we were visiting my grandfather's grave, and I saw him. I wandered off... Crazy, I was a kid, but I wasn't scared. He was a nice man. I figured if he had been cruel or evil alive, he'd be cruel or evil dead—but he'd just been a good man. So, anyway, long story short—too late, I know. He realized I saw him. And he said to come visit him often. He was going to wait—wait for his wife. He hoped she'd wake up and maybe have a good life even with him gone, but he was going to wait until he could be with her again. Your turn. You told me about your folks, but what about your first?"

"No, wait!" Della protested. "What happened? Did his wife come out of the coma? Did she start another life—what happened?" Della demanded.

Mason shook his head. "She never came out of the coma. But..." He paused, smiling at her. "Somehow, she was with him. And he waited to see me at the cemetery again. And he introduced me to her and said he had to tell me goodbye, but never to be afraid. He said what I had was special and needed to be used for all the good it could do."

Della searched his eyes and smiled. "That's a nice story!"

"Yeah. He was a great guy. I'd go and see him when something was going wrong in life, when I was having trouble at school... I loved him."

"That's still beautiful," she assured him.

"You? Come on. I know about your folks, but..." He grinned, lowering his voice to something deep and teasing—and relaxed. He was still surprised she drew so much out of him. But theirs was a strange relationship and he suddenly found himself seeing her in his mind's eye again in a towel. She was a beautiful woman, and he had felt that attraction to her soon after they'd met. He'd reminded himself they were professionals—working. And that had stood him well.

She grimaced and paused a minute, then told him about her past.

"A friend was accidentally struck in the head in a stupid high school rivalry. Anyway…as it happened, he died. We were all devastated, including the poor kid who killed him who was going to have to live with what he'd done all his life. The guys were all throwing stuff at each other, and well, one threw a heavy mug and it hit my friend's head. I mean, it was horrible at first, losing him. And the way I found out. I gave blood a lot, so I went to the hospital to give blood when there was an emergency call. Turned out it was for him… but he couldn't be saved. So later, when I was in college, he saved my life. A killer followed me, and thanks to him…well, I survived and the killer was caught."

"Whoa. Now that's…heavy," Mason acknowledged.

"And the same, really. He was a great friend, good to everyone, and I loved him. As a friend—we weren't dating or anything. But when he knew I could see him—and after the incident with the serial killer—he told me I needed to use what I had. I wasn't a kid, though. I was in college, home and working for the summer. And even then… Well, it was rough at first. Learning not to try to explain to people I could see the dead, or looking crazy when I was somewhere and saw a spirit and wanted to reach out."

"That's hard for everyone."

"But you were just a kid—"

"With help," he said quietly.

"Oh?"

"My father," he told her. "He had whatever this is. I didn't know it, of course, until I realized he was also talking to Mr. Delany—our neighbor who haunted the cemetery. Of course, he realized I saw him and he had a long talk with me, saying he didn't know whether to be happy or sad I'd inherited the ability, but he was a cop…and I wanted to be a cop, too. But after the service, I was recruited by the FBI. I figured it was almost the same thing."

"That's wonderful and admirable. A family of law enforcement!" Della said.

"Three generations. My grandfather was NYPD, too."

"You grew up in the city?"

He nodded. "Hey, not a bad place to grow up! I was raised in an apartment at the north end of Central Park. I spent days playing in teams there, at the museums—and my mom was a Broadway buff. I can't complain about life growing up."

"I didn't imply it was a bad place to grow up!" she assured him.

He smiled. "Guess what?"

"What? Wait! Don't say 'Guess what, chicken butt' or anything like it!" she warned.

He shook his head, grinning. "I didn't travel the way you did as a kid, but I have been to the Orkney Islands before and to Kirkwall, of course."

"What for?" she asked.

He nodded. "I had a great-grandfather from Glasgow and a cousin—Campbell Carter—who fell in love with golf and then all things Scottish. So, the summer between high school and college, my grandfather brought us to Glasgow—then Edinburgh, Stirling, St. Andrews, Loch Ness, naturally, and on up to John O'Groats and on the ferry over to the Orkneys."

She smiled. "Good! You'll know the terrain."

He sat back, smiling. Then his smile wavered. He wished

they were on vacation. A strange date or vacation. He had truly enjoyed the Orkneys from the historic stories about Vikings, kings, jarls, the Ring of Brodgar, the ancient standing stones, and so much more. He wished they could visit St. Magnus Cathedral, founded in 1137, filled with exquisite art chronicling hundreds of years of the Islands in its very walls. But...

As if reading his mind, Della leaned back, growing somber. "And now...the vampire. The Master? Or one of his followers, here in another historic and beautiful place." She turned to look at him. "Did Maryanne say anything that indicated they might know others who followed the Master in any way?"

"We went through all this last night," he reminded her.

"I just wish we could have switched off questioning the way we originally planned. But when Maryanne just started screaming—"

"And we learned about another victim," Mason reminded her. "And you wouldn't have gotten anywhere with Maryanne—any more than I would have gotten anything more out of Tomaso. We've both seen the videos of our interviews. They told the same story—same weird story. They did what they had to do, what the Master ordered them to do—but I never saw two people turn on one another like that. And even now—and I don't care how wonderful the Norwegian correctional system is, they're in for a long, long time—they truly believe they were an inch away from eternity. That's the thing. I think their *Master* was in Norway. I think he's the one I saw in the street."

"How? Because the murder in Kirkwall occurred just yesterday—"

"It's less than two hours in a private jet across the southern tip of Norway and the North Sea," Mason interrupted.

"You believe he has a private jet?"

"Possibly. He has funds from somewhere. It costs to hop around Europe. Just because you're rich, doesn't mean you're not a psychopath."

"True. Well, a profiler told me once that many a CEO was a sociopath or a psychopath. It makes a person capable of making ruthless business decisions. And just because you may be one or the other, that doesn't necessarily make you a crazy killer," Della said thoughtfully.

He nodded.

"That's right. You worked with profilers," she said.

"Six months. Six months well spent. Though profiling is a tool, and it's a tool that isn't perfect. Still, helps a lot."

"Did they profile you?" Della asked.

"I'm sure they did."

"And?"

He laughed. "Whatever they decided about me, they didn't share." He glanced at his watch. "We're almost there. I guess we hit the road running."

Della nodded gravely to him. The Orkney police and medical examiner had been at the scene of the murder. The body had already been taken for autopsy. They hadn't set out last night because it had been late and because the Scottish authorities were already taking all the appropriate steps.

"I'll wake our team members," she said.

"They are pretty great," Mason murmured.

"They are. Is that because they defer to you?" she teased.

"Maybe, hmm. Is it because Edmund Taylor is…tall, perfect and…"

"Hot!" she whispered, laughing. But then her laughter faded. "No, they're just a good group, right? They are different, but they seem to know what's needed most. They don't mind being the supporting figures—none of us does. It makes…"

He nodded, glancing at his tablet. "A good team. And we need to get to it. Our victims deserve justice and we need to get it for them. Elizabeth MacDougall, twenty-three. Scottish-American, traveling back to the land of her grandparents." He looked at Della. "This doesn't sound right, and someone will be devastated—but her parents are deceased and she's an only child. I guess the hardest part of this job anytime is telling a parent that their child has gone before them."

"Agreed. Scottish descent, but our victim was American. Traveling alone. And I imagine she was happy to meet people and that..."

"The Master easily charmed her?"

"Maybe," Della agreed. "I'll wake the others. The pilot is going to call for seat belts any minute."

Mason watched as Della gently woke the sleeping men. They sat up and came forward to take their seats for the landing.

"I'm sorry," Bisset told them. "A great liaison—"

"Sleeps when he can," Mason assured him.

Bisset nodded, then looked out the window. "Well, we'll go by the great circle of stones at Stenness," he said wryly. "To reach the crime scene. The medical examiner wanted the body brought to the new state-of-the-art hospital. The Orkneys had a hike in crime in recent years, coming back down now. The world is fighting to get back to normalcy still after the pandemic."

"Another beautiful place," Della murmured.

"We'll be meeting with Ian Robertson," Edmund Taylor told them. "Northern detective. Scotland is part of the United Kingdom but it has its own parliament, and its laws can be different in various ways. But he's an old friend—we've had to work across the border a few times." He shrugged. "For you, states may have slightly different ways of dealing with things. I wish I could say the United Kingdom has as low of a crime rate as Norway—"

"Well, England had Jack the Ripper, the US had H.H. Holmes, and Scotland had Burke and Hare. People with demented minds exist across the globe. Sadly, that doesn't make them stupid, and they can cause anguish before they're caught," Mason said. "Human beings are capable of the greatest kindness—and the greatest evil."

"Right, well, maybe… Do you think this might be the so-called Master at work?" Edmund asked.

"We will find him," Mason said with assurance. "All of our countries have our best techs and forensic crews looking for anything. But in my mind, our greatest possibility in finding him will be through Angela Hawkins Crow. She was one of the first members of our unit and she's married to our field director. She works in the field, but she's also amazing at maneuvering the computer and research world. She'll go through record after record until she finds out who has been where and when. I believe the fact the *fangs* these killers are using have DNA from dead men who died in prison is going to give us our endgame."

"Except it's going to be a fierce tangle for her," Della reminded him. "Because these people seem to be experts at aliases and fake passports. But she won't just go through records. She'll go through records and video, and she'll get something for us, I know."

"The sooner the better!" Edmund said.

"Of course."

Their pilot came on to announce their landing.

Della leaned close to Mason and asked, "What do you think made this killer choose the Orkney Islands? Curious. I mean, visitors usually head to Edinburgh or Glasgow, or they want to head to Inverness and search for the Loch Ness Monster. It's just curious."

He nodded. "Maybe Kirkwall happened to be where our fellow found one of his followers. From what we've seen, he can spin a lie that appeals to anyone questioning their life. Let's face it, no matter what side of the table people are on at the moment, across the globe we've become divided. So our main monster finds those ready to believe they could be untouchable—no matter what happens. Immortality—that's what he promises."

"Still. Kirkwall. I think there's something behind this," Della said.

They were soon on the ground. As Edmund Taylor had told them, they were greeted by Detective Ian Robertson, a man of about forty, fit and grave. And like Della, he was determined to understand why the strange killings plaguing the globe would come to Kirkwall. His voice was rich with the burr of a Scotsman, and it was good to see he appreciated the appearance of an international group and didn't resent them being in his territory.

"I've gotten us a van," he told them wryly. "We needed to fit. Hope that will work well with you. So, I know you've received the information on the victim, poor lass, and the crime scene photos have been sent to you. We may be far to the north here, but we are quite civilized. Well, with crime like most places, and our teams have worked the scene, searched for clues… But we'll go over it all again. And again, if needed."

"Thank you," Mason said.

"I was gratified to hear you caught killers in Norway, but was disheartened to realize taking down those two didn't end this thing. However, if you can clear Scotland of monsters, you'll be heartily appreciated."

Mason glanced at Della and smiled.

"Thank you. We don't ever mean to step on any toes, and God knows, this is your terrain," he told Robertson. "Oddly enough, we've both been here, separately, but in our younger lives."

"A magical place," Robertson said. "We'll be going through Kirkwall, and then on to the site where she was found."

Driving from the airport, Mason remembered his time here earlier, though he had taken a ferry over from John O'Groats at the tip of the Scottish mainland. The city was populated by about 8,500 people and sat on the harbor. The very air seemed to be a mixture of Norse and Scottish history and custom. The old Neolithic and Mesolithic stones that seemed scattered about, almost casually, here had been awesome to the boy he'd been when he first came.

"I could live here," he said softly, glancing over at Della with a grin.

"Part-time. It gets very cold!" she reminded him.

"Not from a northern realm, eh?" Robertson asked Della from the driver's seat.

"Not even north Florida," she said, grimacing.

Robertson laughed softly, and Edmund Taylor said, "I could do it. Depending on the neighbors. History is harsh. Some Scots never let you forget you're English."

"Really?" Della asked.

Edmund grinned at her. "Don't look at me like that! I have an American friend who moved from Pennsylvania to South Carolina. They never let him forget he was a transplant!"

"I guess we can be harsh anywhere," Della said. "That's something we forget. No matter where we're from, we all live the human experience!"

"And here we are," Robertson said.

Mason saw he had stopped on Main Street in the city of

Kirkwall. Their hotel was fairly large, a popular tourist destination. It was perfectly situated on the harbor, allowing them easy access to shops, restaurants, and the sights of the city.

He was impressed as well to discover he and Della had been booked into a two-bedroom suite with a living/office area that allocated plenty of room for two people to work on computers.

The building was crafted from stone and wood. Robertson must have seen the way Mason was studying it as they left the van.

"The hotel is relatively new—1800s," Robertson said. "I think the builders back then wanted it to stand out nicely next to the building there—from the 1400s. Our buildings reflect many centuries."

"And that makes for a charming city!" Della said enthusiastically.

Robertson smiled at her. Della had something, Mason thought. She hadn't just stolen *his* heart and senses; she had a true warmth to her that was simply compelling. A real asset in what they did, he thought dryly. People who might be suspicious of him might readily believe in Della.

She seemed to know what he was thinking. He reached for her bag from the back of the van and she teased, "Good team—brain and brawn?"

"Oh? You mean I have the brain and the brawn?"

She grimaced.

They all had their things in their Kirkwall lodgings quickly. The first stop was the autopsy. The medical examiner was a Dr. Calleigh Harper, a woman of about forty, serious as she looked up from her work as Robertson introduced the group he was bringing into the room.

"I understand these killers are using saliva from dead men on the teeth they use on the victims after using medical equipment to withdraw their blood. I've sent samples to the lab already," she informed them. "From what I have ascertained, this murder was much like those that occurred in Paris, London, and Lillehammer. And as you can see, the victim was left as if sleeping. Cause of death, exsanguination."

"Was she drugged?" Mason asked.

"I believe so. Rohypnol. Reports are due back shortly that will verify my findings," Dr. Harper said. She shook her head, looking from one person to another in their group. "She simply closed her eyes and her blood was gone. Before she knew it, she was dead and left as you see her. This is…diabolical and horrific. Detective Robertson caught me up this morning. Killers have been apprehended, I understand, but there may be many more out there following a head vampire? That's ridiculous, but just so, I suppose it might well be true. Horribly true." The gentle rolling of the woman's words somehow made it all the more tragic.

Dr. Harper had pulled the sheet from the body of the dead woman. She had been lovely with a head of dark curling hair that lay like a beautiful halo. Her eyes were closed and as Dr. Harper had said, she looked as peaceful as someone who had just fallen asleep and was having a gentle dream filled with sugarplums and fairies.

Mason looked back at Dr. Harper. "I'm afraid the couple apprehended had fallen in with someone they believe can make them eternal. We don't know if the *head vampire* came here and committed this murder, or if it was done by another disciple of this man. And we don't even know if he's really crazy, or perhaps a psychopath with an agenda we haven't begun to understand."

"Whoever he is, wherever he is…you've got to stop him," she said.

"We intend to," Mason told her solemnly. "And we thank you for your help."

"Of course," Dr. Harper assured him. "Please tell me if there is anything I can do that might help in any way."

Robertson and the others thanked her as well, and they started out. But while they were stripping away the paper garments they had donned to enter the autopsy, Dr. Harper came after them.

"Wait, please."

They all paused and waited.

"I don't know if this means anything or not but I understand that in Lillehammer, the killers were focused on popular pubs in the area. There is a new place that advertises it is totally Euro-American, and it's drawing tourists from everywhere and locals, too. You might try—well, this poor girl might have been there, enjoying the evening out. Of course, we have several popular places to go to, restaurants, pubs, and so on, but...the newest places always attract the most attention."

"Thank you," Della told her, glancing at Mason. "Definitely. Are there any traffic cams or ATMs in the area? We might pull footage, too. And, of course, I believe that the UK always has an abundance of CCTV?"

Dr. Harper looked back at her and then at Detective Robertson.

"Yes. There is an ATM nearby, too, a bank," Robertson said. "I'll call and get someone pulling everything from the pub. It's Evie's Euro-American Pub, right? That's the place you're referring to?"

"Exactly," Dr. Harper assured them. "I don't mean to send you on a wild-goose chase or the like, but from what I read in the reports about you catching the killers in Lillehammer, well, it might mean something,"

"Beyond a doubt," Mason said.

Again, one by one, the group thanked her. Detective Lapierre shook her gloved hand with his own and said, "We have
stopped a monster in Norway. He claims he did not kill in
Paris or London. What you have said may well help us here
and back in my homeland, too."

"And in London," Edmund added quietly.

"I can only hope!" Dr. Harper told them.

They were finally back in the van. Mason excused himself to call Angela at headquarters, bringing her up to date
on the autopsy, and the fact that Dr. Harper had suggested a
new pub as a local killer's hunting grounds.

But what he wanted was something only she could give
him.

"I know you're already working on it, but we need to cross-
reference visitors to the prisons where our saliva donors were
incarcerated. Of course, we don't know more yet about other
killers, but I believe one person, one man—the main vampire—is accruing the saliva for the fangs being used."

"I've been on it. And I've asked for any visual as well. Your
head vampire must have a case full of aliases, passports, driver's licenses, and more. But I will sift through it all, Mason.
And I hope to have something for you soon," Angela told
him. "I have everyone here working on this. We're using facial recognition and more, but as you suggested, he's a master
of false identities and disguise."

"The longer he's out there—"

"We know that, Mason. Trust me, we're working, twenty-
four seven. And François Bisset has been seeing to it the proper
law enforcement in all countries is informed each step of the
way—and other nations in the area are on alert."

"Thank you," he said.

"Of course," Angela murmured. "And thank you. And

Della… I know doing what we're doing is new for the Krewe, and you're hopping all over—"

"In style, at least," he interrupted dryly.

Angela laughed. "Hey, it's nice back here at home, too. Anyway, trust me. We are working this to the bone, too, from here."

"Thanks. If we can get an ID on him, we can get him."

"Yep. And we will."

They ended the call. The others were looking at him, even Robertson, who was glancing his way in the rearview mirror.

"When we get the saliva off the fangs, I'd be willing to bet a month's pay we'll discover he's a prisoner—dead or alive—in the US somewhere," he said.

"So," Edmund Taylor said, frowning, "you think the killer is American?"

"I think he's a chameleon. Maybe an American—maybe someone with dual citizenship. Someone who knows his way around the US and the US legal system—and Europe."

"And it might be the main man here," Robertson said.

"Maybe. We can hope. And hope, of course, we get him," Mason said.

"We'll reach the Standing Stones of Stenness in about twenty minutes," Robertson said. "We've got the site cordoned off. A forensic team has been out, but more eyes never hurt. Especially since you've been to other sites these killers chose."

Robertson had nailed it; they reached the area in less than twenty minutes. He parked the car and they headed out.

The body had been discovered by a small clump of bushes near the Loch of Harray.

"Hidden just a bit from the many tourists who head this way," Robertson told them as they walked out. "But meant to be found. You can see the markings where the body lay. We don't seem to have much of a problem with visitors—or locals—leaving behind cigarette butts or beer cans. I mean to a lot of young people, there's nothing exciting about standing stones, even if they are thousands of years old. But… Well, there's also little traffic here at night, so…"

"Grid around the body site?" Mason suggested.

"I'll take north," Edmund said.

"South," Lapierre said, shrugging.

"Mason, if it's okay, I'm going to move toward the stones," Della said.

"I'll head around this area toward the water," Mason said. "Check out the banks of the Loch of Stenness and the Loch of Harray."

"And I'll stand here, and see what I might have missed," Robertson said.

They all moved as they had said they would. Mason watched as Della walked toward the four remaining stones and into the center of the circle. If he remembered his history right—determined by leading archaeologists through the years—there had originally been twelve stones with a hearth in the center of the circle.

He moved toward the Loch of Harray at first, north of the Loch of Stenness. The water, rippling beneath a strong breeze that moved the waves, was beautiful. As was the countryside.

He knew that once again there had to be something to the locations chosen for the killings, even if they were committed by different killers.

Something that meant something to the main killer.

London was…

A huge city, an old city, old Roman Londinium. Nowhere nearly as old as the stones here in the Orkneys, but it had been founded around 50 AD on the Thames. London was huge, however. Paris was also huge—in comparison to Lillehammer and now to this area of Scotland. Julius Caesar mentioned what would become Paris in the first century BC, a time when Rome was conquering the known world.

The ancient Romans had believed in a vampiric creature—they'd called it Strix. It was a demonic creature that lived off blood, particularly enjoying babies.

Lillehammer had been a settlement of one kind or another since the Iron Age. The Vikings had their draugar creature, again, demonic and blood-sucking.

And the Orkney Islands...

The stones spoke of their age.

Scotland was also famous for its legends and lore, including the *baobhan sith*, a vampire-like creature who appeared as a beautiful woman in green, the color of the faeries, but capable of shape-shifting and much more as she sought the blood of others.

But did all that reckon into the killings?

He walked the bank of the water and found nothing. Nothing at all. But as he headed south to the Loch of Stenness, he saw something on the ground.

A cigarette butt. Maybe a careless tourist. Probably a careless tourist.

But he hunkered down to retrieve it, drawing an evidence bag from his pocket and using the bag itself to cover his fingers as he plucked it from the earth.

Yes, from a tourist, except...

As he studied it more closely, he noted that there was something on it. Something red.

Blood.

CHAPTER EIGHT

Della stood in the center of the stones, remembering what Robertson had said. The place was magical. Some of the great standing stones dated back to 3500 BC, she had been told. And Orkney also seemed to have weather at times that added to the feeling of something beyond.

The wind was blowing, as it had when she was younger. It picked up her hair and flew it almost straight out. Standing there, she felt the centuries of human existence sweeping through her. She stood very still and closed her eyes, wondering if there were ghosts that haunted the stones.

There must be, she thought. *All those years…*

But when she opened her eyes, she was alone.

It was still early for tourists—or even locals who enjoyed the stones—to be out. And Mason was with Detective Robertson and the others a distance away, searching the ground by the clump of brush where the body had been discovered spread out.

Standing in the center of the stones, feeling the wind as it whipped around her, she wished they had come just to enjoy the countryside. From her vantage point, she could see the gentle roll of the land leading to the mountains, and see what was left of other massive stones that seemed to reach to the sky. From where she stood, she could see the crystal waters of the lochs, and in the distance the rise of the mountains. All around her, there was the flat land where the stones had once risen in their circle thousands of years ago. The greens of the trees and grass and brush were touched by the beauty of a stunning blue sky, and it truly seemed as if she stood in a place of magic.

Did their killer choose this place? Because while he might be seeking eternal life, the death he created was against everything in nature that was so perfect and beautiful?

She was heading toward Mason's position when she was suddenly attracted by something that seemed to be out of place.

A small white stone set visibly near one of the huge rising stones.

She walked to it, curious, and frowned as she stooped to pick it up. But she paused when she saw an etching in the stone. Reaching for gloves and an evidence bag, she finally picked it up.

She wasn't sure what it was, the texture was almost like marble. It was oval-shaped and about four inches wide and two inches high. She put it in an evidence bag.

And there was no doubt it was from the killer. He had left them another message.

So as the Stones stand for millennium do I, for blood is the life.

She rose, calling out, "I've got something!"

As she did so, she saw Mason had already stood; he also seemed to have found something on the ground.

She hurried toward Mason, and seeing her, the others did the same. He carried an evidence bag that held a cigarette butt. She frowned, knowing the butt would give them DNA but that it might not matter at all. While most people were respectful, there were those who tossed their trash wherever.

Then she noted the red on it, and her thoughts immediately ran to the idea that the color indicated blood.

"Not lipstick?" she asked, hurrying to him.

"I don't think so."

Robertson was with them by then. "Aye, we'll get it to the lab, but my money is with you. That's blood. Della?"

"He left us a message," she said.

Edmund Taylor and Lapierre had joined them as well. Lapierre stared at the baggie Della raised and read aloud. "'So as the Stones stand for millennium do I, for blood is the life.'"

"No one can really be this stupid," Edmund said, shaking his head. "It's just a tease to us, a come-on. He's having a hell of a time taunting us all."

"That may well be true," Robertson agreed, but he offered them all a rueful smile. "Then again, in the past years, I believe divisions in all our countries have been so deep and social media has been so crazy, people believe just about anything."

They were all silent for a minute. "All right, this is my theory which could be proven wrong. I don't think our *head* vampire believes any of it for a second. But! I do believe he convinces his sub-killers, followers, whatever you want to call them, that every word he says is true."

"He's studied legends," Della said. "That's it—that's how he's choosing his places."

"And there you are. The Orkneys by their very essence are filled with legend. From the Picts to the Gaels to Celts and on to the Norse. Gods and goddesses and demons." He looked over at Della, shaking his head. "That stone…a stone against what were religious stones to our Neolithic ancestors." He sighed. "I'd like to get us back to Kirkwall and get a forensic team back out here, widening the field. But I'd also like to get your finds to the lab. A long shot, but we could get DNA or fingerprints that could speed us along."

"Good. And we'll need a plan for tonight," Mason said. "And we'll catch up with our home office again. If our main vampire isn't an American, he's been in America. And I'm also hoping another insight into this matter will be through discovering how the killers wound up with the saliva of dead men."

"I'll drop you at the hotel," Robertson said, nodding to them all, "get to the lab, and be back. We'll meet at the hotel before deciding on our next steps."

"What will you need?" Della asked him. "An hour…an hour or two?"

"Two hours. I'll see what my people have discovered, get the lab to move quickly, and grab a bite. The hotel has fine room service, and there are a dozen eateries nearby…excellent fish—you can see the fleet from the hotel and the street."

"We'll find food and meet in two hours after drop-off," Mason said.

Robertson nodded grimly.

They were quiet as they drove back to Kirkwall. Della thought they were all reflective. And she knew Lapierre and Edmund remained worried.

They'd caught the killers in Norway.

But the killer responsible for the deaths in London and Paris was still at large. Now that they knew there was more than one "vampire," they feared other deaths might occur on their own turf.

They were all disturbed, wondering if the main killer truly saw himself as above all others, and if he might be a man who really believed drinking human blood could give him eternal life.

Robertson dropped them off. Lapierre and Edmund almost spoke over each other, excusing themselves to go to their rooms alone to work with their people. Bisset remained with Della and Mason for a minute, then shrugged and asked if they minded if he took a nap.

"Please!" Della said. "Yes, yes, go get some sleep."

"Hey, they even speak English here," Mason said.

"Well, something like it," Bisset said. He winced. "In truth, the Scottish use of the language is quite beautiful. I must acclimate myself each time to the pirate *R*'s!"

When he headed for the elevator, Della turned to Mason. "I'd very much like to head over to St. Magnus," she told him.

He frowned, curious, but didn't seem against the idea.

"Well, praying we find this bastard couldn't hurt," he said.

"We can certainly say a few prayers. But, Mason, the cathedral is truly part of the heart of the Orkneys. It was begun in 1137 in honor of Magnus Erlendsson and the man is considered a saint by many and a martyr by others."

"And you think he might still be hanging around?"

"The churchyard is old and… Well, someone helpful could be there!"

He smiled and nodded. "I love the story of Magnus, how he refused to partake in a raid in Wales, how his goodness and gentleness made him seem to many of his fellows. He ruled with his cousin Haakon amicably enough until—"

"Until his cousin decided to execute him!" Della said.

"So indignant," Mason teased.

"Well, I am indignant for him!" Della said. "There were two earls of Orkney at the time, and they ruled peaceably enough for a while, but their men started having a problem. To me, it sounds as if Haakon was ready to solve the issue. They were to meet on another island with only two ships each. Instead, Haakon brought a fleet! Magnus spent a night in a church but was treacherously taken the next day. And one of Haakon's men refused to execute Magnus, so Haakon's cook was ordered to kill him with an axe. So, of course, Haakon became earl, but Magnus was first buried where he was murdered. Then his mother asked that he be laid in a church, but that church had been built on awful stony ground and water seeped in, and the place was filled with mold and the foundations turned green—not a great place for honoring anyone with prayer. Then, finally, when the cathedral here was erected in his honor, his remains were brought here and work crews in the last century found them in a pillar and returned them. Oh! The bishop at the time had refused to have the body moved at first. Then he went blind, according to legend, and only when he prayed through Magnus did he get his vision back. So, this poor guy is murdered and his remains went back and forth, so it seems."

"I know the story," Mason assured her, "and heck. Can't hurt. You're right. Maybe we'll find someone."

They walked down Broad Street. The cathedral truly dominated the skyline of Kirkwall, and there was certainly no difficulty finding it.

"Actually, or technically, it's not a cathedral anymore," Mason said as they neared the edifice. "It's a parish church of the Presbyterian Church of Scotland and belongs to the people of Kirkwall—due to an act by James III when the Orkneys officially became part of Scotland."

Della glanced at him, bemused. "How do you know all this history?" she asked him. "It was always a passion for me. I have a cousin who was truly fascinated with my grandparents when we were little, and he made me read everything in the world to him that had anything to do with Vikings and Norway, but...eh?"

He grinned. "I'm just a great historian."

"Really?"

"No. Google," he told her.

She laughed softly.

"I always liked history, too. And my family traces back to the British Isles at some point—though I think someone married someone from everywhere in the years since, but—every time there is a great historic series on cable, I get it in my head to look up what really happened."

"You watch television?" she teased.

"Well, sadly, I don't golf."

It was Della's turn to laugh but she fell silent as she looked ahead.

They were coming to the cathedral, which was open daily. Throughout its history, it had been both Catholic and Protestant, and there were signs assuring the public that anyone of any faith was welcome.

Just like the beauty of the nature around her when she had stood in the stone circle, the majesty of the cathedral touched Della. She knew it was built of red and yellow sandstone, and it'd taken three hundred years to build with major additions even after. Throughout the years of building, there had been rumors of miracles associated with Saint Magnus. To stand at the entry beneath the massive arches and the Romanesque and Gothic features was amazing.

"I'm going to light a candle," she told Mason.

"I'll light one, too, for our victims," he said softly.

She nodded and for a minute felt somber.

They then headed outside to the churchyard.

Like the cathedral itself, it was old, with the graves spanning the centuries.

"There are some amazing souls resting here," Mason said. He was looking at his phone. He looked at her and said, "I downloaded the app."

"Oh, cool!" she told him. "Good idea."

"You know many people are actually interred in the church—or kirk," Mason said.

"Right. But out here…"

She looked around. There were many stones, most seeming to have been erected in the fourteenth to the seventeenth centuries. There were several freestanding sarcophagi as well, and numerous angels and memorials.

"Anyone?" she asked Mason softly. "I know the famous explorer, John Rae, is buried here. The man discovered the northwest passage in Canada. And, of course, every old churchyard has its famous denizens. I was just hoping for…" She let her voice trail.

"Orkney has to be haunted, right?"

She grimaced. "Well, Edinburgh is, and Stirling, and…"

"The little cemetery in no-name America," he said softly. "It just depends on if a man or woman feels he or she needs to stay!"

They wandered the graveyard for several minutes, pointing out different gravestones and memorials, then Della shrugged and said, "Thank you for humoring me."

"We saw something beautiful, and we need beautiful things sometimes," he assured her. He reached out a hand. She took it, and they left the graveyard. As they did so, she realized that leaving there, hand in hand, seemed to be the most natural thing in the world.

They were working and they were professionals, and yet…

She'd heard the term *soulmate* bandied about. It had never meant much to her. In fact, she'd fought against the concept of mistrust when they had first met.

And now…

She gave herself a serious mental shake. They were after a heinous killer.

All the more reason to long for all that was beautiful in humanity.

She was so involved with her thoughts on an intimate and personal nature that she didn't notice the man striding by her side at first.

And it was only after she finally saw him that she knew why she hadn't heard him.

He was a dead man.

A dead man moving along, kilted rather than wearing breeches. His tartan stretched over his shoulder and a brooch with a family crest held the tartan in place above the white linen of his shirt.

And he was grinning at her as he strode along beside them, having accomplished his feat of startling her to the core.

"Beggin' your pardon, lass, but you were lookin' for someone, eh? Well, I watched and saw you were among the magic ones, and decided I'd be finding out just what it was the two of y' be a lookin' to find."

She was so startled she nearly stopped dead in the street.

Mason had her hand.

"Keep walking, Della. Sir, it's a pleasure to make your acquaintance. My name is Mason Carter and this is Della Hamilton."

"Americans," their new spirit friend said knowingly.

"Yes," Della told him quickly.

"Ye haven't quite the look of tourists," he said.

"Because we're not," Mason said, looking ahead as they walked. "We're part of an international team trying to stop a killer," he explained.

"Ah, the poor lass by the great stones!" he said.

"Yes," Mason told him.

"I've heard. People are getting quite afraid here, they are. Those who live here, those who come here. They talk in the burial ground at the old kirk. A monster is at work. Some fear vampires truly roam the earth. There will ne'er come a time, I fear, when men and women all realize the greatest monsters come in human form!"

"We've caught a couple—they were killing in Norway," Della told him. "And we were hoping since you freely go about unseen, you might have been able to see something. How rude! I've not asked you your name yet!"

A tam sat atop the fellow's head of rich chestnut hair. He smiled and looked as if he must have been a friendly and easy-going man in life.

"Sir Gordon, dear lass, Sir Gordon Stewart. Part of His Majesty's fine peacekeeping force at the time when the Islands were becoming part of the greatest land on God's great earth, Scotland!"

"Ah, well, lovely to meet you," Della assured him.

"Likewise."

"Aye, well the pleasure be mine, for the magic ones are few and far between!" Sir Stewart said. "And you were part of that, eh? They talked that a killer or killers had been apprehended in Lillehammer, but warnings were still out and about. There are no monsters," he said firmly. "A witch here and there, perhaps, but that by choice. Evil can only happen then when evil is allowed. How may I be of service?"

"Shall we stop up ahead by that charming little café? I see outside tables, set for the season, I imagine, and if we may…"

"Aye! The café. Leave me with the lass to chat, young Mason, and we'll be quite fine, I do so swear!"

Della glanced at Mason and then at her watch.

"We've thirty minutes left," he said.

"Thirty minutes it will be," the ghost promised.

Della found a table and took a chair, noting the spirit of Sir Gordon Stewart had learned how to manipulate his environment—without her help. He wedged a chair near her out enough to allow him to sit. "Now, lass," he said, "take your phone out and you'll appear to be quite normal."

She smiled, doing as he said.

"You know about phones—and people like us not appearing to be so crazy that they lock us up," Della said.

Her ghost grinned. "Indeed. In the past five hundred years plus, I have learned year by year, and watching man has been…painful and exquisite. Every century brings monsters, and every century brings saints. And if ever I may help put down a monster… Well, I believe that is why I stay," he added softly.

He hadn't died as an old man, Della ascertained. He'd been perhaps forty, if that.

"Sir, if I may ask… I had believed the transition was peaceful."

"Aye, for it was not war that made one country give to another, but simple finances. King Christian, who had created a unified Norwegian and Danish kingdom at the time, granted the earldom to James III because he was broke. He'd offered his daughter, Margaret, in marriage. But rather than summon the promised dowry, the Orkneys—and eventually, the Shetlands—became part of Scotland. I don't believe Margaret and King James were ever a loving couple, but… Well, the world changes."

"One hopes," Della murmured.

"No, I stay because of human monsters," he said. "As many of us do."

"Sir?"

"There was a laird here who believed himself above others, though James himself bore the title of earl, as per King Christian! But he took an innocent lass promised to another, and I knew her mother and her father and her youth and… Well, I did free the lass. But the laird and I both fell in the fight that followed. He preyed upon the young and lovely, just as this monster does now. Then for many years, the monster was powerful. Now, while laws in Scotland and England may be a wee bit different just as they are from state to state for you, such behavior would see a monster behind bars. I do not regret my death—I'd go to battle with such a man again. And just a bit ago—1920, I believe it was—I helped capture a rogue who had killed a fine lass and her lad to steal from them. So…here we are. What may I do for you?"

"Help us find him—or them. It may well be more than one killer, and there may be more than one person or couple involved, each on a separate path. In Norway, it was a couple doing the killing and it was strange," Della told him. She frowned, shaking her head. "They believed it all, the ridiculous tale they'd been told. Enough killing—draining of blood, drinking blood—would lead them to their eternal lives."

Sir Gordon Stewart didn't have a chance to answer. Mason returned with a tray bearing two cups of tea, a basket of biscuits and a plate with different cheeses and meats.

The ghost waited for him to be seated.

"Ah, well then. That is the story of humanity. A man—or a woman—chooses what they believe, and fact may matter and it may not. Aye, 'tis tragic what we're seeing take place and it must be stopped. And I will help in any way. I can't say I know who might be committing such atrocities, but… I believe that there's a film group here."

"A film group?" Mason asked, frowning and glancing at Della.

"They be making a movie, not for the big screen, but for what they're calling a cable channel. There was a lovely young lady I believe to be the lead in the movie, and she was at the cathedral just yesterday with friends from their makeup department. She was so pleased to see the church. They had permission to work by the great stones…but she was so afraid! Then last night, they had something of a costume party, which I believe is something they've been doing now and then. The piece they're working on is *historical*. Something taking place in the 1800s, or so I believe," Sir Stewart said. "And with what happened… There was a man among them in a dark cape, but pretending to be something made his friends yell at him. I don't know what happened then, they all went into the private room they'd taken. I found his behavior quite abominable, too, and moved on down the street to enjoy watching the fleets at the harbor."

Mason looked at Della. "It's him," he said quietly.

"Him? You've seen this man. They were filming in Norway?" Sir Gordon asked.

"No, but one night…there was someone in a cape near our lodging in Lillehammer," Mason said. "I went to find him, but he disappeared when a car came by and scooped him up. Of course, there may be many men with such a cape."

"Legends!" Sir Gordon said, shaking his head. "We have them here, of course. Me own mother swore the banshee was there as she lay adying. And, of course, we have a blood monster—"

"Baobhan sith," Della said, glancing at Mason.

"Aye, indeed," Sir Gordon said. "But…they do come out at night when they're not filming late. Not legendary monsters, here or there, but the film crew. They move along Broad Street and Main Street, along the harbor haunts, so to say. If ye're seeking a man in a cape, he may be among them."

"Thank you," Mason told him. "We had heard about a café—"

"The new café. Combining the best of Europe and America!" Sir Gordon said. "Aye, and indeed, they have spent time there. I shall watch, I shall!"

Della saw Mason was glancing at his watch. They needed to take what they had learned—for whatever it was worth—back to the others.

She believed—whether it was their main vampire or his Scottish lackey—that Sir Gordon was right.

Their local vampire was with the film crew now.

And he was happy to put on a costume—a cape.

"We need to meet with Detective Robertson and our French and English counterparts," Mason told him. "But we thank you. Sincerely."

"Ah, well, 'tis a pleasure to meet such a lovely lass and fine sturdy lad!" Sir Gordon said. "And it will be my pleasure as well to direct you to another human monster! You know where to find me."

His chair scraped as he rose to leave them, bidding them goodbye.

Della thanked him and said goodbye as he walked away.

Mason watched him for a minute and then looked at Della. "He is so right. And we all learn that. Monsters are human."

She nodded. "We see it too often."

"And yet, we do this."

"Because," she assured him, "it feels so good when we've saved the innocent! Right? Seriously."

He nodded, smiling. "This is just…"

"Yeah," she agreed. "We need to get moving!"

She hadn't realized just how much of the cheese and biscuits and meats she had eaten until she looked at the tray as they rose.

Of course, Mason had been dining on all of it, too. She glanced at him.

"Hey, we're terrible. We always forget to eat. So, hmm, go figure! We ate it all."

"Did I leave you anything?"

"I think we shared perfectly," he told her.

He didn't take her hand this time. He had the tray and returned it to a station where he could dispose of their trash and leave the cutlery. Then they started back on the block toward the hotel with Mason glancing at his watch again.

"We'll be just on time," he told her.

"I wonder if Detective Robertson has managed to learn anything."

"Unless their labs work at miracle speed, I doubt we have much yet," he said. "But...after having met with Sir Gordon Stewart, I believe whoever and wherever, they play the same game. They seek out popular places and stalk their victims before seizing upon them—either charmingly or through force. So tonight..."

"Euro-American it is!" she said.

"I'm going to check in with Angela," he told her.

"Maybe we'll get an idea of what we're looking for," she murmured. "Unless—"

"Unless it won't help us any to find the main guy because he has another would-be creature of the dark working here?" Mason asked.

She shrugged.

"But maybe he is here," Mason said softly.

"Maybe. Hey, a name would be nice, just to have—even if we have to crawl all over Europe and beyond to find him."

"Yeah, a name would be nice. I'll call now," he said.

Della watched as he put through the call. They were on the street so he didn't put the phone on Speaker. She watched as he frowned, finally thanked Angela, and ended the call.

"Well?"

"She went through the video logs on every visitor to the prisons where the men were that the saliva traced back to—going back several years. Then she had to cut down the possibilities, then try to do video comparisons. She's come up with a possible."

"A possible?"

He shrugged. "Hard to tell. But if it's who she thinks it is, it all fits. Our head vampire went to the different prisons under different names—with impeccable false IDs each time. She believes, despite the cosmetic differences he had at each stop, he might be a man named Stephan Dante. He has dual citizenship—he was born in America, Slidell, Louisiana, but his father was born in Italy and his mother was born in France, meaning he can hop around the States and Europe when he chooses. But here's where he gets interesting—he was a certified phlebotomist a few years ago, then he took a job as a makeup artist for a production studio. But he was convicted of stealing from the studio and did some time. But he has been out several years. He was released right about the time the strange unsolved murders occurred in the States. He speaks several languages fluently—among them Norwegian, German, French, and Italian."

"Oh, my God!" Della breathed. "Angela has done it. That must be him. I mean…"

"At any rate, she's sending pictures to us—and to all law enforcement involved—of the many different ways he appeared when he visited the prisons. And she's sending his high school graduation picture to get an idea of what he looks like when he's not playing with makeup and costuming."

"Great," Della said. "Then maybe, if he is here… Well, we'll get an idea. Do you think he was the one in the cape below our rental apartments in Lillehammer?"

"If so, he had help. Because he disappeared in a car."

"Did Angela check on everyone involved with the dig outside Lillehammer?"

"Yes. But it was impossible to know if he was ever there

because the records on people hired just to move the heavy dirt are sketchy at best. But even the important archaeologists came and went. She's sent all the information to us. Tonight… Well, let's seriously study all the pics before we head out. But she's also sent us a list of people who came and went. It's extensive."

They reached the hotel and saw Detective Robertson seated in the lobby, studying his phone.

When he saw them arrive, he rose, nodded, and waited for them to sit as well.

"I've been going over the pictures," he said, adding dryly, "It's a pity this guy is a psychotic killer. His talent with makeup and disguise is grand." He looked at them, shaking his head. "We could pass him on the street within arm's reach and not even know it. Anyway, I've seen to…our Orkney victim. Elizabeth MacDougall's cousin arrived, and she said she talked to Elizabeth when she arrived here. Elizabeth was excited to head out for the night. She'd been to Scotland at least twenty times, but she'd never made it up to the Orkneys before. She wanted to see the nightlife of Kirkwall. So we know she did head out at night, and it is likely she headed to the new pub. She would have been pointed in that direction most likely by anyone she met."

"We're ready to hopefully follow in her steps," Della told him. "Did we find any witnesses? Anyone who saw her out before she disappeared?"

He sighed. "We've had her name and picture out there, begging for help. Naturally, our tip line received dozens of calls. She was seen at the new pub, she was seen on the street, and she was even seen drifting above the ground by one caller. So far, we have nothing really substantiated."

"How are we doing on forensics?" Della asked.

Robertson leaned forward and nodded grimly. "Better

along that avenue. We're sending the DNA results from the cigarette butt across the globe, and yes, the blood on the butt belonged to our victim. We may finally have something from that. And as for the stone…it's local limestone, shined to appear to be marble. Etched by a simple tool. Whoever wrote on it most likely acquired it right here in Orkney. What have you seen in the pictures Special Agent Angela Hawkins sent?" he asked.

"We're just getting to them," Mason said.

"Right, of course, I just received them as well." He glanced at his watch. "Detectives Lapierre and Taylor have received them, too. I imagine they'll be down, still going through them."

Della had just started looking at the pictures herself.

The man in them appeared with brown hair. Blond hair. No hair—a skullcap, she assumed. He knew how to use prosthetics—his nose was big, small, straight, and hooked.

At last, she got to the high school graduation picture of their subject. He would have been younger, of course, and yet, if he'd been walking the streets as himself, his facial features would be much the same.

"We were told," Mason said, "that there's a crew here filming a show intended for a cable channel. Do you know anything about that?"

Robertson looked at him, nodding. "Right, indeed. It's been in our news as well, of course." He grimaced and let out a sigh. "It's a detective show. They're playing on the old Burke and Hare story, not using the history, but it revolves around a present-day private eye seeking murderers who are selling human organs on the black market. Of course, the private eye is struggling because it's costume season. They have a made-up holiday going on. Yes, we're all finding dress-up and Halloween fun these days, but nothing here like in America.

They should have filmed in Venice during Carnevale. There you have some costumes."

"But this filming makes it easy for our killer to dress up and blend in," Della said.

She was listening, paying attention to the conversation, and also looking at the pictures Angela had sent.

"The production company is called Lochlean Films. The producer on this—Frasier MacLean—is also the director. I'll call and set up a meet for whenever you'd like," Robertson said.

"Thank you. If our fellow is good, I'd be willing to bet he's made himself part of the film crew," Mason said.

Della paused, frowning as she studied the high school picture of the man who was most likely their main vampire.

There was something about him as a youth…

She looked up and stared at Mason.

"Oh, my God!" she breathed.

"What?"

"Mason, we know him! We interviewed him! He was in Norway, and we talked to this man already!"

CHAPTER NINE

Mason had seen something in the pictures, too—specifically in the picture of the high school student. Something in the shape of the face…

But Della pointed out exactly what he should have seen.

"Sven!" she exclaimed. "In Norway, at Bruger's, he was going by Sven. He spoke Norwegian, and English like an Englishman rather than an American," she continued, shaking her head. "Mason! He was the one who directed us to the couple we nailed for murder in Norway!"

As she spoke, they were joined by Bisset, Lapierre, and Taylor. Each man studied the picture of the young killer thoughtfully.

"We need to reach Wilhelm right away," Lapierre said tensely.

"Indeed," Taylor agreed.

Mason nodded and said, "He can get over to Bruger's—verify the bartender was new to Bruger's—and then he needs to let Tomaso and Maryanne know the master they were serving was the one who led us right to them," Mason said.

"You think he may already have a job here?" Robertson asked. "Evie's Euro-American pub has only been open a few weeks. They would have hired bartenders recently."

"Possibly, but Sven was in Norway when we took down Tomaso and Maryanne," Della said. "I don't think even he could have gotten a new job in a new country so quickly. What was his real name?" she murmured, frowned, and checked the notes on her phone.

"Stephan Dante," Mason said. "And through his visits he's used the names James Miller, Herbert Shaw, and William Franklin. Wilhelm can find out what name he used to enter Norway. And," he said, looking over at Robertson, "we need to get footage from Kirkwall Airport—see who came in during the last forty-eight hours."

"On it," Robertson said, rising. "Going through all the video will, however, take hours—"

"A mountain of searching, yes. But we'll get our tech department on it, too," Mason assured him. "If the authorities can coordinate—"

"I'm on it," Bisset said, stepping away to put through calls.

"Angela found the similarities and ran facial recognition programs—apparently, this man's disguises gave her a hell of a runaround—but she's the best. If he came through the airport, he had to have been caught on video. And she will find out how and when."

"If he arrived at the airport," Della said grimly. "Vikings traveled here from Norway all the time via their longboats."

"Unless he's Njǫrd—the Norse god of the sea—I don't think he'd have time," Edmund Taylor said, grimacing.

"Okay, you have a point," Della told him, offering him a weak smile.

"We don't even know for sure it is him, or that he's left

Norway," Lapierre said, adding, "I'm trying to be the voice of reason and caution."

"Easily solved," Mason said. He already had his phone in his hand and he hit a few keys. "I was going to call Wilhelm to find out if he's working, but...thought to call and ask at the pub first. Except—"

"Wilhelm will have the authority to ask questions about the man," Della finished for him.

"I've got this," Bisset said. "Surveillance footage from Kirkwall already in motion across the world, and I'm ringing Wilhelm."

Mason and the others nodded and waited.

In a minute, Bisset had Wilhelm on the line, but before he could begin to explain, Wilhelm apparently went into a long tirade.

"Yes, we have come to the same conclusion," Bisset said, grimacing at the others. "We need you to find out if Sven left Norway even as we questioned the two who committed murder there—"

Bisset listened another few minutes, thanked Wilhelm, and then started to end the call.

"Wait," Mason said, reaching for Bisset's phone.

The Frenchman hiked a brow, curious, but handed his phone over.

"Hey, it's Mason," he told Wilhelm. "He's gone, right? You saw the pictures Angela sent, and saw what we saw—that good old Sven the Norwegian bartender was really a man named Stephan Dante?"

"Oh, yeah, I saw it. And I headed right over to Bruger's. Sven never quit, he just never appeared for his last shift."

"Well, he's right for what we've determined. Guy could have been a football hero—well-built, great smile, easygoing...people person. In all the wrong ways, so it seems."

"I'm trying to trace his movements from here," Wilhelm told him.

"Great. Thank you. I'd also like you to do something else. I think it's going to be important for you to interview To-maso and Maryanne again. It's very important they know it was their great *Master* who handed them over to the authorities. They might know something they don't know that they know. And if they know they were betrayed by the person who put them in their situation, they just might come up with something else."

"I'll get on it," Wilhelm promised them. "And… Well, I'll be here, but, please—"

"We will keep you in the loop," Mason promised.

"Be careful," Wilhelm warned.

"We will. Just another easy night," Mason said wryly, glancing at Della. "You, too."

"He's out there. He's out there somewhere," Wilhelm said. "And the thing is… Well, here I'll be trying to question two brainwashed idiots. I'm afraid the real deal of a monster is going to be a hell of a lot smarter and more dangerous."

"Forewarned and forearmed," Mason replied. "Thanks." He handed the phone back to Bisset. "I want to get to that Euro-American pub," he said to Robertson, "but I want to meet your friend with the movie production crew."

"Tonight?" Robertson asked. "I'll see what I can do."

The detective excused himself and made the call, spoke quietly, and listened. Then he hung up and nodded to the group around them.

"Frasier will meet us tonight," he said. "I told him we'd explain in greater detail when we saw him, but that we need help." He shrugged. "Needing help sounds a whole lot better than trying to tell a producer we think he may have hired a homicidal madman."

"Agreed," Adam said. "So—"

"He's taken a rental house just a few blocks over. They've been filming in the mountains and at Ring of Brodgar and in the house he's rented. I can take a few of you over. Though—"

Bisset cut in. "I know your concern. We don't want to overwhelm the man or send out any signals when not necessary. I say Detectives Taylor and Lapierre and I head to that pub. You can find us there when you've gotten whatever you can from the producer."

"I could use a good pint!" Edmund said.

"You Englishmen and your beer." Lapierre smiled.

"They most likely have a wine selection," Edmund offered.

Lapierre grinned. "I was thinking of a dirty martini."

They all managed to smile and left the hotel, going in their different directions.

The walk was pleasant. The air was brisk but seemed exceptionally clean. They passed others out for the evening, most laughing and at ease, a few speaking nervously, warning each other not to be apart.

There was a vampire plaguing the city.

There was crime scene tape up on the old building that was Frasier MacLean's "Lochlean Films" home and sometimes work while he was filming in Orkney.

"The tape is for filming, not real, but Frasier likes to keep it up. You get a fair amount of rather bizarre people wanting in on any kind of filming," Robertson told them.

"And it's legal?"

"Oh, aye, the man keeps his permits shipshape," Robertson said. "And he's good."

"You're old friends?" Mason asked him.

"University," Robertson said. "We played football together—real football, you know, soccer, not the American football where your foot almost never touches the ball."

Mason grinned. "Hey. I didn't make up the name."

Robertson tapped at the door, calling out, "Frasier, it's me. Ian."

The door opened immediately. Frasier MacLean was tall and lean, slightly balding, with a quick smile and bright blue eyes. He looked Mason and Della over, glanced at Robertson, and said, "American friends who want to be extras? You've got it! What a handsome couple. Ah, lass, no you are a beauty. Sir!" he addressed Mason. "Sorry, you're a beauty, too, just… Well, you are both welcome in my home. I'd love to have you background in many a scene. My major roles are cast—"

"Sir, we're not actors!" Della said, interrupting quietly. "But thank you so much! It's different help we need."

"Please," Mason added politely.

MacLean looked over at Robertson, frowning.

"You've heard about the vampire killing," Robertson said flatly.

"Of course. It's all anyone is talking about," MacLean said. He frowned. "But… I'm not the vampire killer, I swear it, and I can't begin to believe that my mate here would have suggested such a thing! My murder and mayhem is never real!"

"Frasier," Robertson said, "we have a good idea of who might be orchestrating the so-called vampire killings in several countries. He's a makeup artist, and I know you've thrown a couple of costume parties, and you have used special effects and special makeup effects—"

"Stop," MacLean said.

"Frasier, we're just seeking help—" Robertson began.

MacLean shook his head, looking at the group of them. "No, no, I… Oh, aye! I just hired a man yesterday because my head makeup lass was a wee bit overworked. He happened out on Broad Street right when we were about to start a shoot, going over, hitting hard on the budget, when this fellow approached, and I said we'd take a look at his work if he wanted to use a day as a tryout. He was excellent, and… Well, he's supposed to be back tomorrow. He got on exceptionally well with Lydia Sanderson, our private eye star. The movie is based on books by Lucinda Tyler, dead these many years, but her readers… You don't care. This man you're looking for… Can you describe him?"

Mason, Della, and Robertson all went for their phones, pulling up the high school photo of their suspect, Stephan Dante. "He goes by many nationalities and speaks several languages," Mason said, showing MacLean the picture on his phone first.

"Um, well, this fellow—the bloke I hired—is bald," Frasier MacLean said, frowning. "And his nose was bigger, and I don't think it's the same man. My fellow was American, and he said his name was Theo Wilder."

"He may well be," Mason said. "He's an expert at makeup, as you might have noticed."

MacLean frowned. "And he might be the vampire killer? Oh, my God!" he exclaimed suddenly, clearly distressed.

"What?" Mason asked.

"He was going out with Lydia tonight! He's got her out in Kirkwall somewhere, and… Oh, my God!"

"It's all right—we'll find them," Robertson said grimly. "Did they say where they were going?" he asked.

"Out on the town," MacLean said. "They were here. They couldn't have left more than ten or fifteen minutes ago. They stopped by right before you called, and I said to head on over. He and Lydia were laughing and they said they had to go, they wanted to see all the pubs they could. I know you're a cop, Frasier, but…"

"Call her," Della said.

MacLean did so, looking more distressed by the second. "It's going straight to voice mail."

"Keep trying every few minutes. Fabricate a reason for them to come here," Della said.

"And let us know instantly, of course," Robertson said.

Mason was already calling Bisset, asking him and the English and French detectives to watch out for the man, giving him a description based on how he had appeared on the film set.

"We need to get out on the streets, fast," Robertson said. "Frasier, you call me if they show up here for any reason at all, you understand?"

"I should get out there, I should look for them—"

"No," Mason said quietly. "You need to be here. This is where you can help us the most."

"He's right. Stay here, Frasier, please! We need you at a base where they might come," Robertson said.

They left MacLean and his rental house, hitting the street again.

"This is my fault. I should have said something to him. He could have stopped them somehow, if he'd just known—"

"You might have gotten your friend and Lydia killed right then and there, Detective. Now we have a chance. Let's start moving."

"There are eleven pubs in Kirkwall proper," Robertson said. "Plus, the new one. We're going to have to split up if we're hoping to trace them."

"There's a place right down there. I'll head that way," Della offered.

"Two blocks up and—"

"Robertson," Mason said, "we'll pull up maps. I'll take the north, you take the south, and let Bisset know to stay where he is and send Taylor and Lapierre to the east and west. We'll cover them all, and the streets, and it's early, so..."

"My fault!" Robertson replied.

"No! He has a method in his blood-taking. If he's going to drug her, he has to get her to a pub," Della said. "Ian! Seriously, if this guy is spooked, he'll kill without thought. This way, we have a chance. You are at no fault! This is our best chance yet!"

She hurried off to the pub she'd indicated.

Mason watched her go, longing to stop her. He wasn't perfect, and he wasn't inhuman. He had felt fear, especially when he'd first gone into the military.

But he didn't often feel it for himself, not because he was stupid, but because he was good at what he did and didn't behave recklessly.

Della wasn't reckless, but she was daring. And while he had wanted so badly to protect himself—to never lose another partner—she had become so much more than a partner; in just a couple of days, she was his strange best friend.

He had to trust her. Had to trust her ability. While most police in Scotland and the United Kingdom were not armed, specially trained officers, Robertson among them, did carry weapons. Jackson Crow had seen to it his agents were armed here as they had been in Norway, because they weren't going to be on the hunt for a monster without recourse.

She was smart, wary...

And determined.

"Mason?" Robertson said.

"Right! And she's right. Della is right. Now yes, we move!"

She was his partner, an exceptional partner. And if he was going to keep her, he had to give her all the respect he expected in return.

He moved on. They were close. So damned close. Maybe, just maybe...

★ ★ ★

The call came just before Della entered the pub on Bridge Street.

She frowned at her phone. She didn't recognize the number, and it wasn't in her caller ID, but she decided she needed to answer it. The call was from somewhere in the European Union.

"Hamilton," she said.

"Ah, and there you are, lovely lass, the one and only Special Agent Della Hamilton!" a voice said. It was rich and masculine, deep, and threatening.

"Ah, would this be Stephan Dante by any chance?" she asked. Was it him? How had he gotten her number, and where was he that he'd dare call her?

He had seen them. He knew they'd all split up.

She hit the tiny button on her phone that would record their session. Maybe, just maybe he would think she couldn't do such a thing, not out on the street with just her cell phone.

"Dear God, no. Stephan Dante was a pathetic nerd, bullied by everyone out there, including the popular girls!"

"So, that's it? You're trying to make up for your inadequacies?" Della asked him.

"No, I'm lying. I was popular in high school. And, I'm assuming, that's the image you have of me. I didn't take many photos. I was never a selfie guy."

"So, why?" she asked.

"Maybe I believe I am buying immortality."

"That's a pile of…well, you know," Della told him.

"Ah, the lovely Della. Not even words that threaten of dirt will pass through your beautiful lips. Such a lady to be out by herself on the streets."

"Where's Lydia Sanderson?" she asked him.

"Ah, well, wouldn't you like to know."

"That would be why I'm asking," she said dryly.

"Special lady, I didn't even assign her to an idiot local, but not half so special as you!" he said.

"You don't know anything about me," she told him.

He started to laugh. "But I met you. I know you. Those eyes of yours—beautiful. And I know your veins, too," he added, laughing.

"Oh, yeah. Sven, the helpful bartender!"

"I was helpful. I gave you a pair of murderers."

"Murderers you trained, who were killing at your command."

"I do have my fun. People are so easy. Now, we must agree on the stupidity of man when you get him from the right angle. Of course, put a crowd together and get them going, and you can garner some unbelievable mass stupidity. But… that's not my thing. I like wedging thoughts and ideas and different truths into minds that are soft and impressionable and willing so desperately to believe. Then again, who am I to say all the legends and stories in the books are false?"

"Books. I see. So, you're going with the general rules of a vampire story. And many vampires can be shapeshifters, so that fits right in."

"Do you read, Special Agent Hamilton?"

"What a rude question. Everyone reads."

"Ah, but do you enjoy the imaginations of some of the brilliant storytellers through the ages who have given us vampires norms?"

"I love reading. So, yes, I've read quite a bit. Tell me. Do you sparkle?" she asked him.

He laughed at that. As she listened to him, she looked around, trying to do so as casually as possible.

"Define sparkle. My charm is simply sparkling. Or at least it is in several of my personae. Yes! My personality is sparkling. But then, you met me. Sven was a great bartender, right?"

"I'm sure they're sorry to have lost Sven," she said, deadpan. "Where else have I met you?"

He enjoyed taunting the police. He loved thinking he was creating an ingenious game—and he was winning. She needed to keep him talking.

"Just as Sven. But then again, maybe Sven wasn't alone. I am just about all-seeing, but…hey, not even I can know everything."

"No, you can't. You can't know everything we know."

"Everything you know—well, you know it because you get it from me! Being Sven was fun. Finding that idiot couple was fun, too, and talking them into believing so many kills created immortality—they believed me! Humanity is amazing. Idiocy is amazing. But history helps me here. Every society known to man from before the time of recorded history has had some sort of vampire, a blood-sucking demon. And then books! I do love books. Stoker did so much research on Transylvania, Hungary, and Romania, and the legends to be found around the world, and then you have more modern epics, other authors through the decades…vampires! They're great. Hmm…and just how many of them are there out there? That's what you don't know. Are they already at work in Orkney, or did I come here to partake in choice of blood myself? Ah, well, you will never catch me. I'm already gone."

"No, you're not. You're near here, talking to me," she told him flatly.

He laughed and put on a rich Scottish burr. "Oh, aye, lass, ye be e'er so right! Maybe. Or maybe I am all-seeing and my eye in the sky is watching you. Aye, lass, replenishment! Maybe I am heading home, maybe seeking further afield! But that's not the play at the moment, no, not at all! Think of it this way…you can come after me and others die, or you can use your brilliant mind and save a few lives. It doesn't matter to me one way or the other. If you'd only been a wee bit different, you'd have ruled the world with me throughout eternity. Well, for the next several decades, anyway!"

Save a few lives…

She hung up on him, already racing back to the rental house Frasier MacLean was using, running and dialing at the same time. The first call went straight to Emergency, the second to Mason.

The door was locked.

She banged on it—no answer.

She was glad she was armed; she shot the lock.

The door swung open and she burst in.

The parlor in the old house offered a grouping of chairs. Cameras were still set to record those who might be using the area as a set.

Seated together, slumped, eyes closed, were Frasier MacLean and a brunette, presumably Lydia Sanderson.

They were bleeding.

Bleeding out.

She hurried forward. As they might have suspected, this killer didn't have to stick to his design. When someone was in the way or might provide an escape, it didn't matter how he killed.

But while blood was seeping from the wrists of both the man and the woman, Della believed they were both alive.

Stephan Dante had been waiting, teasing Lydia Sanderson into believing something, and then entering the house as soon as they left.

And then…

"Tourniquets…four of them, fast!" She murmured the words aloud.

She couldn't see any fabric lying around, so she ripped off

her jacket and then her shirt, tearing it into strips with all the strength she could muster.

As she was tying the last of her desperate measures, rescue broke into the house—four EMTS—and she quickly moved out of the way, just as Mason and Ian Robertson returned.

"He was here, right outside, waiting for us!" she said furiously, looking at the two men. "He must have gotten her to hide under a pretext, and then go back in when we were gone, and... I don't know how he got them both. It doesn't look as if they fought... I..."

One of the emergency medical technicians turned and said, "No defensive wounds, but they're both still breathing. There's a chance!"

"He called you?" Mason asked her.

"Right before I could go in the pub. And I knew he had to be near, but... I recorded everything that he said. He, um..." She paused, wincing. "He said that either I catch him or save lives!"

"And you might have saved them," Robertson said, turning to her, his eyes torn with emotion as well. "And we might never have caught him, anyway. There are scores of policemen and women out there now, looking for him!"

"He was here, and he's gone," Della said, shaking her head. "I don't know how he does it, but I know he's headed out of Kirkwall, and he's gone."

"I've alerted the airport, and they will be looking for him," Robertson assured her.

She nodded. "I know everyone is looking for him, but they've been given a description of a bald man. He'll have changed by now!" she said.

"The recording you made. We all need to hear it," Mason told her. "He relishes taunting law enforcement. He has said something in that recording about where he's going next."

"But maybe *we* should all be out there—" she began, but broke off thoughtfully. "He has a camera rigged up somewhere. He said things about already being gone—and then seeing me with his great eyes in the sky."

Robertson nodded, indicating they should step back out into the street.

"There!" Mason said.

Della looked up. There was an obvious camera attached to the eaves of the rental house that Frasier MacLean was using to film his movie.

A camera. Well, yes, they were filming a movie. Easy for someone to set up—easy for anyone to ignore. Not to mention the fact any house might have a security camera.

"We'll get forensics on it," Robertson said.

He went quiet, as they all did. The EMTs were hurrying to their waiting vehicles with Frasier MacLean and his beautiful leading actress, Lydia Sanderson.

"Ian, get to the hospital," Mason told Robertson. "He was your friend, and we all need to hope they both live."

"I may just pace the hallways—"

"But we can all listen to the recording Della made and bring you up to speed. I think Della is right—he's long gone. Stops at the airport and whatever can be managed at the harbor would be good, except I believe he finished the taunting he set out to do here. He was taunting us, and he doesn't truly believe he's a blood-sucking vampire since he left his latest victims bleeding to death. Ian, seriously, we'll get on this. And I'll get the recording to you for something to listen to while you're pacing the halls."

Robertson smiled grimly and nodded. "Okay, thanks."

He left them.

Mason looked at Della. "We'll listen, and get a trace on the phone."

"It's going to be a burner, cash up front, untraceable," Della said.

"Yep, but we'll go through the motions," Mason said. "He may be getting so cocky he doesn't care if we trace it."

She nodded.

They made their way through the police and crowd that had gathered around the house and headed back to their head-quarters first. Bisset made calls to various law enforcement departments. Detectives Taylor and Lapierre returned from their search of Kirkwall and were informed about the events. They were discouraged and tense regarding them.

They all sat and listened to a replay of the call Della had received, re-taping it first, and preparing to send the phone to tech to be traced.

Lapierre swore furiously in French. He spoke so quickly Della couldn't catch everything he was saying, but the gist was he was sick to death of chasing such a monster. He wished that such a monster might have his heart explode so he could drown in his own blood.

Whether they understood him or not, the others certainly got the general picture of what he was saying.

"We will get him," Mason said.

"How?" Lapierre demanded. "He taunts Special Agent Hamilton. Yes, he is probably already gone! And no matter the alerts we give out, he has a different name and a different look at the drop of a hat. He changes like a chameleon! How do you capture a chameleon?"

"When he's busy changing his colors," Mason said.

"He said he was going home," Edmund murmured reflectively. "Where would he consider home to be? The United States? That's where he visited prisoners, collected saliva, and possibly arranged for a few prison murders while he was at it.

Not only that, but he was born in Louisiana. His home, his place of birth, is the US."

"Stephan Dante was born in the United States, his father was Italian, his mother was French," Edmund said reflectively. "And while he may have different citizenships, I don't think any of them matter because everything he moves about on is a forgery."

"I'm not sure about the United States. He knows he can make people believe they can be vampires, and they can be immortal. So. A vampire? Would home be Transylvania?" Lapierre asked.

"He also kept asking if I read," Della said, "so I believe that means he might consider home from any number of books, including, of course, Bram Stoker's classic work."

"Transylvania, Italy, France, or, most probably, the United States," Mason said.

"We have police and airports on notice across Europe and the US right now," Bisset added. "If we're going to be of any use to anyone, I suggest we get some sleep."

"But…" Della began.

She fell silent. They were right. They had to have faith in their fellow law enforcement officers, and she knew Angela would have a team of brilliant technicians on every possible piece of facial recognition working at all airports.

"We are at a harbor," she murmured.

"We have police warned on every inhabited island and on the mainland and beyond," Bisset said. "There is nothing else we can do tonight except hope he decides to call you again, Della."

"Give me five minutes," Edmund said. "Let me get Della's phone to the station where our tech gurus can make sure that it is connected to record automatically, and I believe we can at the least get incoming calls received on Special Agent Carter's line as well."

Della handed him her phone, and he nodded and left them.

She realized Mason was watching her.

And his expression was worried.

"Della, you have to play this one close to one of us at all times," he said.

"Mason—"

"You're careful, you're an excellent agent. You're also relentless and determined. On this, we're all in on any move you make. A killer wants you specifically, Della," Mason said.

She smiled. "Well, he can't have me. And," she added, looking at the others, "I don't intend to be reckless. We want to get this man."

"We're all in agreement. No matter where he goes, we take care. No one should face this monster alone. He has too many tricks up his sleeve," Bisset said.

Edmund returned with Della's phone. "Well, sleep could give us better minds," he said, handing it to her. "Oh, I realize this might be an intrusion on your privacy, but I think it's important that we do this. We have attached Special Agent Carter's phone to yours. That way, one of you can listen while the other is keeping us apprised of whatever might come in."

"That's great," she said. Edmund still appeared a little awkward and embarrassed, and she laughed.

"It's okay. My personal calls aren't all that interesting. It's fine," Della assured him.

"Oh," Bisset said. "I have police at the hotel, too."

"At the hotel?" Della asked. "But we believe he's gone—"

"But he has a special interest now. Safe rather than sorry," Bisset offered.

"I wake up at the drop of a hat, but all help is appreciated," Mason said.

"Sure. Maybe one of us will dream up a solution," Della replied.

They all managed to smile. Bisset locked their headquarters office, and they walked the short distance to the hotel together.

When they reached the suite, Mason bid Della good-night and headed for his room.

"Hey," she called after him.

"Yeah?"

"Are you all right?"

"I'm fine. I'm not the one with a homicidal psychopath calling me and suggesting I'd have been perfect for him for eternity or a few decades."

"He is a homicidal psychopath," Della said. "It's—Mason, it's good I'm in his sights. We can catch him that way."

He was quiet for a minute, and she thought he wanted to argue. He lowered his head and then looked at her.

"I know. Just—"

"Just?"

"We must be behind you at every turn. Close behind you."

"Agreed," she said softly. "Though at this moment—"

"I think we'll know by tomorrow where he's going. He won't wait long before taunting us again."

"You mean killing again."

"All right. He knows where you are and what you're doing. Of course, I feel like an idiot myself—I didn't see a thing in his manner when he was Sven the friendly bartender. But now we do know. And he will keep at it."

They were across the room from one another, but Della could almost feel a lightning heat coming off him, encompassing her in a strange sensation. Maybe not so strange. She'd been a bit wary; she'd chosen to believe in him. And every step of the way…

She'd found herself drawing closer to him in a way she had never known with anyone before.

They seemed locked in silence. She gave herself a severe mental shake.

"If you were an idiot, I was an idiot, too. We walked into a Norwegian bar and met a Norwegian bartender who directed us toward a man who was a killer along with his accomplice. So, here we are. And… Anyway. He will keep at it. Right. Well. Okay, good night."

She started to turn away.

"Della?"

She turned back.

"I can't lose you. And I won't lose you," he said.

She smiled. He went to his room; she went to hers.

In her room, Della felt desperate for a shower. She hadn't discovered any corpses that day, but just the conversation with Stephan Dante had made her feel as if she needed a shower. And the shower was good. She loved a spray of hot, hot water—it made it feel as if her mind were cleared of cobwebs as well as her flesh of the dirt and grime of the day.

She stepped out and dried. Then she wasn't sure of what she was doing herself, or maybe she was.

She walked back out to the parlor section of their suite.

Mason was there, having just showered, wearing a towel as well.

He looked across the room at her and smiled slowly.

"Is this awkward?"

"No, I think it's beautifully natural," she told him.

"Should we talk?" he asked her softly.

"Lord, no!" she said, covering the distance between them.

She'd known from the time she'd first seen him that physically, he was extremely fit. That she found the contours of his face striking, his eyes intense, his mouth…

The way it formed over hers seemed sensuous and sensual to the most extreme levels possible, a kiss, just a kiss, but the wet heat of it...

So much more. The way his fingers first seemed to cherish her face, fall to her shoulders, sweep around her, bring them flush together.

The friction of their bodies caused their towels to fall away. And then he whispered to her, even the feel of his breath like an exotic aphrodisiac, asking, "My room or yours?"

She laughed. "No talking, remember."

"Unless it's to tell me that I'm magnificent."

She laughed softly, their lips apart, their eyes meeting.

"Ah, but... Okay, I won't say you're so-so or anything like that!" she teased.

He grimaced and swept her up into his arms. "My room."

"Because you're the man?"

"Because we're closer to it!"

She laughed, feeling a euphoria she couldn't remember. Maybe she had fallen in love with the mind of the man, maybe she had always known she'd be here as she was with him.

Laughter came easily.

Touching came even more easily.

They tripped at the foot of his bed, falling into it together. Then he showed her just how magnificent he could be with his lips and fingertips and stronger caresses.

And she returned each—passion, hunger, and maybe even the need to bond so completely with another human being increasing with each whisper, each tender brush, each more urgent move that they made against one another. Then they were together, with every movement feeling like a sweet sweep of lightning, until lightning seemed to climax with thunder and they lay together.

Just breathing. And still he touched her with the utmost

tenderness, cradling her against him. She rested her head on his chest, knowing she was happier than she had ever been, just to lie there so.

They both jolted as Mason's phone began to ring.

"Sorry!" he murmured, reaching over her to get it.

She sat up, listening and watching as he glanced at his caller ID and answered.

"It's Mason. François, what's happened?"

A minute later, Mason said, "Thank you. And, yes, of course, I'll tell her. I'll tell her right away."

He ended the call and looked at Della.

"As it has turned out, Della Hamilton, we may not know where our psycho killer is at this minute—but tonight, you did save two lives. Frasier MacLean and his star are going to survive—and what's more, they'll eventually be just fine."

She smiled. "Thank God!" she breathed.

He nodded. "A good night all around," he said softly.

"The best!" she assured him.

"Then let's keep it going," he said. "Hell, tomorrow will come soon enough."

She smiled, opening her arms to wrap around him, wishing the night never needed to end at all.

"Yes, yes, of course."

"No, I guess human beings figure it all out," he said, up on an elbow, looking into her eyes, smiling. "Well, this job came with some perks, huh? The private jet is something, but this…"

She punched him lightly on the shoulder. "There is nothing like the Krewe."

CHAPTER TEN

"Back in the day, Transylvania was part of the Hungarian empire," Mason noted, glancing up from his computer. "And, to many, Vlad Dracul was a hero fighting for Christianity against the invading Turks. And this may be true or not—he was no more brutal than most feudal overlords."

"Impaling people was civil back then?" Della asked.

He smiled at her. They were in the suite, but they weren't alone. Bisset, Taylor, and Lapierre had joined them there that morning.

They were going to have to decide on a course of action.

Pity they were no longer alone. But they were both determined. Finding one another was the best work perk ever, but the fact remained that part of what made them so close was their determination and dedication to do what they did.

And the help they found that others might not along the way.

Back at Krewe headquarters, Angela and others were going through airport surveillance footage, but it was slow going.

They had video from cameras near the harbor, and information from every ship that had set sail from Kirkwall for mainland Scotland.

So far, nothing. But Mason knew Della was convinced their killer, Stephan Dante, had moved on.

He also believed it. Dante wanted to get where he was going, to kill or train new killers, and to taunt them again from a new location.

"I'm just telling you what I'm reading. Anyway, after World War I, Transylvania became part of Romania. But before... So, Bram Stoker never set foot in Transylvania. Sources who knew the man or studied him suggest that in his research reading, he found out that the modern Romanian name for the devil was *Dracul*, and so...a vampire was born."

"And before that," Edward Taylor said, rising from the settee in the suite's parlor to join them at the computer, "you had Varney the Vampire."

"I thought Barney was a large purple dinosaur beloved by children," Bisset said, joining them as well.

"Barney *is* a purple dinosaur. Varney—with a *V*—was a serialized vampire in the mid-1800s in England, a precursor to Stoker's vampire," Edmund explained.

"Ah!" Bisset said. "So, listening to the killer on Della's recording, I do come to believe he's obsessed with vampire fiction. And the legends that stretch across the globe. But I still wonder if by *home* he means America. Whoops! Excuse me, my phone's ringing," he told them, then stepped back to take the call.

Mason and the others watched him as he answered. His look was grim. "We'll be there shortly," he said, and ended the call.

"A young woman has disappeared from Bucharest, a Canadian tourist."

"Romania?" Della asked.

"Bucharest airport is the closest to Bran Castle—*Dracula* castle. Historically, Vlad Dracul didn't even rule from there, but it has the perfect look, and some believe Vlad Dracul was held prisoner there. But the woods surrounding it are everything you would expect. It sits high on a hill, and yes, there are Dracula tours. The Romanians know how to market for their tourism. At any rate, our young lady, Nanette Grissom, went on from Bucharest to Bușteni, Romania, where she was staying in one of the oldest hotels—a travelers' inn since the fifteenth century. When she was to meet her friends to go out on their first night, they couldn't find her. They went to the police, and the police, being forewarned, called us immediately. We can go and catch them up on what we know and help with the investigation. Now, of course, this young lady might have met a handsome Romanian—"

"No. She was there with friends. She would have told her friends," Della said. "Trust me. Friends don't just disappear on friends, not the kind of friends you make a trip to see Castle Bran with."

"She's right," Mason said. "I'll call the pilot—I think we're all ready to travel—"

"*Mais oui!*" Lapierre said. "I mean, yes, of course, we must go immediately."

Mason smiled. "Jeanne, I think we all understood. Let's head to the airport and get going."

He and Della were already packed and so were the others. They just had to stop by their rooms. They'd meet in the lobby.

Robertson wouldn't be coming with them; he was helping the family of the last victim make arrangements to bring her body home.

When the others stepped out, he smiled at Della. "Well, I did read *Dracula* when I was a kid and thought it would be the coolest thing in the world to go to Transylvania. I just never knew that I'd be going and looking for a human monster."

She smiled weakly in return. "Mason, he is ahead of us. Just ahead of us—and he has a victim already. We must get ahead of him somehow."

He nodded, pulling her close for a minute. "I don't know where this will take us. We never know where we'll be. But I know that…"

She smiled. "Yeah, me, too. We are—well, totally a *we*. I don't think anything can change that. Not for me."

He brushed her hair back. "Never for me."

They went down to the lobby and met up with Bisset, Taylor, and Lapierre. Within an hour, they were at the airport and the Krewe pilot had filed their flight plan.

"Have any of us ever been to Castle Bran?" Mason asked, looking at Della. He expected her to say she and her family had been.

But she shook her head.

"I've been there," Bisset told them. "And… Well, you'll see. It's easy to imagine such a story as Bram Stoker wrote. We'll be meeting Commander Anton Alexandru—he speaks English perfectly, as well as French, German, and Russian, and Romanian, of course. A brilliant young man, he rose through the ranks quickly and he's seen what has happened elsewhere…and was moving the minute the girl was reported as missing. He knows the terrain and the people. Of course, we know who is doing this, so it is perhaps most important that he knows the terrain."

"So. Do we believe Dante has this girl, and he's taken her somewhere near Castle Bran?" Edmund asked.

Mason nodded. "We do. If he hasn't taken her himself, he has groomed someone to do so. It might be easier for him to acquire a sick follower to commit murder for him if he's in Sighişoara near Bran Castle," he said.

On that, they were all in agreement. "Well, almost sixteen hundred miles of flying," Bisset said. "I'm going to try to get some sleep."

"Maybe we all should," Mason said, glancing at Della.

"Yes, of course, whoever needs it most must take the beds—" Edmund began politely.

"Hey, these are great chairs, we'll be fine here," Mason said. "We've traveled a lot together and we're good at sleeping anywhere."

Della quicky agreed with him. The others went to stretch out.

Della rested her head on his shoulder and he rested his head on hers. It shouldn't have been comfortable. It was.

Mason closed his eyes, trying to get his mind to rest. There was nothing else they could do now until they landed in Bucharest.

He did sleep. And so did Della. The pilot's announcement they were about to land was what woke him.

Commander Anton Alexandru was at the airport to meet them. He was a tall man in his early fifties with short-cropped dark hair and solid features. As Bisset had told them, his English was perfect, barely accented. He told them they'd been scanning all security tapes, but so far they had found nothing. All they knew was an hour before she was due to meet her friends, she had walked out of the hotel and down the street. Under normal circumstances, an adult wouldn't be considered missing so quickly.

But European law enforcement knew there was a "vampire" at work.

"Of course," he told them, extending his hand toward a large SUV, "this is a land where...legends abound. Bran Castle is an amazing edifice. Though in truth, it wasn't considered a great fortress. Now the architecture is outstanding, but I think you will find our towns to be so also. Much was built in medieval days—and in my mind, our towns do have a magic to them. Due to the situation, you will see Castle Bran. But it is the forests that still surround the hill and the castle that are so amazing. By night, a fog rolls in and... Well, you will see."

"It's beautiful!" Della said, looking out the window.

"We are a beautiful country," Alexandru said, nodding slightly as he drove. "High mountains, sweeping valleys, lakes, rivers, forests, and more. Of course, throughout history that has made this region—under so many different rulers—a land to be coveted. But we are Romania, part of the European Union and part of the United Nations, and we are proud to be the country we are today!"

"Of course!" Bisset agreed.

"And," Alexandru added dryly, "we are famous for Bran Castle and Dracula. I wonder if Mr. Bram Stoker knows wherever the next life may be that he created an industry of tourism for the modern country we've become."

"I imagine it would please him. Although certainly, he must be equally pleased his book has been scaring people now for well over a hundred years," Mason said.

"And I think, from what I've read about the man," Della said, "he'd be happy he helped the region get lots of tourists!"

"So, Monsieur Bisset has seen to it your accommodations are at a lovely and historic hotel, but daylight does not last long. I didn't know if you'd want to head for the hotel or the castle or—" Alexandru began.

"Let's not waste daylight," Edmund Taylor said, glancing as best he could at the others in the SUV. "We believe he takes the women to forested areas—"

"I have alerted our police. They are sending all available

officers out to search as well. You know, Bran Castle had been repaired and refurbished…" He paused for a minute and then said, "And areas are even rented out for private parties so… Well, you can have a vampire wedding if you wish, I assume. We—"

Mason decided he was taking charge. He believed that while everyone had heard Della's recording of Dante, the two of them knew him best.

"The forest," he said. "Whether the man we're seeking—Stephan Dante, the mastermind behind this horror—took the young lady or another man took her, they have a way of working. They drug their captives. Sometimes they hold them a few hours or even a few days. Then they drain their blood. They have medical equipment to do so, but in the end… We need to get looking in the forest. At this point, we can only hope that we may be on time."

"Stop by police headquarters, please," Bisset said. "I've arranged for earbud transmitters—we can split up but be within range if there's any trouble."

"Brilliant, Bisset, thank you!" Mason told him. "And Commander Alexandru, we'll get to the castle tomorrow if we find nothing tonight. We're all human, we'd love to see it, but this killer doesn't function anywhere with a major tour group. He finds his victims and lures them in bars and after-dinner establishments. Drugging his victims is a major part of it. They are found looking as beautiful as if they were asleep. In his mantra to others, they don't hurt the women by killing them, they become sacred for their donations to those who will live forever."

"I have read every brief and file," Alexandru said solemnly. "The forest it is. But even with several score police officers out there, our numbers are small compared to the trees and the brush, the area surrounding Bran Castle, the waterfronts, hills, valleys…"

"With the earbuds, we can split up," Della said.

She was next to Mason and she looked at him. "Earbuds," she said. "And I am a crack shot."

"But if he's out there," Taylor said worriedly, "Della, he has it in for you."

She looked ahead, out the window at the charming town they were passing with its baroque church tower and old stone and wood buildings. She turned to Edmund. "Here's the great thing—if he comes anywhere near me, he's going to want to taunt me. And if he comes across me, you'll know immediately because we'll be transmitting to one another. He won't know that you know—and you'll surprise him."

"Why do I find that to be frightening—but entirely useful logic?" Lapierre asked from the rear seat of the vehicle.

Della turned to him, smiling. "Jeanne, I promise you, I am armed, I am a crack shot—and I'm also an incredible team player. I know you will all be near me. And there's no other choice. Having me out there might save a life."

But it could mean you lose yours! Mason thought.

He knew they wouldn't survive if he didn't respect her abilities. Different situations could arise in the future. They needed to be intelligent and careful.

But not afraid to do the job.

"She's right," Mason said. "Not to mention the fact that… well, I don't believe Stephan Dante is here. I think he has been here, and whatever time he had, he found someone willing to play his game. As absurd as it may seem, there is always a fragile and vulnerable person ready to believe the most ridiculous tale. I believe this young Canadian woman was taken by a so-called vampire—but not Stephan Dante."

"Where do you think he is?" Edmund Taylor asked.

"Home."

"But home to a vampire—" Lapierre began.

"He kept talking about books," Mason said. "Della and I have been over this and over this, and several of the bestselling books referring to vampire lore of modern history place their vampires in the United States." He looked at Della, grimacing ruefully. "In New Orleans," he said quietly.

He believed what he said. It was important they were here; they had a chance to save a woman. If she could be saved, they were the team to do it.

But despite the disappearance of the young woman, he was convinced Stephan Dante was not here.

He had been gone when he'd spoken with Della. By air or sea, he had reached Transylvania that night. He'd met a man, most likely at a bar, someone lost and disillusioned with life, looking for something to cling to, a belief he could be stronger, better, far more powerful than he was.

"The headquarters is straight ahead," Alexandru said. "We'll get the electronics we need."

"The commander and I will retrieve them so we can get close to Bran and get started immediately," Bisset suggested. He was next to Alexandru, who was driving, but he turned to look at Mason, seated by Della in the middle row. "I am not, as you've seen, usually in the field. Today, we are seeking a woman, alive, we hope, and I will be a working member of the team."

"We will all be in earshot, all taking grave care. We know how the women are killed, but we saw what Dante did in Kirkwall when he wanted to taunt us and get away."

"We're all fair game," Lapierre said.

"We'll get the earbuds," Alexandru announced, stopping and putting the car in Park.

He didn't turn off the engine. As he had promised, he and Bisset were quickly in and out of the headquarters.

In the car, Bisset explained he'd arranged for the easiest and best electronics possible. The earbuds were small; the microphones were tiny buttons that pinned easily on a shirt.

They drove through the valley.

Alexandru pulled off the road, stepped out with a large paper map in his hands. They all joined him as he spread it out over the front of the car.

"Water here, pond…stretch of river. Turn to your left and look… Castle Bran there on the hill, and you can just see the restaurant next to it. Then you have scattered homes, most have wood-burning fireplaces that will add smoke to the fog that will roll in soon. There's a small cemetery here, hundreds of years old, pond…another waterway here," he said, pointing. "Police started farther afield. We're closer in. They are near, moving centrally toward the position of the castle. If we—"

"Divide. Della and I can go west through here, taking parallel walks along these trails. Bisset and Lapierre will go there on the eastern trails. Commander, you and Detective Taylor will follow along the direct path toward the hill, either side of the road here."

His plan covered the most ground.

"We can walk all day and find nothing," Taylor murmured. "But we must find this girl! Whatever crazy idiot has her, we must find her."

Mason walked across the road, determined to test the equipment.

"Loud and clear?" he asked, his microphone secure on his shirt.

"Perfect!" Edmund said.

"Della? Jeanne, François, Commander Alexandru?"

Each replied in turn. It was as if they stood just feet away.

"Time to move," he said. "Della?"

They split up, nodding to one another as they started out in different directions. Entering the thickness of the forest on the side of the road, Mason saw the sky was already changing. It seemed incongruous just how beautiful the coming shades of mauve over the deep green beauty of the forest appeared, especially with the mountains in the backdrop and the castle glowing in shimmering pastels in the distance.

He caught Della by the shoulders.

"Be careful!"

She nodded solemnly. "I will be, and you will hear every move I make. And, hey!"

"Yeah?"

"You be careful, too. Dante has his game he plays. But it's true he doesn't give a damn who he kills and how if it's necessary."

"I can stop a bullet as easily as you, I know," he said softly.

She grinned, indicating her microphone. Of course, everything they said could be heard by the entire team.

He nodded, pulling her close for just a minute, kissing her on the forehead.

Then he walked determinedly deeper into the woods, onto the path he was going to take that skirted the water, while she headed toward the private homes and the little cemetery.

Della moved carefully through the forest. It was painstaking, searching for any broken branches or anything that might indicate a body had been brought through the area. The group checked in with one another every thirty minutes.

Nothing.

The hour grew later.

And as it did, the stunning purples and gold that had touched the sky began to become soft, swirling gray. Anton

Alexandru hadn't lied about the forest as twilight came and the evening fog began to roll in. Seeing the castle up on the high hill, the fog sweeping around it as well, Della almost felt as if she'd reached a strange and magical plane. Leaves rustled gently, the air was cool, touching her cheeks, almost as if mystical hands sent light caresses along her arms.

It was just a forest, she reminded herself.

A forest, touched by fog.

"Della?"

She heard Mason's voice through the earbud transmitter.

"I'm fine, moving ever onward toward Bran Castle," she told him.

"All right. I'm still just in. Nothing appears disturbed by the embankment, and no one has been left there," Mason said. "I'm following the water but coming closer to your position."

"I'm right on track. But something is a little different. There is some broken foliage near me, and I see the old cemetery just ahead, I think. I'm starting to see stones…"

She broke off. She'd come through the trees and the brush to an area that was still wild but somewhat controlled.

The small cemetery had to be hundreds of years old, as Alexandru had mentioned. And despite a lack of serious continual care, it was beautiful. Gothic arches rose, offering entrance to family plots or group graves. Stones were ancient, some broken with the odd angles time had created, but baroque angels and charming statues were set abundantly about the graves. There were no fences to delineate the cemetery, but she could see a low stone wall had once surrounded it completely but had crumpled here and there.

A few streaks of gold and crimson now remained in the sky, but the fog was growing heavy, mixing with smoke from the wood-burning fires from nearby homes.

The mist lay low around the graves, seeming to swirl in

strange shades of gray, making it one of the most haunting and atmospheric places she had ever seen.

"I've found the cemetery," she said, knowing the others would hear her. "I can see the castle on the hill and the mountains in the near distance now, and the stones just ahead. This feels…ancient, and haunting and oddly beautiful," she added.

"Yes, the cemetery is very old. Even in such a place, we are a beautiful country. Castle Bran has always been known as a gateway and thus a protector, sometimes achieving that aim, sometimes no," Alexandru said. "I am getting closer to the castle."

She heard Mason ask for positions from Taylor, Bisset, and Lapierre. As she listened, she just stood for a minute, hoping that if there was something to see, she could see it through the fog.

Slow and careful.

Della walked through the graves wondering if she might meet the soul of one of the deceased there. And if so…

She knew a smattering of several languages.

But no Romanian.

She walked around an especially beautiful stone angel.

And that was when she saw the girl.

She couldn't have been much older than twenty. Her hair was long and dark, fanning around her shoulders. She was propped up against the angel, as if just sitting, waiting…

Waiting for a killer? Because she hadn't been laid out yet, not as if she slept… Snow White in the forest!

"Here, I have something—there's a girl by an angel if you can get to me quickly!" Della said, hurrying to hunker down by the young woman. She instantly checked for a pulse and was gratified to discover she was right—the young woman was alive.

"Alive! We need help," Della cried.

"Almost there!" Mason said.

"And on the way!" Alexandru said.

Della checked the young woman for marks at the throat; there were none.

"So, you have come!"

She was startled to hear the rough voice in accented English and turned quickly. A young man stood nearby, holding a gun on her.

Idiot!

She mentally cursed herself. She'd been so hoping the young woman would still be alive that she'd temporarily forgotten about any potential danger.

But Mason had been right: Stephan Dante had been here in Transylvania, but he was already on his way out. And in the little time he had been here, he had found himself a recruit, a young man who believed drinking blood could give him eternal life.

Where else better to meet the real thing than here in Transylvania?

She wasn't beaten yet.

"He said you were perfect!" the man whispered.

His accent sounded Germanic or Slavic; she wasn't sure. And yet, like so many Europeans, he seemed to have a total grasp of the English language.

"He? He who?" Della asked, reaching casually for the Baby Browning in the holster at her ankle.

"The Master!" the man exclaimed. "I knew it was real, I always knew it was real! I came here hoping and he was…he was here. Watching. He only takes those who are chosen, but he shows us all the way. There is no cruelty in setting such sweet lovelies as this free. There is a special place among the clouds for those who give their blood for the eternal lives of others. He wanted you for himself, but he said—"

"How do you know about me?" she asked.

"He described you. He said yours was the ultimate blood. He knows about you—knows about the donations you gave to the living…knows it's special. But if there was danger, I could take you myself. He has gone home. But he thought you might come here. He described you perfectly, your hair, those eyes…"

"Dear sir! In this mist, there is no way you are seeing my eyes!" she assured him. She could barely make out that this was a kid, barely twenty or just over that, lean and tall—and nervous.

He had apparently been about to go for his first kill when she had come upon his victim.

"He's gone home," she said impatiently. "Where is home?"

"Home for the Master…maybe the clouds, maybe the sky… He is the king of all that he sees, all that he rules!"

No help there.

Her fingers curled around the Baby Browning and she aimed it at him.

"Drop the weapon," she said flatly.

"No. You shoot me, I shoot her," he said.

"I don't think so!" A voice snapped out from behind one of the Gothic archways. Mason's voice.

"Drop it now," Mason continued. "Or you're a dead man, no eternity. So far, I think you're just an idiot desperate to believe in something. You haven't killed anyone, and the justice system might go easy on you. I'm not sure about Romanian law. So drop it!"

The young man was shaking so much Della feared he would fire by accident.

"I—I have failed the Master!" he cried.

"Drop it now!" another voice chimed in. Alexandru.

"Now!" That from Jeanne Lapierre.

"You're surrounded, drop it now—or die!"

The last was spoken by Edmund Taylor.

Della was never sure if the young man decided to drop the gun he wielded—or if it just fell from his shaking fingers— but he sank to the ground, sobbing. He was not upset as Alexandru came forward to cuff him; he was just wailing he had failed the Master.

"I think this is our young Canadian," Della said. "We need—"

"I have emergency vehicles on the way," Alexandru assured her. "They'll be just seconds. But I believe she'll be all right— and we made a right move. I believe... Thank you! You...this team, you know what you're doing. And she's alive!"

"So far," Taylor murmured worriedly.

Mason had reached them by then.

He hunkered down by the young woman leaning against the tombstone in the mist, checking her pulse again.

"Edmund, I think she's going to be fine. I believe Stephan Dante teaches his method, which is stalk your prey, watch their habits, find a way to get them a drink—and make sure that drink is well drugged. She'll make it—I truly believe it."

They could hear sirens, loud and piercing against the fog and the coming darkness. Alexandru questioned the young man, but they had fallen into Romanian. Della couldn't even begin to pick out a few words.

The young man was loudly sobbing as Anton Alexandru led him toward one of the police cars that arrived at the location.

And EMTs were there, quickly moving to help the young woman.

Della stood by Mason. Alexandru did all the talking to those who arrived. At last, the scene began to clear and they were left standing among the old stones.

"I didn't get much from him yet," Alexandru told their

group. "He met the *great vampire king* last night at a bar. They invented a story to get their victim out of the hotel—telling her they were the police and one of her friends had been hurt."

"They didn't even pull the charming bit," Della murmured.

"No, it's as if... I don't know, as if they were too hurried this time," Edmund Taylor said thoughtfully.

"The great vampire king wanted us here," Lapierre said.

Mason turned to Alexandru. "How did he drug her? If he said one of her friends was hurt, she would have realized—"

"Oh, the great vampire king did charm her in a way. He told her he was going to take her to her friend at the hospital, got her into a car—and offered her a bottle of water. Then he told this fellow—the man here tonight, born and raised in Sighișoara, drenched in legends about Vlad the Impaler—just to keep her hidden near the castle until he was ready with all the proper equipment to take her blood, and then begin his journey to immortality. Oh, he has a set of teeth on him— fangs, I mean."

"And we'll discover the saliva on the teeth belongs to a dead man who was incarcerated at a prison in the States," Mason said.

"So, Stephan Dante has moved on already," Della said.

"Let me get you to your hotel. I can only imagine what a long day this has been for you," Alexandru said. "But thank you!" he said quietly. "Thank you, eternally. The young woman will live, and that is everything. I will get you to your hotel and head to the hospital."

Della smiled and nodded. She was grateful; they were all grateful.

But other young women might die. Dante remained a step ahead of them.

The hotel was beautiful. She and Mason had naturally been given separate rooms. They didn't go up to their rooms in the charming old establishment at first. They managed to get food, even as the restaurant was closing, and sit with their unlikely team to plan the next day.

"Bright and early again," Mason said, nodding at the others.

"But where—"

"A long trip. Across the pond. We're going to New Orleans," Mason said. Looking at Della he added, "Back to the bayou."

"We don't really know where he's going. We've assumed—" Edmund began.

"Home. He wanted us to think it was Transylvania, and he did come to Transylvania and dupe a pathetic young man. When Alexandru and his people investigate this young man," Mason said, "they'll find out he's recently had a heartbreak, perhaps lost a job, maybe lost a loved one or a pet. He thought the world was against him. Stephan Dante saw that in him and was able to recruit him in a flash. But Dante has talked about books—he's read vampire books. Several in the last years have dealt with New Orleans. The great Anne Rice made New Orleans home for Lestat. Charlaine Harris used Louisiana for her Sookie Stackhouse novels. The area is famous for voodoo and more—though the voodoo practitioners I know today believe in the do-no-harm ethic. The point is in the fantasy, New Orleans is a great home for more contemporary vampires."

"Back to the States," Della said determinedly. "Of course, we have many agents in our unit there, so if you wish to return to your own countries—"

"We're a team," Edmund Taylor said, looking at Bisset and Lapierre.

"As you Americans say, you bet!" Lapierre said.

"Interpol. You may need help. Americans can be tough," Bisset said.

He managed to make them all smile.

And there was better news to come. Alexandru called from the hospital. Once again, because of their timely intervention, a young woman was going to live.

Mason called their pilot so they'd be ready to head out in the morning. They walked up to their rooms, but Della didn't bother to go to hers.

She looked at Mason and he smiled and pulled her to him.

"You okay? It's been a long day," he whispered.

"No, I'm filled with…adrenaline," she told him.

"Enough to keep up with me?"

"You flatter yourself!"

"Well, I mean, someone needs to, right?"

She laughed. They closed and locked the door.

And fell into one another's arms.

CHAPTER ELEVEN

The flight was long, broken up by a stop for fuel. But since the Krewe's jet had been comfortable and furnished by their founder and philanthropist Adam Harrison, it was also a good place to go through everything they knew and to consider their actions before they landed.

It accommodated a place for the five of them, François Bisset, Edmund Taylor, Jeanne Lapierre, Mason, and Della to sit in something of a circle with a desk or table between them, filled with tech and using notepads to create a follow-up to the movements taken by Stephan Dante and his recruits.

Taylor shook his head as he placed two markers near the area on the table that was England. "We do know now Dante doesn't do all the killing himself. When we find him, and we must, I wonder if he'll roll on his subordinates. Or will we have to wonder whether he was the killer in England and France, or if those killers are still out there? When we began this and my superiors suggested a multination task force, we assumed we were chasing one man. Now…"

"If we can get him," Della said. "I think he's so consumed with his own importance that handing us anything will be like swatting a fly to him. What I'm afraid of here is his confidence is so all-consuming he doesn't believe he'll ever be caught. It's frightening, too, to realize the extent of the criminal network behind him, as in those who create the kind of false IDs that have taken him around the world." She reached across the table, setting a hand on Taylor's hand. "Don't worry—we will not forget England. Or France," she said, glancing over at Lapierre.

"*Merci*," he said softly.

"All right," Mason said, setting out a few of his little scraps of paper. "Here we have the US murders that Kat suggested might have been his practice shots. Or those committed by someone he was trying to instruct. I never saw the bodies, but I read her reports." He hesitated a minute and then glanced over at Della. "All right, before we left for Europe, Della and I were involved in the hunt and takedown of a man who wanted to immortalize himself as the Midnight Slasher."

"Maybe he knows something," Edmund said. "If—"

"Whatever he knew," Mason said, "he took to the grave. I was forced to shoot him. And at the time, though he made a few references to the *vampire*, I didn't associate him with any of this. Now, I'm wondering. I think he did meet Dante somewhere. Of course, by the time Della and I became involved with him, Stephan Dante was already in Europe. Our Midnight Slasher wanted the vampire's infamy, but I think he wanted his own style as well. With that said… I think Dante may have started in the United States. Here in Virginia, and here in the Florida Everglades."

"So, now, New Orleans? Because we have missing women following the type, and I imagine because it is a good city for Dante. Is it such an American setting for *vampires*?" Edmund asked.

Mason nodded. "There's that—and while I didn't connect it before, I sincerely believe the Midnight Slasher did meet up with Stephan Dante. We'll get all the info we can on the young women who are missing and set out from there."

"Corpses—on Bourbon Street," Edmund murmured.

"No, New Orleans will just be a base for him," Mason said. "He's going to head out of town—out where we caught up with the Midnight Slasher. Bayou country can be a lot like the Florida Everglades—miles and miles of what is just about no-man's-land."

Lapierre lifted his hands, looking over at Taylor and Bisset. "We will be in your territory. You will by nature be far more familiar with the landscape. We will be your runners. You tell us what is needed for you to accomplish a true discovery, and that is what we will do."

Bisset and Taylor gravely nodded their agreement. Taylor shook his head, still unhappy.

"We need the truth. And if there are killers running free in Europe, we must find out who they are—and they must be brought to justice."

"We will find the truth," Mason vowed to him. "We will do everything in our power to see justice is found for every victim."

He desperately hoped he could deliver on his words.

"The problem with this area is that despite all else, New Orleans is seen by many people in one perspective—they see Bourbon Street and all the partying that goes on. They don't see all the other amazing things the city has to offer. Well, food. Most people do take the time to appreciate the food, but..."

Detective Alan Fremont of the Department of Criminal Investigation for the state of Louisiana had been given lead on the most recent cases of missing persons in the area—specifically that of two young women who had gone out in the evening and never returned to their hotels just the night before. Angela and the team at headquarters had once again seen to it the local law enforcement had been apprised of their latest warnings and information. Fremont had studied the cases revolving around the *vampire* and Stephan Dante; he was ready and able to assist them in any way.

And accept *their* help.

Fremont was a young man, a solid officer of about thirty, leanly muscled, dedicated, and, perhaps most importantly, certain that they were right—Stephan Dante had come to New Orleans.

"I read up on every piece of intel that came through. I was hoping this killer wouldn't come to Louisiana, but New Orleans… We do manage to attract some of the strange, a lot of which is good for tourism, and a lot of what is simply criminal and horrible. People often hit on the voodoo element here, but honest practitioners of voodoo don't hurt anyone. And then we have groups who consider themselves spiritual vampires, those who just come to New Orleans… Well, you know, some damned good books have been written about vampires in the area!"

"Agreed. And Stephan Dante reads and refers to books," Mason told him. "He also referred to home. He was born in the United States—and yes, he headed to Transylvania, but his recruit there was no real killer. Here, I think he intends to kill—if he hasn't already."

"Tell us about the missing girls," Della said.

"Casey Marks and Dina Larkin."

They were seated in a conference room at the local headquarters. Taylor and Lapierre had moved on to Baton Rouge where another missing person had been reported, and Bisset had remained at the airport in Kenner to study arrival footage of recent passengers.

Stephan Dante knew what he was doing when it came to tricking the system. He managed to travel with the freedom of a bird, ever-changing in his identity, never triggering a no-fly list or an alarm of any kind.

"Both young women are twenty-two, they attended Loyola together, and this is their first trip back to the city since they lived here during their college days. They met friends for lunch on Royal Street and talked about going on one of the bayou tours. Bayou tours only leave when they've got at least an hour and a half of light left in the day. They were no-shows when they were supposed to meet friends again for a night out. Casey's boyfriend, who came to meet up with her after his gig—he's a sax player—got worried when she didn't come back to her room last night."

"He's taken them to the bayou," Mason said, looking at Della.

"You're thinking the same area, the wooded area he learned about through the Midnight Slasher?"

"You think this man knew the Midnight Slasher?" Fremont asked. He was intense. A good cop, Fremont wanted any insight that would help catch a possible killer.

"It's a theory, but when we consider things said by both men, we believe Dante was here before, and he recruited a killer here, just as he has done in other vicinities," Mason explained.

"But—you've talked to this man?" Fremont said.

Della leaned forward. "He called my phone. My personal phone. I don't know how he got the number, but he called me and I recorded it. We can play it for you."

"I'd appreciate that," Fremont said.

"Absolutely," Della said, pulling out her phone and letting him hear the conversation that she had recorded.

He listened, shaking his head, staring at Della.

"He—he wants you to join him. Or be his ultimate victim," Fremont said.

"And that may be our way to get him. His overconfidence soars," Della explained. "The word *narcissist* doesn't begin to describe him. He thinks he can slip away and never be caught—"

"He's succeeded so far," Fremont said. He was worried, his statement simply matter-of-fact.

"So far. Not this time. We can't let him disappear this time," Mason said.

"All right, there is a connection there—a frightening one," he told Della. "But if you believe he's in the bayou, I'm willing to go with your beliefs. But how do we start hunting for these girls? The state is filled with bayous, tons of surrounding country, all loaded with alligators, snakes, and more. If you don't know the area, it can be like being tossed in a pit."

"We're aware," Della said quietly. She looked at Mason. "We know the area. We were on the team that took down the Midnight Slasher."

"Ah," Fremont murmured. "All right, so. We believe this man has kidnapped his victims and taken them out to the bayou. But a girl was just reported missing in Baton Rouge—"

"An hour and twenty minutes away in normal traffic," Mason said. "Detective, we believe this man has headed out to an area he learned to traverse while he was training a recruit—the Midnight Slasher. He won't be in the same place because he isn't stupid."

"But he will be out there, somewhere near," Della said. "He'll have carefully chosen his ground, aware we'll be looking for him."

"Okay. We can all pray you're right. How do you want to play this?" Fremont asked, leaning forward.

Mason thought he knew how the fellow had risen in rank at such a young age. He was intelligent, thoughtful—and ready to listen to logic and voices of the experienced.

"Well, we have to get out there," Mason said. "But—"

"We? The three of us? Not enough to begin that kind of a search. If I get a squad—"

"We need a team—not a squad—because we need to be careful. We know this man has two young women, possibly more. We can hope he's holding his victims prisoner. He does that or his accomplices do it sometimes. If he—or they—are threatened, the victims' lives may be forfeit. We don't go in guns blazing. We keep it as quiet as humanly possible."

"So…we need to slip through the bayou like the gators?" Fremont asked dryly.

"Something like that," Mason said.

"All right, then. I'll arrange for an airboat down at the docks. And don't worry, I'll handpick the team. I'll get wires so that we can communicate. As I said, you're talking some hard ground to cover." He hesitated and then said, "If this man is drugging the girls, he could be in any one of dozens of hotel rooms around the city, in surrounding areas… He could be taking them anywhere."

"That's true," Mason said. "It's also true we can't go into every hotel room in the city."

"But he seems to like the great outdoors. He likes to leave his victims in out-of-the-way places where they'll be found—but not found by dozens of people. He's chosen locations where people walk, hike, or enjoy the woods or the wilderness, but he knows the paths that others take. I don't think he'll leave a victim to be found in a hotel room by a housekeeper," Della said. "He likes the beauty of his displays, and then the horror when the truth is discovered."

"I'm on it," Fremont said. "I'm getting us an airboat, and I'll order a team of our best bayou men out there and warn them to be discreet."

"No uniforms," Mason said.

"No uniforms," Fremont agreed. He hesitated again. "There are so many bayous—"

"But Dante will be going for just one," Della said.

"Detective, there are no guarantees. But for the good and the bad, Della has a strange connection with this man, and we have been on his trail. We might be wrong. But our field director and research manager have seen to it that every officer and agent throughout the area have images of this man as himself—though much younger—and as the various different characters he has played."

"We'll get the right people out on the streets, too," Fremont said.

"Thank you, because following the criminal mind is not a guarantee," Della said. She stood. "We'll head to the port and meet you there whenever you're ready. We know where to go. We have to get into the depths by whatever different methods we can. I know it's going to be tough."

"Give me about thirty minutes. Stop and get yourselves some coffee. There's a great place on Broad Street called Coffee Science. Hey, get me one, too. I think I'm going to need the jolt!"

"Will do," Mason said, adding, "Coffee. Yes. Couldn't hurt!"

He and Della headed out. As they did so, Mason's phone rang. "Airport security footage went to everyone, including your headquarters," Bisset said when Mason answered the call. "I haven't studied it all, but—"

"Don't worry. Angela will be right on it with some of her best," Mason told him, and explained what their plans were. Detective Fremont was arranging for radio controls to keep them all informed of where they were and if they found anything.

"All right," Bisset said. "But use the buds and tiny mics we have as well—best if you just come across something. We can all hear."

"Will do," Mason promised.

He hung up and glanced at Della to see if she'd gotten what Bisset had said.

"We have—"

"Security footage," she said. "If he came in, no matter as who—or what he looked like—Angela will find him."

Mason's phone was ringing again. This time, it was Edmund Taylor, checking in from Baton Rouge.

"I was wondering if we should be trolling the nightlife again. Divide and conquer. New Orleans is filled with bars where partiers are out, happy and carefree. Dante teaches his people—" Taylor began.

But Mason interrupted him. "Not this time, Detective. Because Dante knows who we are. He played the congenial bartender Sven to the hilt in Norway, and he knows exactly who we are."

Della arched a brow and he nodded, letting her know the call was with their European counterparts. "We're heading out to the bayou. We're going to *troll* the area where the Midnight Slasher found his place."

"We'll head back that way and join you," Edmund said.

He lowered his volume but put the phone on Speaker so she could hear the conversation.

"Head back this way and join us, but we're going to start out. Detective Fremont is getting us out there, and he'll have a team of his best—men who know the area—out there in plain clothes as well. Come to headquarters here in the city, and they'll see to it they get you out there, too. We'll have radio connection with local law enforcement, and Bisset reminded me we have something even more important, the mics and earbuds he procured for us. Bisset is going to stay on the security footage and correspond with anyone necessary, but he'll hear everything that goes on. We just need to speak up when we want each other to hear without anyone knowing we're communicating with one another. Nothing against the police, just radio communication in a tight spot may not be enough."

"Right. Double communication. I like it. Not against any local cops, but if one of us does run into a killer…well. And we don't have alligators in my woods back home," Edmund said.

Mason looked at Della and nodded. "Are you and Lapierre going to be all right out there?" he asked.

"We're going to be fine. We aren't going home without this guy," Edmund told him.

That was something Mason well understood. "We'll get started. Let us know when they've got you out there," Mason said. "And remember, he knows us. He knows all of us and all about us."

"Discretion is the word, of course," Edmund told him. "But you two be careful out there. He knows us—he wants Della."

"And we may have to play that card," Della said softly to Mason.

Della knew Mason would protest—as would the others. If she tried to get herself caught up by Dante, she was putting herself in danger.

But it wasn't something that hadn't been done dozens of

times before. She'd played many a part to attract the eye of a criminal, and so had dozens of other female officers and agents. Undercover cops and agents of both sexes played roles when necessary.

Bisset had seen to it they had a car upon arrival, and when they left the station and their planning with Detective Fremont, Mason drove to Coffee Science just as Fremont had suggested. After they arrived and parked, they ordered and waited, and Mason expressed his concerns.

"First, we have no idea—this is worse than looking for any needle in any haystack."

"Except—" Della began.

"We're hoping to find our ghostly Gideon—and hoping he might know something?" Mason finished.

She nodded gravely. "Fremont will be with us. And we do need to use the mics and earbuds the way we did before. If anyone encounters him—"

"You're planning on encountering him," Mason said.

She paused, lightly biting on her lower lip before speaking. "Mason, there are two girls out there. Young and innocent of all this. Our first responsibility is always to the victims. And he'll bring me to them. I know he will. Because he does know too much about us. And that's the thing—if those girls are alive, he *will* bring me to them."

"Because he knows it will be the worst torture for you to watch what he'll do to them," Mason said.

"You have to have faith in me," Della said.

"I do. We're also facing a truly heinous killer who is also frighteningly intelligent when it comes to ways to get around the law."

"On my own, I would never do such a thing," she said.

"Oh, great. Now I feel worse—you wouldn't do this if you didn't have faith in me?" he asked.

She laughed softly. "Don't flatter yourself. We'll have Gideon and a team out there. Okay, I admit I wasn't sure at first, but you are the most extraordinary partner. In so many ways."

They picked up their coffee as soon as they were ready and got back in the car.

He reached over and pulled her to him, pausing to study her eyes, and then kissing her gently on the forehead.

"I can't lose you," he whispered.

"And you won't. You won't, because you and I both know what we're doing. We can read one another and... Well, honestly, I will be happiest if we can find Gideon."

"What do we do about Fremont?"

"We're splitting up, covering all the territory we can."

He nodded. "You and I do not split up until we find Gideon. And even when we do, you keep me apprised on the mic about every move you make. Understood?"

"I have no desire to feed a vampire or become one, I promise you!" she told him. "Mason, please, think about it. We have both studied this man. He thinks he so superior to us. You'll be right behind me."

"He'll take your gun. If he doesn't disarm you, he won't take you."

"He doesn't know about the Baby Browning."

"Since he's not stupid, he may figure out the backup is in your boot."

"If so, you'll know. And you'll be right behind me."

He nodded. She knew he didn't like it. He would never like it. But he understood. He knew if she were anyone else, he'd accept the logic even if it was risky.

They had to take calculated risks. That's how they caught this kind of killer.

"Promise me one thing."

"What's that?" she asked him.

"You keep talking. Let me hear you, no matter what is going on."

She nodded solemnly.

He drove in silence then, and soon they reached the docks and found Detective Alan Fremont. He had changed to jeans and a denim jacket, attire that looked just right for hiking—or hunting—in a bayou region.

"You know just where you want to go?" Fremont asked. He seemed curious. "You really do know the area? You were from here?"

"No. I'm from New York. But I was assigned down here for a while," Mason explained to him. "And Della…"

"I always loved New Orleans. I spent a lot of time here. And the terrain…" she said, shrugged, and added, "It's not all that different from the Everglades."

"Alligators," Fremont said. "Guess you're familiar."

"Hey, we've got crocodiles down there, too. Same. Lethal snakes—and now about sixty thousand pythons that don't belong, so…"

"You're not worried about walking in dangerous marshy grasses," Fremont said. "Good. Because in areas, it's not easy. It's mostly residents who come to hunt here. They go after the gators and sometimes deer and nutria, but it's mainly fishing in the area. There's great rainbow trout to be caught and other tasty fish. It's not usually an area for most tourists, though tour boats come and stay out on the water."

"That's good because this guy will eliminate anyone in his way," Mason said.

Della was silent, watching as they moved along the water. They left what some might consider the civilized section of the Crescent City, heading out to the wilderness. But just as she had always loved the Everglades, she loved the land as it changed here, as man's hand upon nature became less and less obvious. Cypress trees and myrtle, oaks dripping with moss.

She'd been assigned here before. While not like a native, she knew the terrain. It was like home. Dangerous reptiles to watch out for, mosquitos that could be annoying—or deadly. She'd learned as a child to leave alligators alone and never go near a nest.

She knew Jackson had asked her to join the team dealing with the Midnight Slasher because she would be careful. She had earlier worked with a team who had assembled to find and arrest bank robbers who had disappeared from Baton Rouge after killing a guard and seriously wounding a teller and a customer.

An alligator slipped silently from the embankment, and startled egrets flew into the sky. The chirp of insects around them and the moss that dripped from the trees gave the area a haunting atmosphere, one that was strangely peaceful, and yet one that invited depths of humid darkness, places where even in sunlight shadows could hide endless sins.

In time, Mason said, "We pulled in here before. The shack where the Midnight Slasher was holding a girl was straight through that grassy trail."

"But you said he won't be there," Fremont said.

"He won't. But he'll be near," Mason said. He looked at Della. "He'll expect us to check the shack. Detective Fremont, if you'll do that, I believe he'll be watching. He'll also be watching to see what Della and I do—"

"How will he even know you're here?" Fremont asked.

"He's been waiting for us," Della told him.

"All right. I'm a decoy?"

"Something like that," Mason said. "I'm—"

"Don't be sorry. I'll be happy to be a decoy if it gets us where we need to go."

"Thank you!" Della said.

"We keep in contact. I'll split from Della, but I'll be close. And your men—"

"Already filtering in," Fremont said. "They're searching, but also waiting for word. I promise you, I picked a good team. Several on this team grew up in the area. They know it the way few others possibly can. We want to find these young women alive."

"Yes," Della murmured.

Della was glad she chose her boots for her daily wear. As much as she did love wilderness areas, there was something there that was a little edgy about stepping into water where snakes and other dangerous creatures might be hiding just below the surface.

They stepped back into the marshy grass that led to the poor trail to the shack. There were others, interspersed with the trees.

"I'm going to head up to that shack. Hey…look. There are still some remnants of crime scene tape around it. You think this guy may be using the exact place?"

"No, but check it out," Mason said.

"You can look for others. Some of the old places have caved in. Fishermen still use a few, and hell, some are older than dirt and part of the landscape. I think maybe, though, we should have stayed in the city. At least we could have grabbed a drink somewhere on Bourbon Street," Fremont said.

"Well, we can get back there," Mason said. "Della and I will choose different paths, cover more territory. At the very least, we'll have checked out the Midnight Slasher's place."

They had both spoken loudly, Della knew, because…

Were they crazy? Could Dante really be expecting them, waiting for them?

Or had they read too much into their own beliefs about the

man? Were they too certain they knew someone who could possibly change his ways, like his appearance, in a split second?

"Lots of hidey-holes out here you might never find!" Fremont called. "Unless you're a gator!"

"We're good! Hey, we'll divide and conquer!" Della called out.

Fremont waved, then seemed to blend into a smattering of oak growing by what was almost a trail.

He'd said it. There were so many possibilities out here.

The killer was using one of them, she was certain.

But then again...

"Mason," she murmured.

"Yes?"

"What if we're wrong?"

"Della, I almost hope we're wrong. We have his image—images—out everywhere. Officers in New Orleans are angry this man might be here. We must have faith in others. Hey, we're team players, right?"

"I just... Mason, maybe we should have played this differently. If he expects we followed him, he might—"

"That conversation, Della. The way he talked about home and books, he's here. And if we hadn't come out—if we had *trolled* the bars on Bourbon Street, tried Magazine Street or Frenchman Street—we might have made him angry."

"And he might have killed the hostages. So, we had to come out here, because he was counting on us realizing he'd known the Midnight Slasher and would come here."

"Right."

She smiled, but he wasn't looking at her.

"We're not going to need to find Gideon," he said.

"But he might—"

"Gideon has found us," Mason said.

CHAPTER TWELVE

The ghost of the old pirate came toward them quickly, his expression grim and somber.

"I prayed you'd be back!" he said. "It's happening again. It's happening here."

"Gideon, where is he?" Mason asked, knowing from the ghost's opening words he knew exactly why they were there.

Gideon shook his head.

"I've tried—so far, I have not seen anything. I didn't see him myself. There were a couple of fishermen out here arguing with one another. They were talking about a man bringing two women out here. The one said they were drugged and doped, and the other said it wasn't their business. The one wanted to call the police, but then the other man pointed out the fact that they seemed to be hanging all over him, maybe they wanted to be out here, maybe they didn't want the world knowing they had something going on."

"Where are these fishermen?"

Gideon shook his head. "Gone. Back to their homes, wherever they may be. My friend Oscar—passed away in the '40s,

World War II—used to love to fish out here and he heard them with me. We tried to follow, but they had an airboat and we couldn't hop on fast enough. And...even if we'd followed them, they might not have said anything else."

"Gideon, where is Oscar now?" Della asked him.

"He's walking through everything that is a trail, resembles a trail—and searching for every shack out here he knows to have ever been built. When he told me what he'd heard, we both thought of the Midnight Slasher, and... I was hoping you'd show up, was afraid you wouldn't, knew you were in Europe, but...a killer has at least two girls out here."

Mason nodded. "That's what we believe. The state police also have people out here, Gideon. We'll find him."

"This killer you seem to know... Does he know you as well?" Gideon asked.

"I'm willing to bet he's expecting us," Mason said.

"But it sounds as if you're getting a big team out here—"

"We can't just rush him, Gideon," Della said.

"Because he has the girls. But that many people... Won't they find the girls?"

"If we know this guy, and he's out here somewhere waiting for us—not us, Della, really—he's set the girls up to die if anything happens to him."

"Della is the bait?" Gideon asked.

"I am the bait—and an experienced agent, not suicidal," Della assured him. "We have buds and mics we're using. Mason will know where I am at every minute. And now—"

"Now, Mason feels better about the whole thing, because you'll be with Della," Mason said.

Gideon smiled at that. "I am glad to be of service, as you know. And I've no lack of faith in Special Agent Hamilton! A pirate for part of my days, there were few like Anne Bonny, Mary Read—or the great Grace O'Malley! Modern

times, other side of the law, but I have seen the brilliance and
subtlety of this fine lady, and I've no doubt we will prevail."

Mason smiled grimly. He thought yes, they might well
bring an end to the reign of the master vampire that day.

He wondered at what cost.

"Where to from here?" Gideon asked.

"Where do you suggest, my friend? You know this bayou
better than any man, I believe, living or dead," Mason told
him.

"Go inland to your left, and we'll be parallel," Gideon said.
"There are a few old shacks, most of them nearly reclaimed
by the vegetation. But that's the point, I believe—they are
difficult to see. But we can run a path that hunters use upon
occasion, again, mostly overgrown, but easy for a man to follow and…your radio?" he asked, pointing to the police radio
attached to Della's belt beneath her jacket.

"My police radio. And I'm turning on the remote, so
we'll—"

"Communicate carefully," Gideon whispered.

Mason and Della both smiled at that, and Della looked at
him. "I will be all right," she said. "You will be right behind me."

"Us," Gideon corrected.

Mason indicated he was starting out.

Anything that Della said, anything that happened near her,
he would hear. And no matter what Stephan Dante knew
about them, he couldn't know about the one ace they had
up their sleeves.

Gideon.

It was time to take down a killer.

Della was glad she had spent time in both the Everglades
and bayou country. Thankfully, the trees flourishing in the

area provided shade, yet they locked in the sweltering touch of the heat as well.

She was glad of the denim jeans and jacket she'd chosen for herself for the day, and her boots. Tall grasses and weeds and vines seemed to tear at her every step. Paths here weren't much; they could be overgrown in a day. She loved being on the water both here and at home, but walking through this much brush and foliage...

Hmm. Not so much.

"Something ahead," Gideon told her.

She nodded, pulling her Glock from the holster at the small of her back as she moved forward.

Stephan Dante might have encouraged this game, positive he had a way to win. He always knew how to disappear. He obviously only chose places he knew well. But when he didn't know them that well, he created his followers, his recruits, and they did the killing and the sharing of their victims' blood.

They were all expendable in his mind. And sadly, they were all willing to sacrifice for their *master vampire*, the king who had tried to teach them how to find immortal life. Others might well kill elsewhere for him while he sat back, relishing his godlike power.

Life and death.

And here...

He'd been born in Slidell. He must have come to know the entire area surrounding Lake Pontchartrain, and New Orleans, down to the Mississippi. In his arrogance, he believed he could disappear at will—and it wouldn't matter how many agents and police officers were out there.

She pulled out her radio.

"Some type of an old structure ahead of me, east of our arrival point," she said.

"Roger that."

Mason's voice came over the remote.

"Something here, too. I'll be checking into it. Thinking we're getting a little far apart, so we'll reposition after we've seen what we each find."

Della didn't reply. There was something almost like a clearing ahead of her and Gideon. She looked at him and arched a brow.

"Bootleggers of the 1920s," he told her. "Hunters use it sometimes, but rarely."

She pretended to use the remote but didn't need to—in the event that it was taken from her, Stephan wouldn't realize her earbuds kept her in close contact with Mason and the team.

"I think this might be the kind of place where we might find this man. People will come by eventually, they will find bodies displayed in their bloodless beauty, but the place is not at all heavily trafficked. He wants them found—but maybe not immediately after he's displayed them.

"Same here. I understand there were families that survived certain years out here, running stills, hiding out. Easy to see how it might have been good business—without much chance of the law descending," Mason said over the radio.

If Stephan Dante was anywhere near them, he could hear the conversation.

And he would know she was alone.

Except, of course, she wasn't. She smiled to herself. Gideon was with her.

"I'm moving ahead," she said.

She nodded to Gideon and they walked across the clearing. Vines and leaves covered the decaying wood of the structure and tree branches growing through it.

But—with her gun drawn—she looked for an entry. The door to the place had long ago rotted from its hinges. But there had been a door and that allowed her to duck under a sagging beam and enter.

There was nothing in what remained of the shelter other than the decaying remnants of years and years of discarded items and refuse. Broken bits of rotting wood lay crumbled on what might have been a low bed or pallet along with bits and pieces of blanket. Weeds grew through the floorboards.

She spoke aloud. "Well, nothing here. Rot and decay. Nature is reclaiming the place."

"There was a rustling sound. Someone is outside, watching, listening," Gideon said.

"Then it's time to put the game into play," she said.

"He's there?" Mason asked.

"We believe. Someone is out there. If so…just keep listening."

She held her Glock out as she stepped around the broken entry of the old shack.

And Gideon was right. He was out there.

"Well, well, well, Special Agent Della Larson in the flesh!"

It was Stephan Dante—as Stephan Dante—no disguise. And as himself, she could see how he had appeared as a handsome and normal young man with charm and an easy smile.

"Why?" she murmured.

"Why?" he queried. "Why not?"

"Because no one has the right to steal life from anyone else!"

"Oh, come on! Man has ripped up man from the beginning of time. Sometimes we call it war, and men—and women— get to go crazy killing one another. We are born to kill. And just as there is a chance there is a god, there is a chance the whole vampire thing might be real—why not kill cleverly? Oh, and rid the world of a little trash as one goes."

She had her Glock on him. He was smiling, unarmed, casual. He was dressed as Della was in denim jeans and boots, and ready to face the elements out here.

He wasn't pointing a gun or any kind of a weapon at her. He probably had one stashed somewhere. And he knew damned well she was going to try to get him to take her to his hostages.

"So, you're going to shoot me, eh?" he asked.

"I try not to shoot people," she told him. "So, if you would be so kind as to tell me where to find the girls—"

"Oh, Della, come on! You are my soulmate, my worthy opponent. If you're lucky, I'll bring you with me to eternal life! But I knew, of course. You're worried about beings so less worthy! But you! You are a worthy opponent."

"Worthy opponent, huh?" Della said dryly. "Okay, I'm worthy. And I don't believe that crock for a single minute."

"Tough nut to crack, as they say. But let's see. Here's the fun part. You have no idea how I know you, oh, so well. But here is what I know. You're not going to shoot me or even arrest me. Not when the girls are out there. Oh, by the way, there are three of them. Little Lyndsey out of Baton Rouge is a sweet and adorable girl. So innocent and naive for a college kid!"

"Sweet and adorable—but you want to rid the world of her?"

"She'll turn into a raving bitch. You can tell. As soon as she realizes her power. That's just it. Life—and death—are all about power. So, what's your pleasure? Shoot me. Or follow me."

"How do I know they're not already dead?"

"You don't. You must gamble."

"Hey, you know, I'm not much of a gambler. Penny slots,

at the lowest possible amount per spin. So, let's see, what's your plan?"

"I want you to see me, see the strength and the brilliance, and join me."

"No. Let's both be honest here. I see you as a narcissist and, of course, a homicidal maniac."

"A genius," he corrected.

"Sorry, I don't see you that way."

He shrugged and grimaced, looking away and then back at her. "Then I want you to die," he told her casually.

"All right. You want me to die. What if I trade me for them?"

"Hmm. I will give that one some consideration. But you must behave to get to the girls."

"Because you know this bayou area is crawling with law enforcement."

"I'd expect nothing less from you. I knew you'd split from tall, dark, and handsome. Mr. Intensity. Because you are you! Independent. Powerful. Taught from the time you were a kid that a girl could do anything a boy could do. No one needs to hold your hand. In truth, though, him? I really—really—want him to die."

"I'm sure he's aware of that," Della said sarcastically. Because, of course, he was. The tiny mic she was wearing let Mason hear every word that was being said.

"He's out there."

"Somewhere, of course. Not even I know where right now. Hey, I'm independent. Not stupid," Della told him.

"And beautiful. Really. From the time I first saw you...well. Now, you still have your chance. Learn to drink blood with me. And if not, Special Agent Della Hamilton, you will be the most spectacular and beautiful display I have ever managed to create. A lovely Snow White just waiting for true love's kiss. Oh, you're thinking that's him, tough he-man Special Agent Mason Carter. Well, when he finds you, no kiss will awaken you. It won't be a nice nap for a hundred years. Death will be eternal."

"Wonderful. Have you thought about that? In death, you will find eternity, too."

"But I won't die! I really do drink the blood, you know. I'm willing to bet you believe there is a god—and others believe wholeheartedly in their gods, too. Religion! I'm a maniac when wars occur over religion all the time? Think about it! Anyway, as I said, since the rest of the world goes on blind faith, maybe I do, too... Believing in something tangible. Blood. The force of life. And taking blood so carefully, leaving behind beautiful angels! That's genius, not crazy. Can't begin to tell you what a high it gives me!"

"You may be the sickest individual I've ever met," Della told him.

Gideon was by her side, watching, listening, nervous, and shaking his head. "Della, careful, you're pissing him off!"

Stephan Dante didn't hear the ghost. He was grinning, highly entertained, as he stared back at Della.

"Sick? Crazy? Brilliant and farseeing. Whatever I am, Della, my love, you'll have to decide very soon to be with me—or against me."

"I want to see the girls," Della said.

"Give me that walkie-talkie thing strapped to your waist. Oh, and hand the Glock over. That's the only way you get to see the girls."

She held still for a long moment.

"You for them," he reminded her. "Or you for me, and they live. The choice will be yours."

She handed him the Glock and her radio walkie-talkie.

"Let's do this," she said.

★ ★ ★

Mason had arrived at the old shack he'd seen deep in the bayou brush. It had been nothing but derelict—no beer cans or cigarette butts littered the place.

It had been abandoned decades ago, he thought, and it hadn't been on the radar of anyone who might see a need to destroy the remains.

Some of the area was private land, and some of that private land had been owned by the same families for centuries.

He was in the cabin when he heard Gideon warn Della someone was just outside.

Stephan Dante.

Knowing he wasn't being watched then, Mason hurried through the foliage toward Della's position.

His temptation was to shoot Dante on the spot if that's what was needed to get him away from Della.

But that wouldn't bring them to the missing young women. As difficult as it might be, he had to let Della play it out.

Bring her to the girls. And then...

Then they had to take the man alive. Because they owed it to Taylor and Lapierre to find out the truth. Had Dante himself killed in France and England, or were there still killers out there who had followed the man's mantra?

He moved into position to see them.

Gideon was standing staunchly by Della's side.

And they were beginning to move.

He pulled out his radio. Taylor and Lapierre would already know what was going on, but he needed Detective Fremont and his local law enforcement to know their play was in motion and to stand down but ready.

He looked at the terrain. Stephan Dante was bringing Della toward something that didn't appear to be a path in any way. They were crawling through thick foliage.

He couldn't help but wish an eastern diamondback, any other rattler, coral snake, or maybe a cottonmouth would sink its fangs into Dante—let the man know just what "fangs" could do.

But the man was from Slidell, and he obviously knew the bayou.

And yet the most experienced man or woman could be surprised.

Dante wasn't going to be bitten by a snake, no matter how ironic such an occurrence would be. And Mason had to control his fear and his temper.

They needed Dante alive.

But more. So much more. He needed Della alive.

As he moved forward, he felt the vibration of his phone. He glanced at it and saw Angela was calling from headquarters. Never taking his eyes off Della, he answered the call.

"She's with him, Angela. I'm right behind. Della is trying to get him to take us to the girls."

"I have a few things for you. Can you follow and listen?"

"I can."

"I found out why Stephan Dante knows so much about the area. His family owned half the property in the area. I'm horrified it took so long, but he was born to an unwed mother who hid him for years—teaching him how to change his name. Then he began to excel in school, and she brought him home where, because he was accomplished, he was accepted. He should have inherited, but the land was sold at auction to pay off back taxes. Federal taxes. His hatred for the government began then, I believe. But I was able to draw up old records—I can show you where he might be heading," Angela told him. "Maps heading to everyone's phones."

"Great, thank you," Mason said. He was moving again as he spoke. The foliage was so dense, the map would prove to be incredibly helpful because he'd have a direction, but it was far too possible Della and Stephan Dante might disappear into the green of the bayou.

"I'm close now," he told Della.

"One more thing," Angela said over the phone. "I found out something else, though I'm not sure how much it helps."

"What? Quickly, please."

"Quickly, and it just may be helpful at some point. His obsession with Della began back when she was working a bank robbery case. One of the men taken down last year went to school with Stephan Dante. When he was a kid, Dante was bullied, and Chase LaRue, one of the bank robbers taken out, was his biggest tormenter."

"Ah, all right, thanks."

"I'm out," Angela said. "Keep me informed."

"Will do."

He pocketed his phone, assuring himself again it was on silent. Then he spoke softly into the mic.

"Team, Angela is sending us a map of all the old buildings in this area. The land we're on now belonged to Dante's family, but it was lost to back taxes. Still, he does know this place and everything ever built in the area. Della, maybe in your talking, mention you took down one of his mortal enemies after the bank heist a year ago. A man named Chase LaRue. Dante does have a thing for you. In his mind, you went to battle for him. He was born to an unwed mother, and had to prove himself to family—and was bullied as a kid—often by Chase LaRue. Use all of it if you can."

Through his earbuds, he heard Della let out a long sigh, assuring him she had heard him.

He heard Edmund Taylor speak then. The man's tone was soft but his words solid. "Got the maps. Mason, you go out straight from our landing just to the west of Della."

"Right. And I've got the map up, too, now," Mason said. "Looks like we're headed toward whatever the building labeled as *stash* is."

"We'll come in from the north and south, and we'll keep our distance until you give the word, Mason," Lapierre said. "Della, we're out here. Just keep talking."

Mason smiled; this time, Della pretended a sneeze.

He kept moving, silently, keeping his distance, but trying damn hard to make sure he could still see snatches of Della and Dante as they moved through the brush.

So, that was it. Dante really did want Della to join him.

She had done for him what he'd never been able to as a child. In his sick, twisted mind, she was his heroine, and he wanted her by his side.

He wondered briefly if the man had just been born with something warped in his mind, or if the life he'd led had caused him to become more bitter each year, and thus, more hateful toward his fellow man.

And yet, he still needed or longed for someone with whom to share…life. Whatever that life might be.

But, though, Dante might dream about a woman like Della by his side, sharing his evil visions of blood and murder, he had to know it wasn't going to happen.

And Mason knew he had to stay close. Because Dante would take her to the young women. And if she didn't drink blood…

If she rejected him…

Then she would die. He would make sure she saw him kill the young women first, and then he would kill her, draining every single drop of blood from her body.

CHAPTER THIRTEEN

"This is ridiculous!" Della said.

"What's ridiculous?"

"Traipsing endlessly through grass and snakes and trees! I don't get you. Just kill me and get it over with!"

"Oh, no, don't worry, I won't kill you now. I don't know why I believed you'd be a suitable consort, other than you knowing how to kill. I liked the fact you thought you were so kick-ass all on your own! That's just the thing—a woman with confidence. A woman who doesn't need a man but is a fitting and worthy partner for a man like me. So, let's see. If that's not going to work out, I want you to die slowly. And I want you to suffer!"

"You didn't want your other victims to suffer? They were all drugged out when you—or your ridiculous sycophants—bled them dry," Della said, staring at him.

Gideon stood by her side, listening, watching anxiously. "That's it. Don't let him see fear. He respects you—he knows you won't cower. He wants you to cry out and beg, but don't allow it!"

"I have no intention of doing so," she said aloud.

Stephan Dante frowned. "Who the hell are you talking to?"

She laughed softly. "Not to worry, I'm talking to my imaginary friend. I'm assuring him you can cut my heart out, and I won't give you the satisfaction of a whimper!"

"Well, we'll see about that, won't we? You're not screaming now. Oh, that's right! You're the eternal savior, the angel of mercy. Oh, how dramatic! 'I have taken an oath. If I lose my life, it's one thing, but I won't let a sweet innocent die!'" He moved closer to her, lifting her chin. "You won't do anything until I finally get you to the girls, will you?"

"No," she said flatly.

He grinned again. "Well, I know your comrades have taken over the shack where you and Special Agent Tall Man shot my buddy, the Midnight Slasher."

"His name was William Temple, if I remember correctly."

"He was the Midnight Slasher. He was my creation."

"You haven't been doing so well with your…creations. Anyway, whoever or whatever he was, he's William Temple, deceased now, and so un-famous that he's leaving the collective memory as we speak. Just as one day… Well, never mind. Yes, I want to see the young women you kidnapped and have tied up somewhere. So, no. I won't fight you."

"Ah, but Special Agent Carter, Mr. Tall Man is out there somewhere, right? And a slew of idiots who think they might know the bayou better than me."

Della stopped walking, hoping to get him to say more.

"Where *are* we going?" Della demanded irritably, swatting a large mosquito that found her hand as she tried to brush branches aside. "There isn't going to be any blood left in me for you if I come across any more mosquitos!"

He paused to laugh. "Oh, the skeeters will leave me enough. And the answer to that reminds me of being a kid—that's for me to know, and you to find out!" Dante said, enjoying his own joke. He glanced back at her as he led the way. "I knew you and your so-called team would set up cops everywhere to try and take me down. But I know this place better than any cop. I know how to disappear in the trees and brush like no one else, trust me."

"I know you *think* you know everything,"

"Ah, but often, I do."

"Which makes this all sadder."

"What's sad? I've taken a few idiots out of the world?"

"What makes you judge young women just beginning their lives as idiots?"

"Easy pickups. I told you. I've spared them. They'd just turn into teasing bitches, crying foul constantly, teasing men… thinking they're all-powerful because of their sex and beauty. Hey, I've made them all angels."

"Oh, please. They might have grown up to do good things. When you take them, they're just young and having fun, something young people do," Della said.

"Idiots—no one who would have done anything for the world."

"Like you're doing?" she asked.

"Honey, come on now. You must agree. You're here with me. I am ruling the world. Look around you. Do you see any of the dozens of the cops running around in here? No. And you won't."

She might not see dozens, Della thought.

But she would see one—or three. Her team was behind her.

And Dante would have no idea Mason, while not having grown up in the area, had studied everything about it when he had followed Mason's trainee, the Midnight Slasher, to Louisiana. And he and the others now had a map in their hands of the acreage that had once belonged to his family.

"Hey, you know, the world is alike in one thing. I don't know of a group of any kind out there that doesn't have a few imperfect eggs."

"You're making excuses for your cops? A bunch of them good ole Louisiana boys born in the bayou?"

"Well, they didn't own the place at one time," she said reflectively.

A branch he had moved slapped back in her face. She had startled him.

"What?" he demanded.

"Oh, come on, please! Of course, we know about you! Unwed mom, you probably bounced around with your mother's friends, started doing well in school, and earned your way into the good graces of your grandfather. Ah, but he did well enough, apparently, and then not, because you should have had a nice inheritance but…well, the government stepped in."

"And you think I'm evil! The taxes…that was pure evil. They took away everything a man—a family—had worked for over generations!"

"I'm fond of roads, public schools, and that kind of thing," Della said. She shrugged. "So, I pay my taxes."

"And I thought you were intelligent—intelligent people figure out how to not pay them."

"Really? Then how did you lose the property?"

"I didn't lose it—and I wouldn't have."

Gideon was still at her side—having a much easier time with the brush than she was. But he whispered to her now, "Careful. You're making him angry. You want him to get you to the girls, you want to let the others know where you are!"

"I guess not because…wow. I mean, how did you do it? Come up with what it must have cost to go hopping from country to country like that?"

"Well, these bayous hide a lot of sins."

"Meaning? Come on, tell me!" Della said. She decided to heed Gideon's warning. "I must admit, I am in awe of the way you've managed all that. But how... Oh!"

"Oh?" he said.

"Prisons! You visited old accomplices or friends in prison. You found out where they stashed whatever it was they stole! And here's another—the amount of fake IDs and personae you have! Astounding!"

"Well, thank you. See? I am a genius," Dante assured her easily. "Okay, so yes, on the one. I visited old friends in prison and made a few new ones. By the way, it's easy to collect saliva. Have baggy, will travel! And some guys in prison believe you're going to get them out. And that means they're willing to share their ill-gotten gains, little realizing the same money can be used to pay the families of fellow convicts who are happy to see that...well, that the original thief never has a chance to regain those same ill-gotten gains. Della, you could be so good at all this! Get your nose out of the air. What has the old establishment ever done for you? You chase killers—but those killers might kill you and what will you get? A nice funeral? Think about all I'm offering you. Think about all I've been capable of doing, and how much more I'd be capable of with you at my side!"

"I don't think I'd like blood," she said.

"Have you tried it?" he queried, grinning.

"No." Della made a pretense of swatting another mosquito. "How much farther are we going?"

"Not that far. Just ahead."

"The old homestead, huh?"

"Oh, seriously. You've obviously figured out who I am. You and your goons have researched the property, right? Would I go somewhere obvious?"

"Maybe. You do have confidence."

"Ah, well, I still might fall to a hail of bullets. But if I die or if I'm taken, the girls die."

"Lead me to them."

He smiled at her. Again, she saw he had begun his flight into this madness. He looked like the all-American young man, eager and ready to have fun while still being kind.

"We're here!" he said.

"We're where?"

He walked a few steps ahead and moved the low hanging branches of an elm. There was a wooden door, with whatever lay behind it well hidden in the brush. It was a cabin, crumbling to the elements and hidden in the denseness of the foliage.

"Ladies first, of course."

Della stepped in. The trees shaded out whatever sunlight tried to filter through the branches and foliage, but her eyes adjusted.

Two young women were seated in chairs set in the middle of the room.

Both were tied to their seats and both had needles in their arms, and tubes that were slowly draining their blood into containers on the floor.

Della didn't know if they were unconscious because of the loss of their blood, or if he had drugged them to keep them silent.

She turned to Dante.

"You told me you were holding three hostages—to donate their blood, of course."

"You never give me credit!" he told her, amused.

"Credit for what?"

"Choices. Life is all about choices, right? I know your boy toy agent is right behind you somewhere. Trying to follow us, though…well, this place isn't on any maps. Oh, in fact, it's not even mine. So…one dying young lady is out there, trying to weave her way through jagged grasses and venomous snakes—maybe a gator or two. He'll stumble upon her or she'll stumble upon him and… Oh, you ethical people! Will he save her, or let her die so that he can try to save you?"

"Let the other two go. Let them go and stumble out to him, too. Then you'll have me."

"Oh, but nothing to drink! Because you are going to drink blood, my lovely. You are going to drink blood. Drink blood, while you watch the lives drain from those you were sworn to protect. Because now, you're going to be sworn to me."

"No. The deal was they go free, and you get me."

"I'm going to need to think about that. But, for now… I like this Glock. Standard issue, eh? There's a third chair against the wall. Go get it and bring it out here. We'll start out with you sitting next to Leslie there. Touch her, if you like. I believe she'll be growing cold. Come on, sit."

"You need to let them both go!" Della insisted.

"Sit. We'll keep talking a bit. We're going to find out what your own life means to you."

Gideon had, of course, followed Della into the old shack.

"Sit. Keep him talking. The girls aren't dead. I would know, I don't know how, but I would know. Keep him talking, give your team time."

"You want me to sit? And we'll talk?" Della asked.

"Sure. You see, I learned how to do what I do. The blood is draining from them slowly. You have a little time to hope you can talk me into someone else's blood. Oh, like tall, dark, and handsome boy toy! You want to save these girls and yourself? You can do it—trick boy toy in here with me having this Bureau Glock aimed right at him. Oh, he's tough. I won't mess around with him—I'll just shoot him dead. When you drink his blood, I'll let them go—and I'll let you live."

"I… Well, I'll sit. And we'll talk," Della said.

Mason would know. Mason wouldn't be tricked. Mason had heard everything said.

She smiled. So, a crazed killer was holding a gun on her. But he didn't know their plan was coming to fruition.

"They're drugged, right?" she asked. "I mean, come on, that is your thing, right? I'm curious. You are capable of being adorable and charming. But maybe, sometimes, no matter how adorable and charming, girls rejected you. So, you learned from experience that women were much more pliable under a drug—"

"I never had to drug anyone for sex!"

"Maybe not, but you learned drugging someone could get them where you wanted them to be!"

"Did you want them to suffer?" he asked. "Maybe there's a side to you I haven't seen as yet—that would mean I could have hope for you!" He didn't try to hide the excitement he was feeling in his voice.

"No, I'm just assuming you had to drug them, not out of any kind of real kindness, but because you didn't want them crying out, warning anyone. And then again, when you're trying to make it appear that a vampire sank its fangs into a neck and drained the blood, you need people to be pliable. Someone struggling could ruin the whole appearance of a romantic death through a long, long kiss on the neck."

He smiled.

"No one knows about me and this place," he said. "So… let's see. Do you live, or do you die?"

He was good at keeping the Glock aimed directly at her chest. One of his hostages was stumbling around in the wilderness and two were here, possibly close to death even now.

But she couldn't reach for the Baby Browning until…

Until she got him to look away, elsewhere.

Mason was close. Listening.

"Okay, now see the rope there? Tie yourself up. And do it right. I'm not an idiot. I'll know if you create a bad knot."

"What? I can't tie myself up!" Della protested. "I mean, you want a good knot? A good knot takes two hands!"

He came and hunkered down before her, the Glock—her own Glock—still aimed directly at her chest.

"You're a clever girl. You can figure it out. Oh, and I know you're aware I prefer my *Sleeping Beauty* method of murder. But if you don't listen to me and do things just right, I'll shoot her right now, shoot one of these girls in the head, and her blood and brains spill all over your ethical little body. Got it?" He stared at her with a half smile curled into his lip as he spoke.

"I'll figure it out," Della said.

Mason was listening, she reminded herself.

And he was close. But there was a dying girl out there, probably close to them, and Mason would be left with a horrible choice.

They had come full circle. They were back in the bayou. She had believed in him before she had even known him.

Now, she knew him. And during the short but intense time they'd been together, she knew his soul, his heart, and so much more.

He would come. And the chance she needed would be provided.

He would figure it out, she determined, without making choices on who lived and who died.

She closed her eyes for a minute. Mason wasn't alone out there. They had a team, and local police and law enforcement were out there…

"Keep him talking!"

It was Edmund Taylor who spoke that time, perhaps almost reading her mind.

"We're all coming in from different angles," he added.

"I'm almost there!" Mason said.

She smiled, glancing at Gideon.

"What the hell?" Dante demanded.

"Oh, sorry. I was looking at Gideon."

"Gideon?"

"Oh, not to worry. Gideon is dead. He's been dead for hundreds of years. Started out as a pirate and became a hero and a great guy."

Dante leaned back, starting to laugh. "New ploy? You see ghosts? And what is the ghost going to do—other than greet you all as you *cross the line*?"

"Well, I'm not sure that's how it works, but if I'm going, yeah, I'd be glad he was there to greet me and to help me along."

"Did you think I'd panic over a ghost?"

"No. He can't really hurt you. He doesn't have that kind of physical strength. But…hmm. You would be surprised by what a ghost can do."

"I know what he can do," Dante said. "You tell your dead friend to get out there and find, oh, so Special Agent Mason Carter. Let him know if he comes here, alone, and unarmed—and doesn't radio any others so they stop looking at old Dante family properties—I'll let another girl go. Then I'll have you, one lady, and him. We'll find out if you do want to live. Or join your ghost!"

"Hey, Gideon, you heard him, huh?"

"I will not be leaving your side," Gideon said. "Mason will know what to do."

She believed him.

Mason would know what to do.

She just hoped he would hurry...

Death, someone's death, was imminent.

Keep him talking, keep him talking, play every angle...

"Okay! Gideon heard you. I'll tie myself up. Yeah, of course, I want to live. But while we're waiting... You talk about idiots! That pair you had working for you in Norway. Now, they were idiots. Did you kill the girls in England or in France? Or did you convince someone in those countries you were a vampire king, and you could get them to a point where they'd earn their way to immortality? Come on, you've got me! Share some info with me."

She had the rope he'd handed her. She made a pretense of trying to figure out how to do decent knots on her own wrists.

"The world is filled with idiots. I'm just cleaning it out."

"But that doesn't answer my question. Did you do all the killing?"

"I do love Paris! I mean, who doesn't love Paris? And the girls there... Well, it is the city for romance. If you were really lucky, I would take you there."

"Because I brought down Chase LaRue."

"Well, you screwed up."

"Screwed up? I was part of the team that brought him—and his accomplice—down!"

Dante stared at her strangely. His face was hard.

"You didn't kill him," he said quietly. "You should have shot the bastard."

"I told you. I try *not* to shoot people."

"Guess what? I don't like to shoot people, either. But I do shoot them when it's necessary."

He waved the Glock in front of her nose. "And Special Agent Tall, Dark, and Deadly... He'll come to that door. And he'll think we can bargain. But him… That's a big dude. I don't like to shoot people, but I'm going to take aim and put a bullet through his head so fast he'll never know what hit him." He laughed. "Maybe your Gideon ghost will be there to greet him and to explain! Oh, wow, and if he's a ghost, he'll still get to see every little thing I do to you!"

"Mason, he'll shoot you the minute you step in!" Lapierre warned.

"Not to worry—I'm there, and I hear him, too. And I won't be playing it his way. The place isn't on the map," Mason said, explaining himself and warning Edmund Taylor and Jeanne Lapierre they might be heading to the wrong area. "I saw them disappear around a tree. Heading that way—from what he's said, I think it's going to be a place that was owned by Chase LaRue. And, of course, Dante now revels in the fact he can take it over—property that belonged to the man who bullied him. I'm heading closer. But he's freed one of the hostages, and—"

He broke off.

He'd heard what Dante had been saying, just as Lapierre and Taylor had heard every word that had been spoken near Della.

She was there, staggering around a tree, gripping it hard to stay on her feet, silent tears streaming down her face.

She saw him. For a minute, pure terror entered her eyes.

"It's okay—I'm FBI," he said softly.

"Help!" she managed. "Help me!"

Then she collapsed into the brush and on down to the ground. He rushed over to her, knowing Dante had wanted him desperate to find a way to save a dying woman—before finding Della and the others on his own.

He crashed through the brush as quietly as he could and knelt quickly, seeking a pulse on the girl. She was alive, yes, but her pulse was weak, faint. She had been bound. Abrasions on her wrists and ankles were deep and red as well. She was pale. Bleeding from the neck, he thought. But she was still breathing shallowly; she was alive.

She hadn't fought him. While she was bruised and bleeding, she had no defensive wounds. His method was to drug his victims so they couldn't fight back.

"I need help out here fast—" he began.

But he broke off. He could hear that someone was near him. Dante was ahead of him and he didn't seem to be working with accomplices. It had to be law enforcement.

"It's me, Edmund Taylor," a voice said. "I think I see you. I'm almost at your location. I'll get the girl and get her to help. You get to that shack or…whatever it is. We'll need EMTs ready to take her, and—"

"Get Fremont on the radio. He'll get help here," Mason said. "I'm trying to make sure she's not still bleeding… She's lost a tremendous amount of blood!"

"I'm coming in close, too," Jeanne Lapierre said. "And I've got the radio going. Fremont is near us, too. He'll know how to get her to help the fastest way. Mason, keep moving."

"I can't just leave—"

"I'm here."

Mason heard the words through his earbuds and through the air. Edmund Taylor had made it to his position.

"I've got the girl," Taylor assured him. "Move in. I think we're running out of time. We'll get her to help and sweep around the whatever that is in the middle of the trees."

"Thank you," Mason said. He nodded grimly to Taylor and started back through the trees. He didn't think Dante would be watching for him. The man had thought he'd known them so well. Yes, they would have figured out who he was.

But in his mind, he was convinced law enforcement would

be searching every property and spit of land that had been owned by the Dante family.

Mason moved silently, taking his time to make sure branches didn't snap, and his travels through the last of the brush, tangling grasses and trees didn't announce his arrival.

There was a door still on the place, but it had been erected from logs, and there weren't windows in the structure, at least none that he could see. Odd. Some light probably filtered in because of the cracks and chips in the wooden walls of the structure. But not at the front, anyway.

Mason made his way carefully and silently around the house, listening to the conversation inside.

"You haven't answered my question!" Della said.

"France, yes, I enjoyed every minute of the lovely lass I met there! She was all sass, a pretty flirt, a tease, until she imbibed my special concoction. And then I walked her out of the bar so easily and to my rental car and then..." Dante broke off with a satisfied laugh.

"You are remarkable. I mean, most men would have needed hideouts everywhere," Della said.

"Have medical bag, will travel. Oh, and it works a few ways. People in general make way for a man walking around with a medical bag. Doctors do command respect."

"Usually," Della murmured.

Mason had made his way around the first corner of the place. The brush grew so tightly around it he had to tear at vines to continue.

But he found a window. Carefully looking in, he saw the two young women in the chairs by Della. Both were slumped over.

Both had needles in their arms.

He saw the glass containers collecting the blood by their

feet and the tubes that carried blood from their throats and down to the containers.

He watched them drip.

Thank God their blood was dripping slowly! But then, how long had they been losing their blood? The containers were filling up.

Dante was hunkered down in front of Della, holding her Glock. Pointing it at her heart.

Gideon stood worriedly by her side.

Mason was afraid to speak; he might be heard inside no matter how quietly he tried to whisper. But when Della pressed Dante for an answer on the killings in England, the man gave her his full attention.

"Ah, London town! London, Big Ben, the Thames! Hey, you know, I do love castles. Castle Bran is so cool, I thought you'd enjoy it, but hey, you figured out I'd never use the standing castle as my display area... You never got to see it, right? You rushed here. Because you could have been my soulmate. Oh, well. So—"

"You brought in an idiot in Kirkwall, too. You're not always the best judge."

"Bear in mind, you have to find just the right people. And to stay ahead, I had to move like wildfire. Which, of course, I did. Really well."

As they spoke, Mason rose in the window opening, hoping Gideon would turn to him.

The ghost did so.

Mason mouthed out a question.

"Could you just shove one of the other chairs?" he asked.

Gideon frowned for a minute, looking worried. Then he squared his ghostly shoulders, looking back at Mason, and nodded.

"Mason is here," Gideon told Della. "Get ready, I'm going to distract Dante."

"In England," Dante continued, "I did the beautiful display. The other, well…was not an idiot! In fact, one of my finest followers. Ah, here's the thing. The world is open and filled with magic for those who read. I mean, what would the movies have been if Bram Stoker hadn't written *Dracula*? And okay, so…they call Castle Bran Dracula's castle, but it really wasn't that big of a deal in his life, and still…what a story came from it. Books! They're filled with puzzles and secrets and wonders."

"That tells me nothing about England."

"You're not reading enough. Or should I say…perhaps not doing the research that goes into a good book!"

He wasn't giving Della a definitive answer.

And they might well be running out of time.

Mason gave Gideon a nod.

The ghost moved away from Della, hunched down, squeezed his eyes shut, and summoned every bit of energy he could from the air.

A chair moved, causing a screeching noise against the floor.

Dante looked away, rising, shocked.

And Mason took aim from the window area and fired.

CHAPTER FOURTEEN

Della dropped the rope, grabbed her Baby Browning from her boot at the same time and sprang to her feet.

Stephan Dante let out a scream of agony.

Mason had aimed perfectly. His shot had caught Dante dead in the wrist. The Glock went flying from his injured hand, up in the air, and down to the floor.

By then, Mason had leaped through the old window opening, and Della had her Baby Browning on Dante as well.

"No!" Dante screamed with rage. "No, no, no! You are to die. I will kill you. I will kill you. I will—"

"What you will do is go to prison!" another voice said.

It was Edmund Taylor who had pushed through the front door and approached Dante without hesitation, a pair of handcuffs ready for the prisoner.

Dante started to laugh, even as Taylor cuffed him.

"Prison! Oh, my friend. I have so many good, good friends there! I'll be out in no time!"

"Louisiana has the death penalty," Mason reminded him.

"Yeah, but I can afford a swanky lawyer. They'll find me

incompetent to stand trial, and I will need mental health assistance! And they'll want me in France and England where there's no death penalty and... Well, Special Agent Mason Carter, I will kill you." He turned to Della. "You go ahead and keep sleeping with him now. Because you're really just a bitch like the rest of them. But when I'm free and he's dead, I'll show you something real before... Well, now I know, you need to be dead, too."

Mason looked at Della. "Maybe I should have shot him in the head?"

"You did the right thing," Taylor said. "Because I need to know—who else killed women in London?"

"What? I killed them."

"They heard you, Dante," Della said. "They heard every word you said."

"But maybe I'm a liar."

"No, you're crazy, sick, twisted, demented—pure evil," Della said calmly. "But you're not a liar. Go figure on that!"

Edmund stared at the man, barely controlling himself.

"Who?" he demanded.

"Me."

"And who else?"

Dante started to laugh. "What? An Englishman! Oh, well, specially granted the power to carry a gun, but hey, no death penalty. You're so damned civilized, and you can't torture anything out of me, so...hmm. Oh! I can see it now! The legal wrangling that's going to go on, the ragged diplomacy among countries, all wanting a piece of me! But prison in England? I will be out so fast you'll never know what hit you."

Edmund looked at Della and she knew. He had to step back out of the room. Or he wouldn't be civilized.

"Forget him, we need help for these girls—" Della began.

But another man stepped through the door, Jeanne Lapierre.

He was followed by two Louisiana state officers and Detective Fremont—and a host of EMTs. The ramshackle cabin was growing crowded.

Mason looked over at Fremont.

"Can they get him out of here? I don't know what legal wrangling will go on, either, but for now I believe the man is a guest in his own great state of Louisiana."

"Officers?" Fremont said.

Silently and grimly, two of the plainclothes men made their way to Dante, ready to escort him out. He started fighting them.

"You two goons! Think you can drag me through all the brush—"

"Yeah, we do," said the one, sliding a leg behind Dante to catch him at the knees, sagging down.

And then the two men started to drag him.

Dante was furious, looking back.

"Don't kid yourselves! I will be free. I am immortal, evil is immortal, and I am immortal! I will see you drown in your own blood while I drink what is left! You will die, you will die, you will die!"

"We all die eventually," Gideon said, staring after him as he was finally dragged out the door.

Della lowered her head, smiling. She couldn't respond with others in the room. But they would get their chance; when they were alone, she and Mason could thank him.

He worried he couldn't do much. Ghosts *could* rattle the proverbial chains, and they could hit light switches. But gathering the energy for any such function was difficult and exhausting, and Gideon had come through. His distraction had given them the chance to save lives and to survive themselves.

The space was small.

The EMTs needed room.

"Can we get the hell out of here now, *s'il vous plait*?" Lapierre asked. "No, no, I don't mean to offend, the bayou is wonderful, but..."

Della laughed. "We're not offended, Jeanne. I think I have mosquito bites on my mosquito bites. Time to head back to civilization."

There would be so much paperwork.

But Della felt good. So good. They had taken down the king of the vampires, and she could pray the young women taken in Louisiana might survive as well.

She and Mason walked slowly as they all started back to the water and the boats. They were in silent agreement, she knew.

They had to thank Gideon.

And they did. Crawling through the overgrowth, they had their chance. Gideon had stayed right with them.

"Thank you. Thank you again, my amazing friend," Mason told him.

"I think you might have managed without me. You have amazing aim, Mason. You could have hit and killed Dante before he knew what was happening."

"It would have been taking a chance. He might have managed to pull the trigger on the Glock."

"And I'd be dead," Della said.

Gideon shrugged, but he was smiling. "This is a hell of a team," he told him. "You have a Frenchman on it and an Englishman and... I don't know Bisset, or the people at your headquarters, but I have seldom been so impressed. In so many years!" he added.

Della and Mason smiled at one another and then at Gideon.

"The fact remains. You, Gideon, were an outstanding member of this team."

"Then I am grateful. And I am equally ready to be of service at any time. This has all made sense of my life, and my death. For now… I have some friends I must brag to! I will, of course, see you again."

He started to leave them but then stopped himself, grinning. "The best thing about being the dead member of the team is I don't have to do any of the paperwork." He frowned. "There is one thing."

"The killings in England," Della said quietly. "I just wish I could have gotten him to tell the truth, to give us a name."

"Well, we do know he was the active killer in Paris," Gideon said.

"I know. But Edmund Taylor is, of course, worried there might be more *vampire* bodies in London. Though nothing has been reported since Dante moved on to Norway."

"Still, if someone has gotten away with such a thing…" Gideon murmured.

"He will show himself in time, or…" Mason paused and shrugged. "Angela can pull records out of thin air. We will discover this man somehow. Forensic teams here and in Europe are still working on any minuscule item they might find."

Gideon nodded.

He lifted a hand to them. *"Au revoir, à tout à l'heure!"*

He disappeared into the brush. Mason looked at Della and smiled and took her hand.

"I'm still shaking, I think."

"Thank you, too."

He grinned. "For saving your ass?"

"For having the faith in me to do what we needed to do to bring him down."

He nodded. "It's not easy. But… Well, I am a professional. Oh, yeah. So are you!"

She grinned.

They cleared the heavy brush. The others were waiting, but she didn't care. Hand in hand, they ran the last few yards to the waiting boat. Even as they boarded, they saw the EMTS heading out with Dante's last victims.

Later, they'd be able to contact the hospital and hope that the news they received regarding Dante's last victims would be good news.

But for now...

Della took her seat on the airboat. She closed her eyes and felt the air and the wind as it ripped around them. Full circle. They were headed back to New Orleans.

"Taylor, what about the first girl?" Mason asked.

"Fremont was right behind me. He had the EMTs ready to move at a moment's notice and they did. They might not have known Dante would use his old enemy's property out here—or even known it existed—but they do know what they are doing and where they are. You weren't gone three minutes before Detective Fremont made it to my position."

"Everyone's timing was great," Mason said.

Lapierre laughed softly. "We may have proven to be backup, but..."

"The best damned backup in the world," Edmund Taylor supplied.

"No one is anything without backup," Della said.

"Still, you are our heroine, too!" Fremont said. "And tonight, we will toast to you—and ourselves, of course. Onward! To New Orleans. And paperwork," he added dryly.

Della closed her eyes again. She loved the cool touch of the wind.

She enjoyed the caress of nature, eyes closed, feeling Mason's body heat at her side.

It was a very good day.

★ ★ ★

Paperwork took the rest of day into the evening. They'd be at it again in the morning, trying to untangle everything that had happened. Bisset worked the information line, making sure law enforcement in the countries involved knew everything that had happened.

It was ten o'clock when they were finally free for the night.

But for New Orleans, that was early. Mason truly wanted nothing more than to head straight back to a room with Della, but he knew the others were eager to celebrate. While he would have preferred a venue on Frenchman Street, Edmund Taylor had never been to Bourbon Street and Bisset and Lapierre were both intrigued by the fact it was famous across the globe, so he gave in. But first, dinner at one of his favorite places, Antoine's, and then a walk down Bourbon.

Naturally, Della insisted they stop at Lafitte's. She knew a lot of the history of the area and the building and she regaled Bisset, Lapierre, Taylor, and even Detective Fremont, a Louisiana native, with her attention to truth and detail.

When they left to head down to the music venues and the bars, Mason whispered to her, "How the hell do you know details about Lafitte's?" he asked.

She grinned.

"Google! I looked it all up—because I want to talk to Gideon again. I want to find out what is and isn't true!"

"Ah! Hmm. Remember, truth, like beauty, is often in the eye of the beholder!"

She smiled and nodded. "Ah, but in our business, there are also facts. And then again, I do love to study history. Because it gives so much." She frowned, looking at him. "What are you hiding?" she asked him.

"What?"

"You're hiding something."

"Seriously? Okay, yes. A surprise."

She laughed. "You're not talking about bed tonight, right?"

He grinned at that. "I don't think anything can still be a surprise, but sometimes the best presents are something you know someone wants."

"Oooh. Presumptive!" she teased. "So—"

"Patience is a virtue."

"What made you think I had any virtues?"

"Ah, well, you're going to have the virtue of patience until later! I think you impressed Detective Fremont with all your knowledge about the places we went, especially Lafitte's!"

"Trying to change the subject?"

"Yes."

"Okay. History. And fiction. Hey, Lafitte's is supposedly the oldest structure used as a bar in the United States, and no, its namesakes didn't own the place, but supposedly again, one of their partners in crime did and smuggled goods went through the place. You know—Jean and Pierre Laffite stood there! Anyway, it's an exceptional building and nicely run. There's the little courtyard, and I intend to find out if Gideon was ever there!"

"But probably not tonight!" he whispered back. "We do have our international friends, and they are ready to keep moving!"

They stopped in to see several of the bars, all offering great music with styles ranging from NOLA jazz to blues and, of course, rock. It wasn't surprising that dozens of young women flirted with Edmund Taylor; as Mason had once pointed out in teasing her, he was an impressive man.

And while Jeanne Lapierre was older, he had his share of laughter and flirtations, too.

It was very late when they decided they'd end the evening

together at a late-late-late-night restaurant off Bourbon Street. Food—and then sleep!

It had been fun, an enjoyable night with enjoyable people.

Detective Fremont excused himself and answered his phone while determining whether to join everyone or head on home.

He smiled after listening to the call and informed them early on that all three of the Louisiana victims were in stable condition.

They would make it.

After that call, Detective Fremont left them, pleased, relieved, and thanking them, and telling them that he was about to keel over.

Della thought she should have been ready to keel over, too. But adrenaline was still rushing through her. She loved the French Quarter and loved showing it to their teammates. Especially since they hadn't been before, because they were Europeans—and Lapierre and Bisset Frenchmen!

It was when they had ordered—breakfast had seemed the correct meal since it was nearly three in the morning—that Bisset lifted his cup of coffee and looked around the table.

"Cheers, bravo! Della, an American expression here. Boy, do you have balls! You're beautiful, of course, but fearless."

"No, trust me, I can be afraid," she promised.

"We all need to be afraid," Mason said quietly. "Fear can keep us alive."

"Ah, but there is fear that debilitates, and fear that is controlled. Fear that is weighed and... Special Agent Mason Carter! Not sure you know what fear is!"

"Ah, but I do."

"You walk in where you need to be—in the most intelligent manner, of course."

"Well, um, thank you."

"That leads us to the detectives. Lapierre and Taylor. Gentlemen, may I just say I will be glad to be your liaison at any time, anywhere within my ability."

"Best backup ever!" Edmund Taylor said, lifting his coffee cup and grinning.

"Best team ever," Mason said.

"We were a good team. And I am grateful this horrible man will face prison in several different countries, grateful for Norway, Scotland, for Romania, France..." Bisset told them.

His voice trailed.

"But according to what we learned when Dante thought only Della was with him, he had a follower in England. So, there is still a *vampire* killer at large in England," Mason supplied. "We have people at the Krewe with some really special abilities, a psychiatrist who has worked with criminal minds for years and is brilliant. We'll get him talking to Dante and see what we can find out. If anyone can get him to talk—"

"I really don't think anyone can," Edmund said. "Of course, I'm open to your people trying anything, but..."

"Whatever it takes, we'll find the truth," Mason said.

"What?" Edmund asked, confused.

"Team. We're a team. Bisset already knows... He had to go through a few channels to become permanently assigned to us. But we're officially a Euro-team—an experimental Euro-team. But a team, under the jurisdiction of Jackson Crow and the Krewe and Detective Taylor, we'll keep working this case. We'll go to England or wherever we need to go. We'll find the killer Dante twisted in England, no matter what it takes."

"Team," Edmund said, looking at all of them.

"To the team!" Della cried, lifting her coffee.

"To the team!" Edmund agreed, but then he paused. "So... tomorrow..."

"Tomorrow, we start to finish the endless paperwork. Jackson Crow is sending down Patrick Law—Special Agent *Doc-*

tor Law. If anyone can get a name out of Dante, it will be Patrick. He may want Della to go back in, or he may find it detrimental. But after that…"

"On to England?" Edmund queried.

"Not right away," Della said.

"What?"

"A trip to Castle Bran. There's something in history we need to learn, something in the research Stoker did from afar… Remember our conversations. We caught up with him—but we might have known more if we'd gone to Castle Bran," Della said. She looked around the table at the group.

"All right, team!" Lapierre said, and he raised his coffee cup again.

Soon after, they parted ways, and it was easy. There was no need for long goodbyes.

And finally, Della and Mason were alone. It was ridiculously late. Or early. But Angela had seen to it they had a stunning hotel room with a Jacuzzi right in the bedroom. Stripping away each other's clothes was wonderful, like stripping off the stain of a man like Stephan Dante.

Stepping into the bubbling hot water together…

"Exhaustion should be kicking in," Mason said. "I mean all the heat…"

"I am exhausted," she assured him.

"Sleep…"

"Oh, really?"

"No. I'm just trying to be polite."

Della crawled on top of him, feeling the delicious slide of flesh against flesh and the quick constriction of his muscles… and organs.

She smiled, smoothing back a lock of his hair and taking his face in her hands before whispering sensuously, "This is not the place to be polite."

"Oh, well, then, good! The hell with it!"

They laughed. And they made love. And nothing had ever felt as sweetly like the best celebration of victory ever.

The next day, they spent hours on paperwork. But then it was complete.

They'd leave for Europe again the next day. Mason let Della know Jackson had offered him time off.

He'd asked that they have vacation time later; they weren't sending Edmund back to England alone. Not with what they knew—and didn't know.

Della was just closing her personal computer, making the last of her personal notes, ready to head back to the room with Mason—for sleep, real sleep, before taking on jet lag again—when Edmund Taylor almost ran into her at the exit from the station.

"Tomorrow, we're off," he said.

She nodded. "Tomorrow, we're off. Edmund, we'll get him. I've met Patrick and he's a brilliant psychiatrist—and agent. He'll see Dante alone first and let me know if he thinks I can spur him into anything or if he can get something on his own. Anyway, I promise you, we'll do everything we can. I know England is your home and it's natural to…"

"Want a killer there, right," he agreed. "Thanks for last night. It was the break we needed. And thanks for—being a team!"

"I think we're going to be a better team than ever!"

"Hope so. One day—on a vacation—I want to come back here. Love the place!" he told her.

She smiled. "I do, too. Hey, who knows where we'll wind up when!"

"Yeah, well, I want to get out to the bayou again," he told her, just as Mason joined them, ready to head out, too.

"The bayou is great—especially when you spend time there for pleasure," Mason said.

Edmund Taylor nodded. Then grinned and gave Mason a light punch on the arm.

"The next time we're out there," he said, "you can introduce me to your friend, Gideon. I'd really love to meet him."

He walked on by them. Della looked at Mason. They laughed, shook their heads, then headed out together.

The world could be so senseless, but now and then...

Some things just did make sense!

EPILOGUE

"Fact, fantasy, folklore—and fiction," Mason said, turning to smile at Della.

She smiled in return. "There is something here, maybe something we need to put together. And, hey, now we can say we've been to Castle Bran and, well…"

They stood on the ramparts of Bran Castle. While it might not be "Dracula's Castle" in fact and history, the castle featured displays with fascinating information—and looked over beautiful countryside in the shade of the Carpathian Mountains.

Neighboring villages were charming, medieval, brought into the modern world in colors that added to their historic charm.

But they hadn't come for the beauty.

It seemed that even after Stephan Dante had been captured, they'd been waiting for the next development in the case.

Detectives Edmund Taylor and Jeanne Lapierre had moved on to London, along with François Bisset. They were poring over every detail of the killings that had taken place there.

Della and Mason would join them, flying out of Transylvania the next morning. No matter how hard she tried, she couldn't help thinking that with all the mind games Dante played, there was something she would see or perhaps even realize at Castle Bran.

"So...hmm. Thinking it all out. Vlad Tepes was born circa 1431, and his father was a member of the Order of the Dragon, and thus he took on the name Dracul, or Dragon," Mason said. "At the age of seven, Vlad was sent to be a prisoner, a hostage, of the Turks to guarantee his father's loyalty. Then his brother was killed and his father was assassinated. At seventeen, Vlad was released...and left to avenge his father—who was hated by his own people—and then... I guess that his horrid imprisonment under the Ottoman Empire left him bitter, and when he finally gathered forces and help from the Hungarians, he managed to take over Wachovia and started a true reign of terror against the Turks, and thus—Vlad the Impaler, monster and hero, came into being. Okay, so, many historians are of the opinion that he never entered Castle Bran, and we know that Bram Stoker never set foot here—"

"But Bram Stoker was the ultimate writer, creating all kinds of incredible fiction by researching all kinds of historical fact," Della said. She wasn't sure herself what they were looking for. Stephan Dante was imprisoned and seeing Patrick Law an hour a day. Patrick had suggested that Della not give in to the man—he wanted to tease and tempt and torment her, and if given time, Patrick believed he could get through to whatever truths the man had that might lead to another killer.

Not at all sure why, Della had been determined to come back to Romania. The truth—or the information they were seeking—lay somewhere between fact, fiction, folklore, and fantasy, which defined their journey to Bran Castle."

"Okay, vampires, bats… Stoker probably knew that one of the biggest bat caves in the world is in Romania."

"And the boundary lines of the Ottoman Empire, Wallachia, Transylvania, Hungary, and Romania changed through the years, with the Iron Curtain only falling in 1989," Della murmured. "But while Vlad the Impaler might not have been here…hmm."

"I was thinking of… Well, fact or fiction. His first wife threw herself from the ramparts of Poenari Castle rather than face imprisonment by the Turks," Mason said. "But! Others say she killed herself because she knew that her husband really wanted to marry his mistress."

"Right, great, so…no one knows which is true," Della murmured. "Wait—I think in one of the movies that was made about Dracula, his beautiful wife threw herself from this very parapet."

"No one knows which is true," Mason agreed. "Just as no one knows what happened to Vlad's remains. It's believed that he died in battle. He was supposedly buried on a small island in the floor of a fantastic eleventh-century church, but archaeologists disproved that. The story I believe the most is that the Turk's displayed his head on a spike in Istanbul. I can imagine their anger. It's estimated he killed between forty and a hundred thousand people—of course, some of them his own—in the short seven years of his reign." He shrugged. "We see man's inhumanity to man on a daily basis, and still, it's difficult to imagine fields of people impaled—and in a way that made sure they didn't die immediately but suffered as long as possible. Patrick would have had a field day with the man's mind, I'm sure."

"Imprisoned, growing up abandoned and bitter, and into a world of brutality," Della said. "Marrying…and…maybe he did love his wife and maybe she threw herself to her death because she didn't intend to be taken by his enemies. Hmm…"

"What?"

"I think I know!" she said.

Mason looked at her, his eyebrow hiking. "Um—the name of the man Dante took under his wing as a second killer in London?"

She sighed with exaggerated aggravation and told him, "No! Mason, think about it. Okay, yes, it's a long shot, but the best that seems to come to mind. Dante preyed on those who were weak. Who had been bullied or had something happen to them that twisted their minds."

"Right, so?"

"I think we're looking for a man who might have lost his wife or his beloved to suicide—over something that he might have done himself, or because of something unfair that fell upon them. We need to get to the records, to tell Edmund and Jeanne to start searching through any possibilities. We need to—"

"Call and get everyone looking in that direction," Mason said, pulling out his phone. "Conference call," he murmured to Della. "Angela and Bisset. They'll get moving. And then…"

Angela and Bisset answered him and Mason put forward Della's theory. He nodded, ending the call. He reached out and pulled her close to him.

"The sun is setting," he said softly. "Let's take a second for all that's beautiful in life."

She smiled, turning in his arms to face him.

"Well, hmm, you're beautiful."

"Well, um, thanks, but not… Hmm, doesn't make me much of a manly man!"

She laughed, leaned against him, and turned within his arms again.

The sun was falling. Tomorrow, they'd join the hunt with Edmund, Jeanne, and Bisset. They would hunt monsters again, those that lurked in the minds of men.

But now…

It was beautiful.

And it was okay to know and love all that was beautiful…

She grinned to herself.

…including Mason!

★ ★ ★ ★ ★

New York Times *bestselling author*
Heather Graham brings Blackbird to the streets
of London to hunt down a copycat killer!

Read on for a sneak peek of
Secrets in the Dark

PROLOGUE

The king was dead.

Or, rather, at this time in history, incarcerated.

Of course, the "king" believed that he would "rise" again—after all, a vampire was immortal.

But the Vampire King had taught Ripper well. Just as the world was filled with different countries, presidents, kings, queens and prime ministers—and, of course, great dictators—the world should equally be filled with kings of the underworld.

And with learning, a man could rise to greatness, become king of his own domain.

Ripper smiled to himself, watching the world go by around him. He wasn't lurking in the shadows. He was sitting amongst the neon lights of the busy bars in Brixton, watching.

Just watching.

He'd learned from his master to watch, and to listen. And there was a lot to watch. Of course, the area was popular amongst all age groups, but it attracted the young and the beautiful.

He'd learned as well to mimic a variety of accents. If someone was fascinated by Scots, he could roll his *R*'s like no one else. Irish was an easy one to slip into. Welsh a bit harder, and then, of course, there was proper British and such twists as those made famous by rock bands, like a Liverpool bit.

He was anything anyone wanted him to be. He could even imitate Americans—from a hard-toned New Yorker to a fellow with a Southern drawl or even a man with a Western twang.

All in a day's work.

Well, of course, there was work, too. Which meant he could only watch so late on certain nights. But tonight...

Ah, but tonight was his. And he learned from experience— from watching the master at work as well.

He'd learned how to play the game, how to maneuver, what to do and what not to do.

In short, his reign was just beginning.

And that all-important lesson he'd learned?

Not to get caught! After all, he would be king in his own right. And the man history knew as "Jack the Ripper" had never been caught—though every few years, there was a new theory, a new belief that forensic measures might not have given the world the truth.

But that would never happen. And like that Jack, this Ripper would never let himself be caught.

No, he would never let an obsession rule him. Emotion would never come into the picture. He had learned all the tricks of the trade, including the one he'd learned all on his own. Never let anything but cold, cool calculation rule his actions, never...

Never, never! But then, he'd known deep in his heart from the beginning that he was his own man, with his own plan and agenda. He'd made a start before he'd met the vampire. But back then…

Well, he had feared the slightest rustle of sound. He hadn't had the confidence he had now, hadn't mastered his craft, so to say. Now…

He had been a good student. The best student. And he was smart enough to utilize all that he had learned, including the fact that he must not make mistakes, that mistakes and obsession could lead to behavior that wasn't the most calculated and smart.

And now…he had such a dream, such an agenda!

Maybe he'd always coveted the idea of being king.

King of the Rippers!

Three stunning young women were walking by his table. Laughing, chatting about coming to Europe to find a prince.

He pretended to look at his watch, as if he were waiting for someone. And as they came nearer, he started to rise, almost knocking into one of them.

"Oh, I'm ever so bloody sorry!" he said.

"No, no, it's all right!" the closest girl in the trio said, smiling. She was an attractive blonde, perfectly configured with wickedly long legs, generous breasts and, best of all, a trusting smile.

"Sorry, me mate just had to stand me up and I'd figured…" He paused, shrugging and indicating the table where he'd been seated. "Well, unless you'd like to join me!"

Three might be a challenge, but…

"Sorry! I'm Brad Terry. And this…" He paused again, indicating the environs of Brixton. "This is my home ground if I can give you any pointers. You are American."

"We are, straight out of Kansas," the blonde said. "I'm Shelly McNamara and these are my friends Ginger Cannon and Tess Garcia."

"Nice to meet you. And thank you," one of her friends, the brunette introduced as Ginger, said. She glanced at the blonde, Shelly, and said, "we'll leave you to get pointers for us. Tess and I will try the place right across the street if you want to join us."

Ripper smiled. He'd listened and watched enough to know that Shelly McNamara's friends were giving her leeway to flirt with him and decide if she wanted a bit of a British fling or not. They were leaving her alone but offering her a safety net.

Pity for her and them that it wouldn't be enough.

The two friends waved and started off. Ripper looked at the young woman, Shelly, and gave her his most innocent, charming smile.

"What will you have?" he asked her.

Whatever it was, she'd have more.

So much more...

As she sat down, smiling, eager and adventurous, he thought that his night was going to go beautifully.

Yes, the king was dead—incarcerated.

But then again...

Long live the king!

CHAPTER ONE

Della Hamilton looked out the window as they drove from Heathrow Airport to the center of London, Detective Edmund Taylor driving and her partner, Mason Carter, seated behind her.

She took a moment to close her eyes and imagine that they were there for a fun vacation, to enjoy the sights.

She loved the city of London. A history buff, she'd been fascinated as a teenager to visit with her parents, to roam the halls of the Tower of London and ride over London Bridge, visit the remaining Roman sites, stare at the legendary Big Ben and marvel at the beauty and the stories to be discovered within the hallowed ground of Westminster Cathedral.

She hadn't been back since she'd been a college student, and on that trip, she'd revisited a few of her favorite historic sites, but she'd also spent time in Chelsea, Covent Gardens and other areas for the nightlife and fun with friends.

Now...

Now, she was Special Agent Della Hamilton and part of a unique unit within the FBI. She and Mason had been assigned to a new "assistance" force, and thus they headed to Europe when the need arose. They had started out on a case in which a killer had skipped from country to country, his method of killing unique. They'd been able to trick him into being captured when he'd returned to the United States and, through his taunting, they had learned that he had more followers—doing some of the killings attributed to him—than they had previously expected.

And so now...

London. A city of over eight million people, busy with their day-to-day lives, most good citizens, hard-working human beings. And yet, like anywhere in the world, there were those among humanity who were not quite so decent. In fact, they might be described as purely evil.

"We've had some bloody whack jobs in this city," Edmund Taylor said, his eyes on the road, his head shaking as he stared hard ahead. "Just in the last decade we had a man who killed his victims, chopped them up—and ate their brains. And other body parts, I believe. He was incarcerated, released and killed again, once again chopping up his victim and eating their brains until he was rearrested. We have no death penalty and he was sentenced to a secure mental facility, but..." He paused, shaking his head, and Della had to wonder if he wasn't wishing that, in certain cases when a killer escaped to kill and kill again, there might be a death penalty in Great Britain.

But Edmund just shook his head and continued with, "All throughout its history, there have been incidents that defy anything resembling normality. Going all the way back to Jack the Ripper. Latest case in point, our so-called Vampire King—a man I am entirely grateful to see incarcerated and behind bars, thanks, of course, to Blackbird and the two of you."

From the back seat, Mason leaned forward to speak. "Blackbird! We're a team. And working as a team, we got Dante. But the man is claiming that he didn't do the killing in London— and when he made those claims, he didn't know that Della was in contact with all of us and that his words were recorded. But those victims he was referring to were killed by his method— the victims were drugged, carefully exsanguinated, and left as sleeping beauties."

Edmund nodded. "We don't know just how many killers there may be—but we've gone through every bit of evidence we have, which is sadly not much. Dante was good about teaching his people that forensics are at a point these days where a single hair can identify a killer. And he also made a point of leaving bodies where they'd be discovered but not before the elements around them had compromised whatever might be found. He isn't saying more, right?"

"One of our agents who is also a criminal psychiatrist has been working with him," Mason said. "And, so far, he knows what we surmised. You were with us in the bayou. He said he killed in France, but not all the victims in Norway—or in London. Dante was great at finding those people who were seeking something in life that they didn't have. Some looking for any excuse to kill and some believing in whatever ridiculous story he told them. Hopefully, any of the true idiots he had among his followers never got to the point of murder— and are scared to death now that he has been taken and, in the United States, may well face lethal injection. Of course, every country where he killed wants a crack at him, but..."

"But?" Edmund asked.

"I think even the most peace-loving countries in the world want a man like him removed with no possibility of parole or escape," Della provided flatly.

Edmund didn't respond, but watching him, she knew that he might agree.

"I'm always conflicted," she told him. "There is no undoing an execution if it's later proven that someone was innocent. But sometimes, when evidence is overwhelming, and a killer does get out and kill and kill again… I guess we wouldn't be human if we didn't wish it could be stopped."

"Of course," Edmund murmured.

She turned and glanced at Mason. He was serious, a thoughtful frown creasing his forehead. She was glad that he was her partner for so many reasons. She had been hesitant about him at first—before they'd met on a case, he'd been working solo for a year because his partner had been killed in the line of duty. That did something to any law enforcement officer. But while he hated to kill, he was a crack shot and an excellent judge of when deadly force was necessary and when a suspect could be talked down. He had an extreme sense of justice. It also helped that he stood an intimidating six foot five, was incredibly fit and blessed with ink-dark hair and eyes so dark a blue they could appear almost black in shadows.

And it helped, of course, that in the Krewe, it was all right to fall for one's partner. Krewe members were simply different—some said special, others said cursed—and for their work, it was important that they shared that difference.

They were simply a minute portion of the population.

Like many others—in law enforcement in general—she and Mason had also made the most of all their off-time. There was always a fine line that had to be observed. They cared. They cared deeply for the victims, for ending violence that was humanly possible to end. They also knew that they had to stop and smell the proverbial flowers when they could— they needed that space to stay sane and as prepared as humanly possible as well.

It was natural that she couldn't help but wish it was a vacation.

But it wasn't. And since it wasn't, she was grateful that she was with Mason—and Detective Edmund Taylor. They were becoming their own "special" unit, unofficially termed Blackbird, while they were officially the Euro Special Assistance Team.

Edmund Taylor was, in Della's mind, a top-notch detective. They'd met in Norway, on their hunt for the "vampire" who had struck in England and France before turning to the Scandinavian nation. While the FBI had long had liaison offices across the world, they were unique in their ability to join in on an investigation—when asked, of course. Interpol had provided them with François Bisset, their go-between for all countries, and they worked with the detectives involved in each case. While this was a new case, it was also an old one.

Because no one knew what magic or hypnotism the confessed killer Stephan Dante had used on others or just how many other killers he had created and/or trained.

Edmund knew the case. He was somewhere in his early forties, but he had worked long and hard with Scotland Yard to earn his position with homicide and in this case, what they were calling "special services." He was solid and serious most of the time, just an inch or so shorter than Mason and a man who evidently worked his frustrations out at the gym and could still smile and find humor upon occasion, letting his guard down when he was among friends. He was a handsome man with a headful of light brown hair and eyes so soft a brown they might have been almost amber.

"Yeah, us!" he said lightly then. "We caught the killer—who let us know that we didn't catch all the killers we need to catch. But…we're on it. We've been on it. Night is coming, so…did you two want to get to the hotel and get some sleep, or—"

Laughing, Della interrupted him. "No, we're ready to hit

the ground running. That's the plan with us having our own pilot and private plane. Of course, poor Gene, our pilot, needs to be ready to fly at the drop of a hat, but he gets lots of downtime, too. And he wants to see the sights, so…anyway, no! We had plenty of sleep on the plane. Do you have any ideas? I'd assumed we'd go over files—"

"Which we will, tomorrow. Two of our victims—supposedly taken by the *vampire* killer—were last seen in the Brixton nightlife area. I thought you might need a pint or two as well after your long journey."

Della glanced back at Mason. "We just flew in from Bucharest, so hardly a long journey. Since Dante had insinuated that we might find clues at Castle Bran, we went to the castle, and, called you—as you know—so…"

"Yes, indeed. We need to find possible suspects—and then, as you suggested, discover if any of them lost a wife or loved one to a suicide—as suggested by our quickie trip to Transylvania and discoveries regarding Vlad Dracul. A suicide they just might blame on themselves. But we're struggling to find suspects, going back over all the paperwork… Anyway, I'm not going to feel sorry for you for a long journey since…" He paused to grin. "Since you did get something of a holiday in there, and the castle is beautiful and the Romanian countryside even more so. But we can have a relaxing drink and dinner—and perhaps spot something or at the very least, chat with a bartender or two."

"I think we can function well with a pint," Mason said. "Has anything happened since we made our way here?"

Edmund shook his head. "But I was there when Dante was taken down in the Louisiana bayou—I heard what he said. The victims killed *already* have families, and—"

"Don't worry. We understand. The victims deserve justice,

and truth in that justice. And we need to make sure there aren't more victims," Mason said quietly.

"Exactly," Edmund murmured. "And if there is someone out there—something we all believe—we have to stop him before he starts on his own *reign* of whatever kind of terror he's planning."

"Yes," Della said quietly. "So, a pint it is!"

They'd headed out from Bucharest in the midafternoon. But even though the flight was short, time at the airports and driving was turning day into night. A fog was sweeping in, as one so commonly did in England, and the sun was dying in the western sky.

It was beautiful and eerie.

But not so eerie in the Brixton section. Restaurants and pubs blazed with lights. Visitors and locals were hurrying about. The night was temperate and pleasant and many were dining at outside cafés or sipping drinks at sidewalk tables.

Edmund luckily managed to park right on the street. They all exited the car and for a minute, stood looking around at the many lights.

Couples and groups walked about, laughing, teasing, chatting, some arm in arm, all out for a good time, for camaraderie with old friends and new.

"Hopefully, the news about Stephan Dante has kept women from casually hooking up in bars."

"Men and women have been casually hooking up in pubs since forever," Edmund said. "I've wanted to do a press conference, but the powers that be... Well, no one wants a panic. And at this time, all we have is what Dante is saying and we have no proof and... Well, no press conference. But thankfully, they still think I should be part of this special force and that we should continue to investigate."

"The sad thing is that something is going to happen before

the powers that be decide a warning is in order—and that's probably the way in every western country, not just England," Mason told him. "Hey, we get on it, and we move fast."

"All right, well. Welcome to England! So…would you have a dark ale or light?" he asked. "Oh, let's head there, to Bixby's—great bar food and wonderful taps."

"It's a plan. It's also where one victim was last seen, right?" Della asked.

Edmund nodded. "Aye, but… Hey! I'm not lying. Great bar food and clean, clear taps!"

Bixby's was a large establishment with plenty of inside seating and even more on a large courtyard just outside. Those tables offered views of both the interior and exterior of the restaurant with a bar central in the courtyard, with still more tables spilling out onto the sidewalk and the street.

"Great table!" Mason assured Edmund as they were seated.

It was a great table just inside where they could see what was going on where they were—and out the door to the street. They could watch the flow of humanity around them, couples, groups and the occasional loner.

Della found herself studying the couples as Edmund and Mason ordered after she had waved a hand, indicating she'd be happy with anything they chose.

There was a young couple near them, both smiling, holding hands now and then, sharing their food, either new lovers or old who were very much in love! They were speaking French, she thought, overhearing a bit of the conversation.

She didn't believe that the killer they were seeking was French.

He was American or British.

Another couple intrigued her at first; they were joined by an older couple, and it appeared that they were young newlyweds out with the wife's parents.

"Fish and chips. Better here than at home," Mason said. "Or, maybe I just think that they're better because we are in jolly old England."

"No. Fish and chips are better here," Edmund said lightly. "Hey, no insult. Creole cooking is it in Louisiana, and when not in Cuba, Cuban coffee is best in Miami."

"Ah, we all lay claim to our culinary delights," Della murmured. They were having dinner. There was no guarantee that anything was going to happen here tonight.

Here—or anywhere.

"The biggest problem we have is that, of course, everyone assumed that there was just one killer—that's why they had me and our Interpol liaison Bisset and Jeanne Lapierre from France joining you two and Detective Wilhelm in Norway. We don't have a list of possible suspects, though tomorrow, we'll go back through the files. Within them now, we may just find those we cleared at the time because Dante was here and working and they could twist the truth...all the witnesses had alibis that seemed truthful, and then when the murders started in Norway, well..."

Della was half listening and half watching people as they came and went. A group moved and she noticed one of the courtyard tables closest to the sidewalk. A pretty blonde sat there, laughing as she chatted with a young man who appeared to be in his early thirties. He had slightly shaggy light brown hair and an easy smile. She wasn't sure why, but she didn't think that they'd known one another forever—they had the look of two young people flirting and enjoying the get-to-know-you part of a relationship.

And they most likely were just a young couple getting to know one another.

"Excuse me!" she murmured.

She stood and pretended to head out and look down the

sidewalk as if she were trying to see if a friend might be arriving.

But as she passed by the table, she heard their conversation.

The girl spoke with an American accent; she probably hailed from somewhere in the Midwest.

The man spoke with an English accent, as if he'd been born and bred in London.

"Well, we could meet up with your friends, or…" the young man said.

The blonde giggled and ran her fingers over the back of his hand. "My friends are genuinely nice, and I think that you would enjoy them. Then again…how quickly we could move, so much we could see and do if we were alone!"

Della wasn't sure why, but alarms rang loudly in her head. She wasn't sure that she thought anything out, she just hurried back to the table and picked up her pint of ale.

She meant to explain, but just as she picked up the glass, she saw the couple rising. She hurried back, weaving through tables, anxious to reach them before they could leave the restaurant.

She pretended to look elsewhere and slammed into the young woman, making sure that her ale flew into the air… and fell due to the force of gravity, soaking the pretty young blonde.

"Oh! I am so sorry!" Della cried. "I am truly sorry, I've ruined your night, oh…!"

The man stared at her for a split second. "I'll go get something," he said quickly, stepping around her and heading for the bar in the center of the courtyard.

By then, Edmund and Mason had come up and Edmund quickly did the speaking. "Hello, miss, we are so sorry, but forgive me—" he paused to flash his badge "—do you know the gentleman you were with, or did you just meet?"

"Uh," she said, frowning, staring at the badge. "I—uh—did I do something wrong? If so, I'm deeply sorry, I'm loving being here, this trip has been a dream—"

"You haven't done anything wrong," Mason quickly assured her. "We're just—"

He broke off. He had twisted around to watch for her companion. "He's not getting a bar rag—he's gone," he said. "I'm going after him."

"Oh, my God, what did he do?" the young woman whispered.

"Maybe nothing, maybe nothing at all!" Della said quickly. "But we're advising young women against being alone with men they've just met. There have been unusual murders in the last year and—"

"They caught the guy! It's all over the news everywhere. They caught the Vampire King!" the girl said.

"He had followers," Edmund said quietly. "And if we've ruined your trip in any way, we're heartily sorry, and yet—"

"You really are a detective. I'm not being pranked or anything?" she asked. "Did my friends put you up to this? I mean…you," she said, looking at Della. "You're American. This is England. You can't have any authority here—"

"I am an American. FBI, on special assignment because we don't know that the *Vampire King* was the only one doing the killing," Della explained quickly. "And if you're disturbed, we are sorry, but in my mind, disturbing you—"

"I'm not just disturbed. I'm wearing beer," the girl said.

"And again, I am sorry. I'll be happy to pay for your dry cleaning—"

The girl suddenly shuddered. "No, no, I'm sorry, I'm being ugly and I don't mean to be, it's just that he seemed like such a nice guy and…"

"I think if he was just a nice guy, he'd have gotten the rag and come back," Edmund said. He reached into his pocket and gave her one of his cards. "I swear, I am with Scotland Yard. And please, I'd greatly appreciate a call if anyone does anything suspicious near you—"

"He didn't come back!" the girl whispered. "He—he didn't get a rag and come back!"

"You have friends here in London with you," Della said. "Do you know where they are? May we walk you to wherever they are?"

The girl looked at them and swallowed nervously. Then she nodded. "I'm Shelly McNamara. My first trip with college friends. That man... I..."

"You're young, beautiful, on your first European trip, and it seemed you met a great British guy and there's usually no reason for that to be anything but fine," Della assured her quickly. "Again, I'm sorry that the world has come to this, but...please, don't go with strangers alone. Make sure that if you're going to be with anyone, that someone knows exactly who you are with and where you're going to be. Please. For your own safety."

"Walk me across the street?" the girl asked.

"Of course," Edmund said.

Edmund lifted an arm, indicating that he would follow her. Della paused briefly, looking for Mason. But he hadn't returned.

She felt a chill, wondering if her intuition had been right in any way.

The young man had seen her, and surely Mason and Edmund, and he had disappeared. He'd been charming the girl—until they might have attracted the attention of others...

Mason was good. He could move quickly. But the man had apparently found a back way out. Brixton was brimming with its night crowd. There were people, restaurants and pubs everywhere.

She should have gone with him. But she had been the one who had splashed the girl with ale. And Edmund had the proper credentials for this country and...

Maybe the man had just been a student with a warrant out on a petty drug charge or the like and had simply needed to escape any brush with the authorities.

Mason would find them.

She hurried after Shelly McNamara and Edmund. Shelly's friends were inside the pub, sitting at the bar, listening to a tale from the young woman who was serving drinks there. They smiled, curious when Shelly arrived with her friends.

"You're wearing beer!" one of the girls said.

"My fault—I ran into her," Della explained quickly.

"And he's a cop—a copper here, right? Or a bobby?" Shelly asked, looking at Edmund.

He smiled and said dramatically, "They call me Mr. Detective—Detective Inspector Edmund Taylor. And, of course, ladies, we're all at your service."

"What happened to lover boy?" one of her friends asked.

"That's Ginger. Ginger Cannon and my other friend here is Tess Garcia," Shelly said in way of introduction. "Oh! And you must see this lady's badge! She's Special Agent Della Hamilton, FBI."

"In England?" Tess said.

"Attached to a case," Della said briefly.

"Vampire King!" the pretty bartender, who had gone silent in the middle of her story when they'd arrived, spoke up.

"He's been caught, right? The news went on and on about him. Well, of course. Creepy and scary as hell. So, what about lover boy?" Tess persisted.

"Gone. And I'm starting to like myself in good British ale. You can get me another," Shelly said.

"Well, I think I could do that. Nice to have met you all and please, enjoy London, but take care," Edmund said.

"Whoa!"

They were all startled when the pretty bartender, who had turned to the television just as a soccer match was interrupted by a newscaster cutting in with "breaking news."

Every London paper had received a letter—claiming that Jack the Ripper was back in the city.

They all paused to listen.

"Naturally, the police were informed immediately and many believe this to be a hoax, but just an hour ago the station received an anonymous letter, a single type-written page, mailed to the station from nearby warning, Jack is Back. We don't know how serious this threat to be, but with recent murders in and around our great country, we felt that it was only right that our populace and our tourists be warned immediately."

She went on speaking, describing the recent capture of Stephan Dante and warning that everyone, especially young women, needed to be careful.

Watching the screen, Edmund shook his head. "Jack is back. Great." He seemed to forget Shelly McNamara and her friends. "Of course—"

"It could be a hoax," Della said. "And I'm sure that it's with the police and a forensic crew by now, and maybe they'll find out that it is a hoax, or, at the very least, discover something about whoever sent it."

"A hoax by an idiot, or a warning from a protégé!" Edmund said. He realized that the three girls at the bar were watching him, but he no longer seemed to need to project a cordial image for his city.

"Please! Be careful," he said.

He started out of the pub and Della was quick to follow, turning back to the three young women with a smile. "So sorry about the beer. Do be careful!"

Close on Edmund's heels, she saw that Mason had found them. He was shaking his head with disgust.

"Never even got to follow him—he raced out through the kitchen. He was gone when I hit the alley, but I tried both directions and… It may be nothing," he said.

"Probably nothing," Della said. "Just a guy with a petty crime behind him afraid of authority."

"But something about him bothered you," Mason said.

Della shrugged. "Yes. But… Hey. Intuition can be wrong."

Edmund was watching her. "I saw him so briefly," he said. "But… I don't know. I got the feeling I had seen him before and I don't know in what context."

"We can keep looking," Della said.

"We can. But…"

"He's gone. Wherever he hides out, he's there. He's gone. We're not going to get him tonight. Damn. We have a tab open across the street!"

"Paid it," Mason assured him. "Well—"

He frowned, breaking off as his phone buzzed faintly. "Philip," he said, glancing at his caller ID.

Della and Edmund watched him, frowning, as he listened to the caller.

"Philip is—"

"I know. I was there, in Louisiana, remember?" Edmund reminded him. "Special agent with the Krewe, psychiatrist working with Dante."

If they'd been alone, Mason would have put the call on speaker, Della knew.

But they were standing in the street surrounded by Brixton nightlife.

He ended the call and looked at them. "We must take a quick hop home. Edmund, you're free to come, or work the case from here. Philip has gotten a lot from Dante—including the fact that he did kill women in unsolved crimes where the officers came to suspect that they were his *practice* killings. He had details, so... Anyway, Philip thinks that we might get a great deal more on a suspect if he observes Dante talking to Della."

"Private jet with sleeping quarters there and back?" Edmund said. "I'm with you. Unless, of course, you two want to be alone? I guess that—"

"We'll be fine with you in the plane," Della assured him quickly, looking at Mason and laughing. "We're to be at the airport by seven a.m. The pilot has been informed."

"So...let me get you to your hotel. I guess we all need some sleep," Edmund said.

There was nothing else to do that night. There really hadn't been much that they could have done, except...

Della couldn't help but feel that something had happened.

And as they hurried back to Edmund's car, they could hear people talking about the emergency news broadcast.

Jack's back.

"You may have saved a life tonight!" Mason told her softly. She smiled and nodded.

Maybe. And yet...

It also felt as if they had just missed something.

They reached the hotel and there, they showered and fell into bed. Without words, Della turned into Mason, anxious that night to make love.

To see the beauty in the world.

In his arms, she slept.

But in her dreams, she suddenly saw the man's face again, and in her mind's eye, he smiled and whispered, "Jack's back!"

She woke with a start, but Mason pulled her back into his arms.

"We will find this man, too. Get some sleep. Tomorrow, you face Dante again."

She was tough, she assured herself. She was a good agent, trained, savvy and she knew it.

But it still felt good to pull his arms more tightly around her, knowing that there was support, in the field or in their minds, that only they could provide for one another.

It would all become much harder because...

She knew in her heart that it was no hoax. Jack was back.

Don't miss
Secrets in the Dark

from New York Times *bestselling author*
Heather Graham,
available July 2023
wherever MIRA books are sold!